IN
INK

DAVE SIVERS

ISBN: 978-1-9997397-2-0

DAVE SIVERS

Dave Sivers grew up in West London and has been writing all his life. His books include the popular crime series featuring the Aylesbury Vale detectives, DI Lizzie Archer and DS Dan Baines.

The Scars Beneath the Soul and *Dead in Deep Water* were both top three bestsellers in the Amazon Kindle Serial Killers chart. His other works include the Lowmar Dashiel crime fantasy novels. *In Ink* introduces DI Nathan Quarrel.

Dave also writes plays and other material for the amateur stage and is a founder of the annual BeaconLit festival of books and writing. He lives in Buckinghamshire with his wife, Chris.

To keep up with Dave's news and upcoming releases, subscribe to his newsletter at www.davesivers.co.uk.

For Chris.
Always.

1

The rhythmic beat of the music helps you concentrate your mind on the task in hand. It is the perfect accompaniment to the buzz of the machine as you guide it in its delicate work.

Rap, specifically grime: it hasn't always been a sound you appreciated but, when you were doing your apprenticeship... well, that was when you really started to get it. The stories the artists told, the rawness and darkness to be found in some of the lyrics. And those rapid, syncopated breakbeats. It's ideal for this work.

Today it's Stormzy. Okay, not exactly obscure, but you like it.

The machine itself sounds a little like an angry wasp as it glides over the surface, puncturing the skin between 50 and 3,000 times per minute as it penetrates the dermis by about a millimetre and deposits a drop of insoluble black ink into the skin with each puncture. And, with each puncture, your painstaking work of art has been emerging, literally drop by drop.

Those numbers are important, the precision of it all as beautiful as the image you're creating.

You've been at this for the best part of five hours now, and the job is almost done. When it's finally finished, you think you'll feel a little bereft, but incredibly proud at the same time. This work – *these works* – are what you got into this business for in the first place. Well, not so much the works themselves, you suppose, but the inspiration that guided you towards tattooing was always going to culminate in what you're doing here and now.

In the beginning, it was that motivation that mattered. Now the art – the quality of the finished product – is every bit as important to you. Your most important work should also be your finest.

You hope your subject will like it. You're used to conversation while you work, but this client has said nothing throughout.

Even the moans and whimpers have subsided.

Not that you can blame them for that. You know that, working so close to bone, it hurts like hell. Meanwhile, silence is fine by you. You suspect you know the sort of conversation you'd be having.

Those peripheral thoughts drift away as you give the final detailed touches your full concentration. Even Stormzy seems muted. The air in your workspace seems heavy, as if even the building is holding its breath for the finished product.

When it *is* finished, the realisation almost takes you by surprise. It's a little like snapping out of a trance. You withdraw the needle and allow the machine to buzz for a few seconds more before switching it off.

You meticulously clean out your needle, then spray a green soap solution over the tattoo before wiping it down to remove excess ink and blood. Finally, you apply an aftercare salve to the tattooed area to soften and moisturise the skin.

You step back and look at what you've done, and pride swells in your chest. You haven't felt this way since your very first – incredibly basic and simple – tattoo. This one says exactly what you wanted it to say, and it says it beautifully.

You take up a mirror and hold it so the subject can see.

"Well," you say, "what do you think?"

The response disgusts you. You don't expect them to say anything. But the eyes say it all. Horror mingles with stark terror and fresh tears leak out, spilling onto your precious work. The salve will protect it, though.

Behind the silver duct tape sealing the lips, the client attempts to scream, hideous animal noises. Their body attempts to thrash against the straps binding them to the workbench. It's ineffectual. The head can't move, of course. The vice has held it tight and still, so you could work without any unhelpful movements.

You shake your head, sickened by the pathetic self-pity of this person. They'll just have to have enough pity for both of you, because you feel none at all.

You hold the mirror closer, feeling a smile tug at the corners of your mouth.

"See?" you whisper. "The truth is written all over your face."

2

Detective Inspector Nathan Quarrel wouldn't go so far as to shoot the day down but, when his first order of business was to visit a crime scene that included a dead body, he couldn't say he much cared for Mondays.

It was not long after 7am, and the centre of Tring was barely awake. As Quarrel had guided his aged and battered Volvo estate along the small market town's High Street, he'd passed a couple of dog walkers and a jogger in shrieking pink Lycra, a shade his eyes could have done without at such an hour. He imagined the newsagent's would be open, but he knew nothing much else would be opening up before 8am at the earliest. Then the town centre would really begin to wake up.

Quarrel drew the car up by Church Square, with its unusual pavement maze in the shape of a zebra's head – a reference to Lord Walter Rothschild, a passionate zoologist who had ridden around Tring in a zebra-drawn carriage. The aristocratic Rothschild family, dominant in the global finance and banking industry in the 19th century, had arrived in this corner of Hertfordshire in 1872, transforming the town and providing employment, housing and improved social welfare for its residents.

On the far side of the small square stood the town's war memorial and the entrance to St Peter and St Paul Church. His colleague, Detective Sergeant Katie Gray, had fleetingly belonged to a choir that sang there, roped in by a friend, and Quarrel had gone to the concert, his 6ft 4in frame squeezed into a pew behind a pillar in a packed church on a stormy night. Rolling thunder had added to the atmosphere. 'Percussion by God,' Katie had described it afterwards.

He glanced at Katie, beside him in the passenger seat and already undoing her seat belt. "Ready for this?"

She rolled her green eyes. "Oh, yeah. You know me. Always up for viewing a cold corpse. Let's hope this one's not too gruesome."

Quarrel didn't consider himself big on humour, but he always found Katie's squeamishness mildly amusing. She was, after all, a murder detective and a self-proclaimed former goth. He'd had her accompany him to three post mortems and then given up. Seeing her green-faced, with sweat on her brow and her arms wrapped around herself, like she was literally trying to hold it together, had made him feel bad. These days, if he needed a second pair of eyes at the mortuary, he'd take one of his detective constables, either Ricky James or Aliya Nazir. Usually Aliya. Nothing seemed to faze her.

They got out of the car and donned protective clothing – overalls, latex gloves and paper shoes.

Quarrel wasn't an especially religious man, but he always found something reassuring in old churches that had watched over centuries of changes. This one was no exception. St Peter and St Paul was a 15th century Anglican church, its solid bulk built from local flint and Totternhoe stone. A low brick wall enclosing the church and two of its three graveyards, opened onto a brick path leading past mature trees to the front of the building.

Local uniforms were already in place, and familiar blue and white crime scene tape had been liberally applied, flapping like bunting in the morning breeze.

Overhead, the sky was dark and brooding. This had been a weird year for weather so far: a positively spring-like February, while much of April so far had felt more like winter. As usual, he found the drop in temperature had coincided with feelings of anxiety and discomfort. There'd been talk on the forecast of heavy showers in these parts. Quarrel hoped they'd hold off until the Crime Scene Investigators and the pathologist had their way with the scene.

Quarrel and Katie showed their ID to the young policewoman barring the entrance to the site. She raised the tape to admit them.

"PC Cole," she said. "Me and PC Harrison over there" – she pointed out a stocky male officer guarding another access point – "were first on the scene."

"So what have we got?" Quarrel asked.

"White male, late forties, early fifties, propped against a wall at the back. There were showers overnight, so he's a bit bedraggled, but his clothing looks good quality. But—"

"Not Man at M&S then?"

PC Cole smiled. "I quite like some M&S stuff, but no. My dad's a solicitor and spends a small fortune on his clothes. I'd say our victim shopped in the same circles."

"Any idea who he was?" Katie asked.

"None. I didn't like to rummage in the pockets in case I compromised any evidence."

"Good," Quarrel acknowledged approvingly. He glanced about. "We've beaten the CSIs to it, I assume?"

"I'm assured they'll be on their way. And Dr Stoddart."

"New one on me. Pathologist, I take it?"

She nodded. "Dr Hussain retired, and he's the new man."

"Okay. And who found the body?"

"A Mrs Vaughan. Lives in one of the retirement apartments just across the road. Apparently she doesn't sleep well and is in the habit of an early morning stroll around the town. Her route takes her past the back of the church, and she spotted the body. We escorted her home and told her to stay there. I assume you'll want to talk to her, sir."

"In a while, yes." He liked this young woman's efficiency. "So what can you tell us about the body? How do you think he died?"

"That's just it. Nothing obvious. But—"

"So do you think he maybe was taking a short cut through the church and came over funny? Leaned against the wall for support, had a heart attack, and slid down and died?" He looked at Katie. "They told me it was a *suspicious* death."

"Oh, it is, sir," Cole assured him. "That's what I've been trying to say." Quarrel realised he'd interrupted her a couple of times with his questions, but she said it with no trace of annoyance.

"So what is it?"

She gave the smallest of shrugs. "See for yourself, sir. If you go round the back, you'll find him. You'll see what I mean."

Quarrel thanked her, and he and Katie skirted the church building, which backed onto a footpath leading to a large car park. Just off the footpath stood the impressive archway to the former rectory, now serving as a commercial office building.

A couple more uniforms were here. The enterprising local cops had used a tarpaulin and some traffic cones to cobble together a makeshift screen until the CSIs arrived with their purpose-built tents. Already a couple of early morning passers-by had stopped beyond the church wall, rubbernecking at the police activity, doubtless speculating on what was going on. The uniforms had done their best to preserve the dead man's dignity.

The man himself sat behind the screen, propped against the wall, just as PC Cole had described. To Quarrel's eye, he'd been posed, rather than having naturally come to rest there. But that wasn't the most remarkable thing.

"Jesus," breathed Katie.

Cole had made an efficient job of describing the man. Quarrel was no expert, but the clothes did look high-end, the jacket a Belstaff Trialmaster, his walking boots good leather with a decent shine on them.

"Outdoor clothes," Quarrel commented.

He continued to study the dead man, Well-cut hair, thin on top, a fair bit of grey permeating the dark brown. Yes, Cole's assessment of age – late forties to early fifties – was probably about right. Although Quarrel wondered how old she thought *he* was. He knew he looked a lot older than his forty-two years, with an untidy straggle of steel-grey hair that almost matched his eyes, and craggy, lived-in features.

But age hardly mattered at the moment. What had shocked Katie Gray, and arrested Quarrel's attention, was the tattoo.

Nathan Quarrel had seen plenty of tattoos on corpses. He'd never seen one all over a face before now.

He moved in for a closer look, noting that Katie seemed in no rush to follow suit. The design, all in black ink covered the face from forehead to chin and, as a work of art, was impressive. The style reminded him vaguely of the Victorian Pre-Raphaelite paintings. A fair-haired youth in an ornate smock carried a bundle on a stick over his shoulder. The sun was at his back and a little dog capered at his heels.

At first glance, it was a carefree, joyful image. Yet there were four things wrong with the picture.

The first was the wide cuffs of the youth's diaphanous sleeves, their openings finished in solid black. Whether by coincidence or deliberate design, they covered the area around the eyes, creating a sinister circus clown effect. Then there was the cliff edge on which the youth trod. His pose looked as if he was about to take another step, oblivious to his danger. Thirdly, the image was upside down for some reason. But these things paled into insignificance compared with the silver duct tape covering the mouth. It marred the picture, as well as telling Quarrel all he needed to know.

"Well," he said, "the tattoo doesn't exactly fit in with his ensemble, does it?"

Hesitantly, Katie leaned closer. "It looks pretty new, too. The skin's a bit puffy. I'd say he died before the swelling, redness and oozing really got underway."

He looked at her, surprised. "I didn't know you were an expert."

"I'm not. I've no interest in having a tattoo myself, but a couple of my mates got them in their teens and I remember the various healing stages. This poor sod didn't get far with his."

"We're thinking he was tattooed against his will and then killed?"

She nodded. "That's what the tape's suggesting to me. The experts will need to look for signs of other restraints. But I suppose the whole experience might have induced a heart attack, rather than it being a deliberate murder."

He turned to look at her with interest, the wind catching at his own hair. "You're thinking this could have been some sort of prank gone wrong?"

She bit her lip. "Pretty unpleasant prank, if it was, to permanently disfigure someone like that. And no, I don't really think that at all. I just think we should keep an open mind."

"Agreed." Quarrel had been thinking exactly the same, but Katie always made a good sounding board. They'd both learned a long time ago to accept nothing at face value.

"Why do you suppose it's upside down?"

She frowned as she studied the tattoo again. "Well, it looks like a Tarot card."

"Really?" He shook his head. "You're full of surprises this morning."

"My brother. I must have told you he's a bit alternative?"

"Does water divining, doesn't he?"

"Well, dowsing. It's not just about water. He's also into feng shui, homeopathy, and a bunch of other hippy shit. I don't really mind. It's not like he shoves it down your throat all the time, although he's got quite a thing about electromagnetic impulses—"

"The tattoo?" he reminded her.

"Sorry, Nate. Yeah, so he's interested in Tarot too. Got a pack and was learning about it, so he could do readings. I don't know how far he got, but we did have a chat about it. It seems the cards have subtly different meanings when they're upside down, or reversed, to use the jargon. It gives the interpretation of the card the opposite meaning. So good news becomes bad, or vice versa."

"Do you know what this card is?"

"Sorry. I didn't take that much notice when he was showing them to me. You know me. Down to earth gal. But maybe I can find something online." Her phone was already in her hands, her thumbs working the keys.

While Katie conducted her Internet search, Quarrel straightened up, massaging his lower back, which didn't enjoy too much bending these days. He always tried to tell himself it was a feature of his height, rather than his advance towards middle age. He looked around. This man hadn't been tattooed here, that was for sure, and Quarrel very much doubted he'd died here, either. No, it was most likely he'd died elsewhere and then been brought here.

"I've got something,"

"That was quick."

"I searched for 'Tarot, dog, cliff'." She held her phone towards him, so he could see an image not dissimilar to the one on the dead man's face. "The Fool," she said.

He raised an eyebrow. "Really? I knew there was a Fool card, but I sort of assumed it would be like a jester. You know, cap and bells, like a Joker card."

"I think there can be a number of different representations. Let's see if I can find a meaning." She turned the phone back towards her, thumbs busy again. "Okay. It says here The Fool card is numbered zero. Apparently, that's a number of infinite potential. The Fool's like a blank canvas, if you like. His journey will shape his character."

"What does that mean, exactly?"

"The card usually signifies the start of a new journey. You can never tell what lies ahead, but The Fool offers optimism, freedom, opportunities. That sort of thing."

"He appears to offer a drop off a cliff edge, in this case," Quarrel remarked drily.

"I suppose it means all these opportunities carry risks with them. I'm just reading what it says," she added with a hint of defensiveness.

"So what about – what did you call it? The Reversed Fool?"

"Oh, yes. Hang on. Here we are. Yep, the Reversed Fool emphasises his more negative characteristics. It can suggest that you're literally acting like a fool. Like this youth on his cliff edge, you don't see the dangers under your nose. You're living in the moment, not planning for the future, and should beware of being taken advantage of."

"So the Reversed Fool is a sort of warning. Maybe that's what this tattoo is. But to him, or to others?"

"Or some kind of statement. You'd really need a proper Tarot expert for all the ins and outs."

"Your brother, maybe?"

Katie smiled and shook her head. "I don't think so. Mick's more of a dabbler. But I'll bet he knows someone who can tell us more about what this means. I'll ask him."

"The picture on your phone's in colour. This is just black ink. Maybe it's quicker. If there's a meaning to the choice of image, I guess this still makes the point."

A pair of crows swooped down into the churchyard, cawing. The sound seemed like an omen to Quarrel, sending the faintest shiver through him.

"Because it does mean *something*, doesn't it?" he said. "Got to. Whether his death was intended or was just a by-product of what was done to him, this," he indicated the tattoo, "is some sort of message." He glanced up at the dark sky. "I don't like messages. Often, they don't stop at one."

Footsteps were approaching down the side of the church. Moments later, three figures appeared, similarly attired to Quarrel and Katie, each carrying a case containing their equipment. Quarrel recognised the crime scene manager, Debbie Brown. Sharp, almost foxy features. Red, designer glasses with thick lenses. A few wisps of brown hair poked out from the sides of her hood.

"Morning," she said. She pulled a face. "Well, this is a rubbish start to the week."

The three CSIs put their bags down. Debbie's colleagues opened theirs and started busying themselves with the contents. Debbie herself stepped closer to the body.

"Bloody hell," she said. "It's like Halloween."

"About six months too early," Katie commented, "and I reckon this is some sick bastard's idea of a trick, rather than a treat."

"It's nice work," Debbie observed, "but yes, I think I agree with you." She looked Quarrel's way. "Any idea who he was?"

"I haven't been through the pockets. Thought I'd let you do the honours."

"Too kind."

Quarrel stepped back to give her room, and she hunkered down in front of the body, reaching out a gloved hand to open the jacket. She slipped her fingers carefully inside the man's right-hand pocket and withdrew a mobile phone. Katie produced an evidence bag, allowed Debbie to drop it inside, then sealed it.

The left-hand pocket contained an expensive-looking leather wallet, which Debbie opened, checking through it.

"Cash and credit cards, so it doesn't look as if he was robbed."

Quarrel wasn't surprised. The whole point of the attack on this man was the abomination on his face, not the contents of his wallet.

"Here we go," Debbie said, holding up a driver's licence. The photograph, even without the tattoo, was plainly of the victim. "Alastair Murdoch. Aged..." She did mental arithmetic. "Forty-nine. From Aldbury." A picturesque village only two or three miles from here. "What else do we have? Ah, some business cards." She peered at one. "He was an accountant. Offices in Hemel."

"Whereabouts?" Quarrel asked.

"Marlowes. Firm's called Piper Murdoch."

"Short stroll from the station," Katie remarked. Hemel Hempstead police station was in Combe Street, just off the Marlowes, the town's main drag.

"I wonder what time he would have been due to start work," said Quarrel. Then he dismissed the thought. "But he'll already have been reported missing, most likely. I'm thinking, whoever dumped him here, they probably did it in the small hours. Not too many people about, especially round the back here. And a Sunday night, especially, with work in the morning. But this artwork doesn't look like something you could knock off in an hour or so."

"It looks painstaking," Debbie agreed.

"Someone abducted him from somewhere, took him to a home, a workshop, wherever he did the tattoo, did all that work, and then brought the body here." Quarrel shoved his hands in the pockets of his old leather jacket. "We're talking hours. Someone must have missed him. Someone must have reported it."

"Unless he lived alone," Katie pointed out.

"True enough." Quarrel always imagined Aldbury as a family village, but he supposed it must have its fair share of people living alone. "We need to find out."

"I suppose we're assuming Mr Murdoch was alive when the tattoo was done," Debbie said. "That tape must have been to keep him quiet during the work, or why spoil the picture?" She looked from Quarrel to Katie. "What *is* that about, anyway?"

Katie explained the Tarot card theory.

"So we're dealing with a nutcase," Debbie said flatly.

"I'd certainly say we're not dealing with someone who follows accepted norms," Quarrel said. "This work screams 'agenda' at me."

"A nutcase," Debbie repeated. "Do you think there'll be more?"

"I sincerely hope not. This could be very specific to Mr Murdoch here. We don't want to run away with the idea that there's some Tarot card maniac running around out there."

Debbie looked singularly unimpressed. "If you say so."

"Morning!" chirped a male voice, startling them all.

They turned to look at a young-looking man in a crime scene suit, who seemed to have appeared from nowhere. Quarrel hadn't heard his approach, and he didn't think either of his colleagues had.

"Hello," Quarrel said. "You would be…?"

"Ah," the newcomer said cheerfully. "Dr Jordan Stoddart. Pathologist."

Quarrel regarded him doubtfully. Dr Hussain had looked about ninety. This guy looked more like nineteen. And he had a ring through one nostril. Quarrel knew how long it took to train a pathologist, so either this was an imposter, or Jordan Stoddart was considerably older than he looked.

"I know what you're thinking," Stoddart said, fishing in a pocket. "There you go." He showed them ID. "I'm cursed with a baby face. I still get asked my age in pubs. Women my own age won't go out with me because they feel like cradle snatchers."

"You'll have to tell us your life story over a drink some time," Quarrel cut him off. "What we need right now is your first impressions of the body."

"Of course. Sorry."

"I'm DI Nathan Quarrel, by the way." Quarrel introduced Katie and Debbie.

The pathologist grinned. "Well, Inspector, I hope you don't *quarrel* with me!"

Quarrel made his face smile. "Good one."

Stoddart squirmed. "I suppose you get that all the time, right?"

"Quite a bit."

"Sorry," Stoddart said again. "Note to self: try not to be an arse. Pleased to meet you all. Now, if you could just give me some room?"

3

Once there was no more Quarrel and Katie could do at the church, they left Debbie Brown and her team to continue taking photographs, and combing the area for evidence. The CSIs had set up a proper crime scene tent, and Dr Stoddart, who seemed competent enough once he got down to business, had estimated the time of death as Sunday afternoon, between 5pm and 7pm.

"That's based on body temperature, taking account of the fact that he's clearly been here overnight in damp conditions."

"What about actual cause of death?" Quarrel had asked. "No real signs of violence."

Stoddart had lifted one eyelid, then another. "Bloodshot eyes," he observed, "so quite probably asphyxia." He loosened the tie and shirt collar. "No bruising to the neck or throat to indicate strangulation. Possibly he was smothered. But I'll know more once I get him to the mortuary. As soon as the CSI guys have finished whatever they need to do with him here, I'll have him taken there. Will you and DS Gray be attending the post mortem?"

"I certainly will. Maybe not Katie." He'd handed Stoddart a card, glancing at his colleague, who looked relieved. "Give me a call when you've sorted out a time."

For Quarrel, the first order of business was notifying Murdoch's next of kin of his death. You always wanted to do this as quickly as possible, so that the news could be broken sympathetically. It had been bad enough back in the day when families occasionally got the bad news through some fleet-footed and over-zealous journalist, eager to be first with a close-up of a weeping spouse or parent, and asking banal questions about how they felt. These days, there was also the risk of a loved one's death being all over social media while the police attempted to get in touch.

Often, it was straightforward. You'd go to the deceased's home, knock on the door, and someone would answer. So Quarrel and Katie had driven the two and a half miles to Aldbury and tried that, but they'd drawn a blank. No one was at home. What was more, Katie had checked in with the station on the way here and established that no one had reported the dead man missing. Of course, his spouse or partner could be away, visiting family, or on business. But, whatever his domestic arrangements, it was possible that this was where Murdoch had been snatched from.

Or had he in fact been held in his own home while the tattooist had done his work?

At least the house gave them some insight into Alastair Murdoch's life. Aldbury was the quintessential English 'chocolate box' village, with quaint cottages, several manor houses, and a fair-sized duck pond at its heart, with a set of stocks and a whipping post nearby, both still in decent repair. No wonder so many film crews had used the village as the perfect setting for film and TV drama.

Murdoch had lived in what estate agents would probably have described as 'an enchanting double fronted detached character cottage', a decent sized property with Georgian windows. It stood in Trooper Road, handy for The Valiant Trooper, one of the village's two pubs, if Murdoch had liked his pint.

A two-year-old VW Passat sat in the drive. Peering through a window, Quarrel observed a beamed ceiling and mostly antique looking furniture. It all looked calm and orderly, but it wouldn't be long before Debbie Brown and her team were in here, turning out drawers and sprinkling fingerprint powder around.

"Let's split up," he proposed. "Knock on a few neighbours' doors and see if anyone knows who to contact. Otherwise we'll try his work. They must have a next of kin listed on his employee records."

So he took the house to the right while Katie went left. He found himself confronted by a timber door that had to weigh a ton, with an old fashioned bell-pull. He yanked on it and was rewarded by a solid clang from within.

A friendly-looking woman, probably in her seventies, opened up. She sported an apron with cartoon sheep on it, and a pair of yellow rubber gloves.

"Sorry," she said, flapping the gloves at him. "Caught me washing up." She was evidently the woman that dishwashers forgot.

Quarrel showed his ID and introduced himself. "We need to speak to your neighbour's family. Mr Alastair Murdoch? I think he lives there." He jabbed a thumb towards the Murdoch house.

Her face clouded. "Alistair? Why? Is he all right?"

He sidestepped the question. "Is there a Mrs Murdoch?"

She shook her head. "No, no. Amanda died. It must be four years ago. Just horrible. Breast cancer. But what's happened?"

"Are there any children?"

"A boy and a girl, but they've both fled the nest. Hannah got married a couple of years ago and lives up in the Midlands somewhere, Derbyshire, I think. Rob's a bit more local, I'm not sure where. I don't think he's married."

"Have you got contact numbers for either of them?"

"Sorry, no. But what's this all about? Is Alastair all right?"

"Did you see him at all yesterday?"

She pondered. "I saw him come back from church around quarter past eleven. I was out myself from just before noon until about 6pm. I didn't see him again."

"You've been very helpful, Mrs…"

"Sands. Frances Sands."

He met Katie back outside Murdoch's home. She had a similar story. Neighbours knew Murdoch had been widowed, knew his kids, but had no contact details.

"If all else fails, we can get into his phone," Katie said. "He must have had the children's numbers stored there."

"Not that we want to break the bad news over the phone, if we can help it. This Rob sounds the best bet, if we can track him down."

"The neighbour I spoke to thinks he's in the car business. Mercedes or Audi, they think. Maybe BMW. Probably turn out to be Hyundai or Kia."

"Still, it's something, I suppose." He'd retained one of Murdoch's business cards. He slipped it out of his wallet, checked the address, then looked at his watch. "Let's see what we can get out of his workplace. You'd hope someone would be in the office by now."

Someone was. Quarrel broke the bad news as gently as he could, said the death was being treated as suspicious, and urged Murdoch's partner, Gillian Piper, to keep it in-house for the time being. Piper Murdoch's personnel records were in good shape at least, with home, mobile and work numbers for both children. Katie jotted all the details down. Quarrel was grateful that there was no stalling over data protection.

"So you and Mr Murdoch were business partners?" Quarrel asked Piper.

"Quite a while now. We were on the same accountancy course, became friends, kept in touch after we qualified. Then, it must be a dozen or so years ago, I'd set up on my own, the business was booming, and I asked him if he'd like to come in with me. I can't believe he's gone." She was a petite blonde, probably of similar age to Murdoch. Her eyes filled with tears.

"I'm sorry for your loss," said Quarrel. And he was, even if he did feel that the stock condolence slid a little too easily off his tongue.

"When did you last see him?" Katie asked.

"Friday. We both finished about 6pm."

"How did he seem?"

"He was just Alastair. Oh, he always seemed a little lost. I don't think he ever recovered from Amanda's death. Never seemed to be really looking forward to weekends, unless he was seeing one of the kids."

"And was he?" Katie prompted.

"I don't think so. He talked about a bit of gardening, a walk or two, washing his car. Same old, same old, he always described it. It's such a shame. He was a thoroughly decent man. He'd been a parish councillor, a churchwarden... I

18

remember when he did jury service a couple of years ago, how proud he was to do his civic duty. Scrupulous about paying his taxes, despite us accountants being supposed to be all about the loopholes."

"Can you think of anyone who'd want to harm him?"

"No!" She almost laughed. "He wasn't the sort to have enemies. He had a really sweet disposition. Very popular." Fresh tears fell, and her face clouded. "Christ, poor Rob. His son. This will kill him."

"And the daughter, I presume," Quarrel suggested.

"Obviously. But it's only a few months since Rob's best friend was killed."

"Killed?" Quarrel echoed, all ears now.

"Hit and run. To the best of my knowledge, they're still looking for the driver. By all accounts, the lads were really close, mates since school. And now he's lost both parents."

"You've been helpful," Quarrel said. "We'll need to take a statement from you and maybe ask more questions, later. Just a couple more things for now, though. Was he at all interested in tattoos?"

Piper scoffed. "Alastair? Really not his style."

"What about Tarot cards?"

She frowned. "Is this a joke?"

"Just answer the question, please."

"No, obviously. He'd have laughed at that sort of mumbo jumbo. Tattoos and Tarot? Are you sure it's Alastair who's dead?"

"We've yet to do a formal identification, but there's no doubt." He looked her in the eye. "I can see you're very shocked and upset. Will you be okay? Is there anyone—"

She gave him a shaky smile. "I'm fine, really. It's just…" She shook her head. "Everyone will be upset. He was well liked here. We might pack up early today."

He held out a hand for her to shake. "We really are sorry for your loss."

*

It turned out that Rob Murdoch didn't work for a main dealer after all. He was head of sales for a business in St Albans that offered 'all makes servicing' and specialised in 'quality pre-loved cars'. The forecourt featured a number of shiny German prestige brands, nestling with the odd Jaguar, some Range Rovers and a few run-of-the-mill vehicles.

Rob Murdoch was with a customer when Quarrel and Katie arrived. They agreed to wait, asked for somewhere private they could speak to him, and were shown into his small office. They gratefully accepted the receptionist's offer of coffee and, while she was off sorting the drinks, settled themselves into chairs.

While they waited, Quarrel allowed his gaze to roam the room. Pictures of cars, and a couple of posters for the business, on the beige walls. Dark, nondescript carpet that probably hid a multitude of sins, should an oily mechanic drop by. Nothing personal on an incredibly tidy desk. It all spoke of a focused mind, something maybe inherited from Rob's accountant father.

The coffee arrived, and Quarrel was taking his first tentative sip when a slim, twenty-something man with slightly over-long, floppy brown hair breezed in, all apologies for keeping them waiting. He wore a blue and white striped shirt with a conservative blue tie, and his charcoal grey trousers appeared to match the jacket on the back of the chair behind the desk.

"Rob Murdoch," he said, offering a hand. Quarrel and Katie each shook it, introducing themselves.

"So how can I help?" Rob asked. "No problems with any of our cars, I hope, because we do all the necessary checks—"

"No," Quarrel assured him. "It's nothing like that. I'm afraid we've got some bad news for you, Mr Murdoch. You might like to sit down."

He did so, fear of what he was about to hear naked in his eyes. "Is it Dad?"

Quarrel thought it interesting that the son would jump to that conclusion, but then Alastair had presumably been his oldest close relative. It made sense. If, say, a grandparent had died, Alastair himself would presumably have broken the news.

"I'm afraid so," Quarrel confirmed, watching the younger man's face for his reaction, hating this aspect of his job even as he did so.

Rob Murdoch's face duly crumpled. He didn't burst into tears or fall instantly apart, but his shock and distress seemed genuine.

"Is he…" Rob swallowed. "What's happened?"

"I'm afraid a body's been found that we strongly believe to be your father's. Alastair Murdoch."

"Found?" Now Rob looked confused. "Found where? You mean he wasn't at home? Oh, God. What was it? A heart attack? Are you sure it's him? I mean, how can you be so sure? I only spoke to him yesterday. He was fine, fine. I…" He tailed off.

"We'll need someone to formally identify him," Katie said softly, "but we've no real doubts. He had his wallet on him with his driver's licence. The photo on the licence looks like the deceased. I'm so sorry for your loss."

"Oh, Christ." Rob clutched his hands to his head. "Oh, Dad. What happened? Where was he? When was he found?"

Such a barrage of questions was not unusual in Quarrel's experience. He often suspected it was as much about hoping there'd somehow been a terrible mistake of identity, as about a natural need to know exactly what had happened to a loved one.

"I have to tell you, your father's death is being treated as suspicious," Quarrel said.

Rob's eyes widened. "Suspicious? What does that mean? You mean he was…" He took his hands away from his head and held them out as if in supplication. "No. No, not Dad. There must be a mistake. Who'd murder Dad? Maybe someone lifted his wallet, and it's the thief you've found. I mean, those pictures on licences and passports… They could be anyone, half the time. You check, maybe you'll find my dad's reported his wallet stolen. Or maybe he'd just report the credit cards to the bank."

"Mr Murdoch," Quarrel said gently, "you really need to stop this now. DS Gray and I are really, really sorry, but we're as sure as we can be that the body we've found is your father's, subject to formal identification, of course. I'm afraid I can't go into too many details yet, as we're in the very early stages of an investigation. But you can help us now by answering some questions. Is that all right?"

Tears stood out in the younger man's eyes, and his lower lip wobbled. But he nodded.

"Yes, of course."

"You said you spoke to your father yesterday. About what time was that?"

He shrugged. "Oh, I don't know. Probably around noon. It's a sort of Sunday morning ritual. I give him half an hour after he gets back from church."

"Aldbury Church?" Quarrel knew it. 13th century with an iconic lych-gate.

"St John's, yes. Sunday Communion is 10am except the first Sunday of the month, when it's 8am."

"He'd been a churchwarden, I understand?"

"Yes. How did you know?"

"We spoke to your dad's business partner, Mrs Piper, when we were trying to get some contact details for you."

Rob nodded. "Gill knows? How's she taking it?"

Quarrel didn't want to be sidetracked. "So he always went to Sunday Communion?"

"Yes. Well, almost always. He'd have to be pretty poorly not to drag himself along. He and Mum both had faith, you see. It helped them, I think, when Mum was dying – you know she died?" Quarrel nodded. "I think it comforted him afterwards, too. He was lucky, I suppose."

"You're not a believer?"

"I was never big on religion. Less so when Mum got ill. Less still, after today, I suspect. What's the point of omnipotence, when a man like my dad can..." His voice broke.

"How did he sound when you spoke to him?"

Rob swiped at his eyes. "The usual. Interested in how I was. A bit of news about Hannah, my sister – oh, Christ, does she know?"

"Not yet. Would you prefer it if we—"

"No, no. I'll do it." His lip trembled again. "God knows how, though."

"When you spoke to your dad," Quarrel got back on point, "did you sense he was worried or frightened in any way?"

"I wish you'd tell me how he died."

"We'll give you more information as soon as we can. If you could answer the question?"

Rob Murdoch's brow furrowed in thought. "No," he said. "Honestly. He was the same as always. Dull. I don't mean that unkindly, but he seemed to lose all purpose after Mum died. They were real soulmates. Oh, he's conscientious – about work and other commitments, but pretty rudderless in his private life. I should have spared him more time."

"How long did the phone call last?"

"An hour. Up to lunch time. He was having soup." A sad smile fleeted across his face and was gone.

"Did he mention his plans for the rest of the day?"

"I honestly can't remember but, as I said, his Sundays were always a bit ritualised. Provided it wasn't too wet, he'd go to church, take my phone call, have a bit of lunch. Then he'd wash his car. Then go for a walk."

"Always the same walk?" Quarrel was thinking of the outdoor clothes Murdoch had been found in.

"Usually. It was one he and Mum always enjoyed. Up Tom's Hill Road and up the hill towards the Ashridge Estate, up to Bridgewater Monument. Then down the hill, past the golf course, through the wood, and along the road past Tring station. Then back to Aldbury."

Quarrel had done that walk himself a few times, beginning and ending at the Greyhound pub. It struck him that, if anyone wanted to abduct Alastair Murdoch, his incredibly regular habits would have made their job easy.

"Has he ever said anything that suggests someone might want to harm him? Or maybe he's made enemies, or fallen out with someone?"

"No, honestly. I mean, he's mentioned now and then that clients wanted to get round the tax laws and were a bit miffed that he insisted on everything by the book. One of them took his business elsewhere, I think. But we're not talking underworld figures here. At least, I don't think so."

"How miffed is miffed?" Katie wondered.

"I can only go by what he said. No names, obviously – Dad's hot on confidentiality. But he didn't give me the impression there'd been blazing rows. Miffed as in disappointed, I suppose. The client who found a new accountant didn't make a big drama out of it, either, as far as I know. Just moved on, presumably to a dodgier accountant."

Quarrel thought it was worth checking out, all the same.

"No one else who might have a grudge?"

"Dad was one of the good guys. I can't imagine anyone wanting to hurt him."

"Okay." Quarrel paused for a beat. "A couple of slightly unusual questions. Has he had anything to do with tattoos or tattooists?"

Rob shot him a quizzical look before considering the question. "No. He wouldn't have got a tattoo, ever, if that's what you mean, unless he's had a mid-life crisis I don't know about. He took a dim view of them. Went ape when Hannah got a butterfly tattoo on her ankle. Said she'd disfigured herself. And we're talking a very tiny motif."

"Could he have done a tattooist's accounts, though?"

"Not personally, unless it was a very successful tattooist. He and Gill do the higher end clients. The associates deal with smaller businesses and so forth. But what have tattoos got to do with anything?"

"What about Tarot cards? Does that mean anything to you?"

"*Tarot* cards? Tattoos and Tarot cards?" He actually laughed. "Oh my God. It *isn't* Dad. I don't know who you've found with his wallet—"

"Please," Quarrel interrupted. "Please don't clutch at false hope, Rob. We've good reasons for asking these questions, even if neither of them sound like they could possibly relate to your father." He watched the spark of hope die in the other man's eyes and felt wretched. "I'm sorry to be so blunt."

"Tarot cards," Katie said. "I take it you don't think they held any interest for your dad?"

"I know they didn't. He always dismissed anything like that as occult shit. At best, some sort of con trick. At worst, the slippery slope to Hell."

That sounded a bit extreme to Quarrel's ears. Alastair Murdoch might have been an upright citizen, but maybe he could also be the sort of religious zealot who got on your nerves.

"Okay," Quarrel said, "so he wasn't into Tarot himself. But did he know, or come into contact with, someone who *did* take it seriously? Someone who'd not take kindly to being ridiculed?"

Rob Murdoch stood up, walked over to his office window, and stared out at the cars on the forecourt, as if their solidity could wake him from this nightmare and put things back the way they were before the police came calling.

"This is insane," he said with his back to them. He turned to face them. "If there's been anything like that, Dad's never mentioned it." His eyes narrowed. "What aren't you telling me?"

Quarrel didn't answer immediately, weighing the question. Rob would have to view the body for identification purposes soon enough, and would have to be told about the Tarot tattoo before he saw it. But this was one of those weird cases the media were going to sink their teeth into and sensationalise. He wanted to control the message for as long as possible and, even if he swore the family to secrecy, there was always the chance they'd tell just one person, who'd tell just one person – in strictest confidence, of course. Finally, some enterprising confidante would want to share what they knew with the media, hoping for a finder's fee, or at least their fifteen minutes of fame.

"So the answer's no, as far as you're concerned?" he said.

"Dad wouldn't have any truck with fortune tellers. But he wasn't the kind to laugh in their faces, or tell them to piss off, either. He'd have politely made it clear that he wasn't interested."

"I think that's all for now," Quarrel said, rising.

Katie did likewise. "I know this is a shock, Rob," she said gently. "Are you okay? Do you want us to get in touch with anyone for you, or organise you a lift home?"

"No," he said decisively. "No, I'll be okay, I think."

"You're sure? Only, delayed shock…"

"I'll stay here for a while. Get my shit together. Then I'd better phone Hannah. I really ought to tell her in person, but she's up in Derbyshire. Bakewell. It's the thick end of three hours' drive, and I'm not sure I'm up to it."

"You're sure we can't contact the local police? Get them to break the news for you?"

"No. No, it's my job. When will I hear from you again?"

"Soon," Quarrel said.

4

At the Combe street police station, Quarrel and his team had been busy, trying to build on what little they knew about the case so far. Now they gathered in the major incident room that had been set up. A photograph of Alastair Murdoch and his Fool tattoo was the only image attached to what they called the 'Wall of Death' here – basically a large whiteboard. As the investigation progressed, more pictures, notes and, it was to be hoped, lines connecting them, would be added.

Quarrel stood at the front of the room, DCI Rachel Sharp at his side. Sharp was of similar age to himself, her blonde hair worn short and businesslike, her slim figure encased in a smart navy blue trouser suit. She was a bit of a workaholic, but found time to go to the gym every evening. She and her partner did long walks and the odd London theatre trip at the weekends, when work permitted. Sharp was the kind of boss that supported her DIs, but let them get on with their jobs.

"Okay," she said, when the chattering and fidgeting had subsided. "So this is a new investigation into the suspicious death of Alastair Murdoch, a forty-nine-year-old Aldbury man, whose body was discovered in Tring this morning. You already know the peculiarities of the case, and I know a number of you have been putting in some hard work in the last few hours. I'm going to hand over to DI Quarrel, who'll be leading the enquiry."

She nodded to Quarrel and returned to her seat at the front. Quarrel took a pace forward, letting his gaze roam over the faces in the room: Katie Gray; DCs Ricky James and Aliya Nazir; PC Libby Statham, a trained and competent family liaison officer; and a handful of other uniformed officers who had been attached to the team.

He began by outlining the grim discovery in the churchyard this morning, pointing to the photograph on the board for emphasis.

"Aliya," he said, "any luck getting a picture of Alastair before this happened to him?"

"Yes, guv." She waved a sheet of paper at him. "I got a decent pic from his firm's website. It's enlarged quite well, too."

"Could you pop it on the board? To the left of the tattoo picture, I think."

Aliya brought the sheet forward. She'd seemed a little sad lately. She'd confided in Katie about a relationship breakup she'd taken badly. While she busied herself with the ball of sticky putty at the bottom of the board, Quarrel continued.

"Forensics have combed the churchyard," he said. "Found a few odds and sods, but can't say with any certainty that they're relevant to our case. Bits of litter, a few fag ends. It seems unlikely any of it'll lead us to our killer. They did find a couple of shoeprints near the body which could be useful once we have some actual suspects. Size nines."

Aliya had affixed her photograph and was returning to her seat. He added a note about the shoeprint to the board.

"A team's been into Mr Murdoch's home," he continued. "Nothing to indicate he was attacked there. Well, no sign of a struggle. No half-eaten meal or half-drunk cup of tea to suggest he was rudely interrupted in anything. So it seems probable that he was taken from outside the home. I'm not surprised. He was dressed for the outdoors, including walking boots, and I understand from the son that he did the same walk most Sundays. Apparently he was a creature of habit. Had the killer been watching him, studying his routine?"

He looked Ricky James's way. "Ricky, could you and one of our PCs..." His eye fell on Sophie Monahan at the back of the room. "Sophie, I think. After we break up, we'll get a map and I'll show you the route for that walk. I'd like you to retrace his steps and see if there are any signs of a struggle along the way. If we're really lucky, the killer might have left something behind."

Ricky wore faded jeans and a tee shirt stretched over his beer belly. His hair was close shaved, his stubble pure designer. Quarrel had long suspected the thirty-ish DC tried to model himself on some of the TV cops he saw. It wasn't a look he quite carried off. But underneath the casual persona he cultivated, he was a thoughtful, conscientious detective.

Ricky grinned, half-turning round. "Got your walking boots with you, Soph?"

"No, but I might pick them up, after that rain."

"Do that," Quarrel said. "I don't want you ending up in the fracture clinic." He turned to Katie. "Katie, you were going to speak to your brother. See if he could suggest an expert on Tarot cards we can speak to?"

Katie pushed her long black hair back from her face. "Yep, and he's given me a name. I also did an Internet search, but it just left me more confused than ever. Just because someone's got a Tarot website, doesn't mean they know any more than the next person. Mick reckons this woman – Lucy Andrews – knows her stuff and also knows a lot of other people who could help, if need be. She lives in Leverstock Green, so she's quite handy for us."

"Right," Quarrel said. "So speak to Ms Andrews. See how much she can tell us about The Fool. Don't let her involve anyone else for now, though. We don't want investigation by committee, especially a committee of Tarot card readers. I'm interested in exactly what message that tattoo is trying to send. Because I'm pretty sure it's a message, and a deeply personal one. You don't spend hours tattooing something like that on a random stranger." Quarrel turned to the two images. "That message, whatever the hell it is, will help tell us why this –" He tapped the website photo of a smiling Murdoch. "– was turned into this." He indicated Murdoch's dead, tattooed face.

Ricky James raised a finger. "Guv, you said you didn't think this was random. So do you reckon our Mr Murdoch knew his killer?"

Quarrel considered the question. "Not necessarily, Ricky, but it's a good point. What I am sure of is that the killer knew something about Alastair, something that made him want to put that image on his face and then kill him."

"Maybe he just didn't like accountants?" Aliya suggested.

"'Let's kill all the lawyers?'" said Katie.

"Shakespeare?" Quarrel guessed.

She nodded. "Except Alastair was an accountant, not a lawyer. But Aliya might have a point."

"It's a good point," he agreed. "But even then, why *this* accountant?" He turned the thought over in his mind. "Aliya, do a follow-up at Piper Murdoch. Find out which clients Alastair had been dealing with recently, and whether everything was in order. And the son, Rob Murdoch said there'd been a client or two who wanted him to bend the tax laws in their favour. One even took his business away when Alastair wouldn't play ball. Who were they?"

"They might be a bit coy about it, mightn't they?" Aliya said.

"They might, although Gillian Piper was a good friend and was keen enough to cooperate earlier. And we want names at this stage, not accounting secrets. If they do get awkward about it, remind them this is a murder enquiry. Now, what's next?" He consulted the list he'd made earlier. "Oh, yes. Libby."

"Yes, guv?" PC Libby Statham practically sat to attention.

"I want you to make contact with Rob Murdoch as family liaison officer. Offer him every support. And talk to Derbyshire Constabulary. See if someone can offer similar services to the daughter, Hannah. We need eyes and ears on the family. I very much doubt they had anything to do with this, but you never know for sure. Presumably there's an inheritance coming to them. This tattoo could just be an elaborate distraction."

Ricky James stuck up a hand. "We should see if there's some sort of register of tattooists. That looks like professional work to me, not just someone doing a bit of amateur scratching. Maybe the work's distinctive enough that someone'll recognise it."

"Excellent point, Ricky. It was the next thing on my list. Could you look into that before you go for that walk?"

"Well volunteered, Ricky," grinned Aliya. Ricky made a face at her.

Quarrel took a step back. "As for me, I'm going to see what else is worth adding to the Wall, then touch base with Debbie Brown and our new pathologist. I want to see if there's any new forensics and get a time for the post mortem. Any other points?"

"Just one," DCI Sharp said. "We ought to put something out to the press. Just that we've found a body and we're treating it as suspicious? I'd imagine we don't want to mention the tattoo at this point."

"I'd say not," Quarrel said. "If any of our local nut jobs come confessing to the murder and don't know about that pretty big detail, we can easily weed them out." He paused. "Oh. One other thing. One of you – was it you, Aliya? – referred to the killer as a 'he'."

"That *was* me, guv," Aliya admitted.

"Any particular reason for that assumption? I'm not having a go at you. Just curious."

She frowned. "Not really. You're right, guv. Of course, it could have been a woman, although she would have had to manhandle the body from a car, presumably, to the church wall. But then, I can think of a few women strong enough for that. Say a firefighter, for example," she added slyly.

"You think I should put Laura on the suspect list?" Quarrel asked, deadpan. His partner, Laura Shaw, was a crew manager with Hertfordshire Fire and Rescue.

"Maybe not for now," Aliya said.

*

Leverstock Green had been one of a number of neighbourhoods subsumed into Hemel Hempstead after the Second World War, when Hemel had been developed as a new town. But it retained its original village centre and still regarded itself as very much a village, with a village hall, village shops, pubs and school, a village cricket club, and a football club.

Lucy Andrews lived in Pancake Lane, just around the corner from Holy Trinity Church, where Katie Gray had attended a friend's wedding last year. The road was not the widest, and flanked by hedgerows interspersed with mature trees, the house detached, faux-Tudor and quietly impressive. Either the Tarot reading business was booming, or someone in the household had a decently-paid job.

Katie had phoned ahead, and Lucy Andrews had been delighted to help Mick Gray's sister, and the police. Katie had half-expected the forty-ish woman who answered the door to be wearing a diaphanous, hippyish dress and have mad hair dyed bright purple or magenta. Instead, she wore her well-cut light brown hair medium length, and had teamed slate grey trousers with a lavender cardigan. A string of small pearls adorned her slender neck. She could have passed for a Conservative MP, or the wife of one.

"I'll make us coffee," Lucy said. "Unless you prefer tea?" Her accent wasn't quite cut-glass, but hinted at County set.

"Coffee's good. Black, no sugar." Katie leaned against the island in the middle of an impressive open-plan kitchen diner. "Nice place."

"Thank you. I made a sponge cake yesterday, if I can tempt you?"

Katie's stomach rumbled quietly. "I wouldn't say no." She watched the woman spooning ground coffee into a cafetière. "Were you affected by Buncefield?"

The village had made the headlines for all the wrong reasons in 2005 when the largest explosion in peacetime Europe had occurred at the nearby Buncefield oil depot. The blast had measured 2.4 on the Richter scale.

Lucy shrugged. "We had a couple of broken windows. We got off lightly. Some people had fallen chimneys, and some had more serious structural damage. A number of families were temporarily displaced. Where do you live?"

"I'm in Berkhamsted now, but back then I was in King's Langley with my parents." Katie had been not long out of uni and looking for her own place. "I still remember being woken up by what sounded like a huge door slamming. Our loft hatch burst open. That was almost four miles away."

"The smoke could be seen from Lincolnshire. That's about seventy miles." She poured boiling water over the coffee grounds, stirred the cafetière, then opened a round cake tin. "But you wanted to talk about Tarot?"

"That's right. In connection with a murder we're investigating."

"Really? How intriguing." Lucy carefully lifted a formidable-looking Victoria sponge from the tin, set it down on a board and picked up a knife.

"As I said on the phone, I'd appreciate discretion. We're anxious to control the flow of information at this stage."

"Understood, Sergeant."

"Please. Call me Katie."

"Let's sit at the table." Lucy nodded towards the large oak table in the dining area and handed Katie a mug of coffee and a plate bearing a huge slice of cake and a fork.

Katie chose a seat, and Lucy took the chair next to her. She pointed to a number of decks of cards in the middle of the table.

"I looked out a selection of Tarot decks," she said. "There are many different styles, and I'm afraid nothing's simple. There's no standard number of cards across all decks and, while the types of cards, the suits and their meanings are pretty much the same, the illustrations can vary greatly. The decks might be themed around nature, animals, fantasy, even dragons."

"But you say the meanings of the cards are the same? And I'm guessing The Fool features in every deck?"

"Yes. It's The Fool you're interested in?"

Katie briefly described the morning's macabre discovery in Tring.

Lucy blanched. "How horrible."

"I've got a photograph, if you can bear to look at it. I don't want to upset you, or put you off your cake..."

"I'm sure I can cope. And, as I said, I'm intrigued."

Katie removed the photograph of Alastair Murdoch's dead face from her briefcase and placed it on the table between them. The silver duct tape had still covered the mouth when the picture was taken.

"Poor man," Lucy Andrews said. "I'm guessing he didn't choose to have that tattoo?"

"That's certainly our theory."

"Well, it's The Fool, all right. And the design is after the Rider Waite deck. It's quite old-fashioned, and not many serious Tarot readers use them nowadays – but it's still one of the most popular in the English-speaking world today, in the sense that most readers will own a set." She reached for one of the decks and spread a few cards in front of them. Katie could see that they were a similar style to the tattoo that had desecrated Murdoch's countenance.

"The cards were drawn by an illustrator called Pamela Colman Smith," Lucy said. "But she took her instructions from A E Waite, an American-born British poet and mystic. They were originally published in November, 1909 by William Rider & Son of London. The following year, a guide by Waite, called *The Key to the Tarot*, started to be included with the cards. It gives some of the traditions and history behind the cards, descriptions of their symbols, and some information about interpretations."

Katie took that in. "But you say they're not much used any more. So do you think there's a particular significance in the choice for our murder case?"

Lucy smiled. "There are two possibilities I can think of. One's pretty simple. The other might sound a bit bonkers."

"Okay. Simple first."

"Well, it's entirely possible that your murderer has chosen the Rider Waite design just because they like it. They may not even know that much about Tarot, and maybe got what they do know off the Internet."

"And the bonkers?"

The smile faded. "You could be looking at a traditionalist, possibly a member of the Hermetic Order of the Golden Dawn or one of its offshoots. Your tattooist could be a Ritual magician, or even a Chaos magician."

Lucy was right. It did sound bonkers.

"Could you expand?"

"The Hermetic Order of the Golden Dawn was a secret society devoted to the study and practice of the occult and the paranormal in the late 19th and early 20th centuries. It was actually known as a magical order, but in Britain its focus was on invoking the intervention, or even the presence, of a deity, and on spiritual development. It's inspired many present-day concepts of ritual and magic, such as Wicca, and it's been one of the biggest influences on 20th-century Western occultism."

She sipped her coffee. "The original Order were all Freemasons, and their organisation was based on hierarchy and initiation like the Masonic lodges, although women were admitted on an equal basis with men."

Katie was scribbling notes. "But you're talking as if all this is in the past tense."

Another smile. "Yes and no. No temples from the original lineage of the Golden Dawn survived past the 1970s, but quite a few organisations have since revived its teachings and rituals. I can email you a list, if it would help."

"That would be great. So what's a…" Katie checked her notes, "a Chaos magician?"

"Chaos magic is a more contemporary practice. It developed in England in the 1970s. It draws on the philosophy of an artist and occultist called Austin Osman Spare, who died in the 50s. Spare developed magical techniques like automatic writing, based on his theories about the relationship between the conscious and unconscious self."

"Automatic writing?" Katie half-wondered if her leg was being pulled. "Does that really work?"

"He presumably thought so, and I guess his adherents do too. The thing about Chaos magic though, is it's all about getting results, rather than what practitioners see as the symbolic and ritualistic trappings found in other occult traditions, religions, and so on."

"But this tattoo. Surely that's *all* about ritual and symbolism? Doesn't that rule out Chaos magic?"

"You'd think so. But in fact a Chaos magician may experiment with various ideas – a sort of pick and mix approach – so each magician's working practice is different, with many authors explicitly encouraging readers to invent their own magical style."

"Would that affect their interpretation of the Tarot cards?"

"Yes," Lucy said. "They may well have their own interpretations of specific card meanings – more about the magical working they are trying to create than anything else."

Katie looked her in the eye. "And what about you? What do you believe?"

Lucy smiled. "Let's look at the cards before I answer that. A standard Tarot deck will have two types of cards: Major and Minor Arcana. The Major Arcana are stand-alone cards, each with its own unique meanings. They include our friend The Fool, The Devil, Strength, Temperance, The Hanged Man, and Death."

"And Minor Arcana?"

"They're similar to a deck of ordinary playing cards, divided into four suits – Wands for creativity and passion, Cups for emotion and empathy, Swords for thought and observation, and Pentacles for health and wealth. Each suit contains ten cards numbered from one to ten, and each suit also includes four face cards – Page, Knight, Queen, and King."

"And how do they predict the future?"

Lucy smiled again. "The truth is, most Tarot readers believe that the future is fluid, not fixed. We focus more on identifying possible outcomes for the person we're reading for, to arm them with information that can help them with decision making. I start a reading by dealing a series of cards from the deck and placing them in an arrangement called a spread."

"What's that?"

"Two of the most common spreads are the Three Fates and the Celtic Cross. I prefer the Cross. It consists of ten cards representing elements like past and future influences, personal hopes, and conflicting influences. Either way, each card in the spread is interpreted by its face value and its position in the spread. The position represents a different aspect of the question we're addressing."

"And the Three Fates?"

"That's a spread of three cards: the first represents the past, the second represents the present, and the third is the future. For me, it's a bit simplistic. It may be okay for a quick answer, but the Cross gives me a proper in-depth understanding, plus I get longer to work with the client."

"And there's some mystic power at work that makes the right cards come out?" Katie hoped her scepticism didn't show.

"Some readers think that way. That some supernatural power in the cards accentuates their talents. I prefer to think of the cards as simply a medium to help me to sense the subject's problem and help them understand it. To me, the cards have no actual power. They're just an aid to the reader."

"Is it possible that the killer's done some sort of reading, and The Fool is just the first card in the – what did you call it – spread?" Katie suddenly felt colder.

Lucy looked at her sharply. "You think that's the case?"

She shook herself. "No. I don't think anything right now. I was just speculating out loud."

Katie looked again at the cards and pointed to one in particular. "There's our Fool." The tattoo was more than a half-decent representation. "What can you tell me about him?"

Lucy smiled. "I'll try not to make this too much of a lecture."

"I don't mind."

"Well, the Fool stands for new beginnings and opportunity. That cliff edge at his feet is like a step into the unknown. The card represents a call to follow your heart – to trust where the Universe is taking you. You need to leave behind your fears and anxieties and be ready for new experiences and adventures. It's a time of great potential and opportunity if you just go with the flow." She picked up the card and held it up to Katie. "This is the card for you if you're struggling with worries or self-doubt. The Fool encourages you to acknowledge your fear, take a chance, and see where that first step will take you."

"Okay. That's for the upright fool though?"

"You've done some homework."

"Just a quick Internet search."

"But you're right." She turned the card upside down. "This tattoo is what we call The Fool Reversed. It accentuates the flip side of the card's meaning. So, if you've got a new idea or project, maybe something is holding you back. Maybe it's a fear of the unknown. Or the Reversed Fool may mean you're being reckless and taking too many chances. In trying to be spontaneous and adventurous, you're ignoring the consequences of your actions, putting yourself and others at risk. It can be a metaphor for bad choices, indecision, even downright stupidity. But it can also signify that ultimately knowledge is indistinguishable from ignorance."

Katie had taken a forkful of cake. It was delicious. She finished chewing and swallowed.

"Wow," she said. "That does all sound a bit negative. So maybe whoever did this thought our victim had been reckless or stupid?"

"Maybe," said Lucy. "As you can imagine, you can interpret the card with various degrees of subtlety. If your tattooist is sending a message, it's probably a deeply personal one, not a one size fits all."

Katie grinned ruefully. "I had a nasty feeling you were going to say something like that."

Lucy grinned back. "Can I spoil your day just a little more, then?"

"Be my guest."

"Well, the first thing I ask myself is whether The Fool has any significance at all."

"Surely it must."

"Most likely. But what if your killer's playing some sort of game? He or she was always going to do a Tarot tattoo, but left the choice to fate. They drew a card at random and The Fool Reversed came out."

"Oh, terrific." Katie took a reflective sip of her coffee. "I suppose you've got a point, though."

"Or they've chosen a Tarot representation of The Fool, but they really have the notion of the court jester, or 'licensed fool' in mind. Underneath the cap and bells and the pig's bladder on a stick, there could be a sharp mind – at least, that's how Shakespeare often depicted him. He was the man who could speak truth to power when others feared to do so."

"Like the Fool in *King Lear*?"

"Exactly. Though it didn't just happen in literature. When the French fleet was destroyed by the English at the Battle of Sluys in 1340, no one at the French court wanted to break the news to King Philip VI. In the end, it was the court jester who broached the subject by telling Philip that the French knights were much braver than the English, because 'the English don't have the guts to jump into the sea in full armour like our men'."

"But the card's reversed. Maybe the message is that our man didn't speak truth to power?"

"Maybe," Lucy Andrews agreed. "I'm really sorry, Katie."

"What about?"

"I'd have loved to give you something definitive to go with. I suspect I've muddied the waters still further for you."

Katie shook her head. "No, it's great. Maybe when we know more about our victim, we'll see more clearly how he relates to some of what you've said." She drained her coffee cup. "Please don't mention this to anyone else."

"Don't worry. I'm a Tarot reader. I'm like the confessional – good at keeping secrets." She smiled. "Perhaps I can do a reading for you?"

Katie checked her watch. The day was getting away from her. "Maybe another time."

5

Hemel Hempstead Hospital was located in Hillfield Road, just ten minutes' walk from the Combe Street police station. It was late afternoon and Quarrel had gone with his instinct to have Aliya Nazir accompany him to the post mortem. Rob Murdoch had been along to the hospital's mortuary earlier, supported by Libby Statham, and had formally identified his father's body.

Quarrel had been feeling bad that he knew Aliya had been unhappy in recent weeks, and that he probably hadn't been very supportive. As they walked, he asked her how she was doing.

"Only I couldn't help noticing you've not been your usual self," he added awkwardly.

She laughed. "Don't worry, sir. I know you know about me and Joe. It was me who asked Katie to tell you, so you'd understand why I was a bit off song, without me having to blub about it in your office."

"Joe? That was his name?"

"Yeah. It just didn't work out. What with the job and my bloody family…"

"They didn't like him?"

She sighed. "They didn't *know* him. Being white and non-Moslem was more than enough information for them. Oh, nothing *too* heavy, but the sniping when I was going to see him put me on edge, and then there were the cancelled dates when work got in the way. He couldn't hack it."

"He's a fool," Quarrel said. "He should have tried harder."

"Yeah, you're probably right. Anyway, some good's come out of it. I'm sick of Mum trying to engineer meetings with men she thinks are suitable – and disapproving those she doesn't. So I'm looking for my own place. It's about time."

Quarrel knew she still loved living with her parents.

"Anything looking promising?"

"It's early days. But, once I've got somewhere, I'm going to find myself someone in emergency services who understands about the job. It seems to work for you and Laura," she added.

"Yes, I'm very lucky." Quarrel wasn't a great one for talking about his private life, so steered the conversation round to Aliya's visit to Piper Murdoch.

"Alastair Murdoch might have mentioned to his son that some clients tried it on about tax dodges," she said, "but he didn't really deal with them himself. The only exception was some ageing rock star. Jimmy Steele?"

"Oh, I remember him," Quarrel said. "Goth Rock in the 80s and 90s."

"I'll take your word for it," said Aliya, who'd only been born in the early 90s.

"He was a contemporary of The Cure. Not really my stuff, to be honest. I think Katie Gray might have gone to see him in her Goth period." He frowned. "So what happened with him and Alastair?"

"Gillian Piper chose her words carefully, but it sounds like he'd invested in some complex tax avoidance schemes. The trouble is, there can be a thin line between avoidance and evasion, and some of these schemes have been deemed to be illegal. Alastair told Jimmy he wasn't prepared to do his accounts on that basis. Reading between the lines, Steele thought he could sweeten Alastair with some extra dosh on the side. Alastair took umbrage at the suggestion that he was corruptible, and there was a rather vocal row. Jimmy Steele stormed out, slamming doors and shouting about how Alastair had better watch his step."

"Gillian didn't mention any of that when I asked if he had any enemies."

Aliya shrugged. "I think it had genuinely slipped her mind until I asked the specific question. I don't think they took it that seriously. She said Jimmy always had a taste for the dramatic."

"True," Quarrel said. "And interesting. There was a lot of occult and supernatural stuff in his act, as I recall. His public persona was that of some sort of mystic. I can't remember if Tarot was involved at all. I don't even know if he believed in any of it. For all I know, it was all a gimmick dreamed up by his agent." They stopped at some traffic lights, waiting to cross the Marlowes. "I seem to remember he liked his tattoos though."

"He did," Aliya agreed. "I did a quick web search and came up with some pictures. Snake tattoos on his arms and a big angel of death thing across his back. But none of it looks at all similar to the work done on Alastair Murdoch's face."

"Still, someone ought to go see him," he said as the lights changed and they stepped into the road. "Maybe I'll take Katie along. Give her a fangirl moment."

The hospital mortuary was on Verulam Wing, at the south-east end of the site. Added in 1992, it had been kept fairly up to date, although it was light years from the space-age facilities often seen on TV crime shows. Dr Jordan Stoddart was waiting for them with his assistant, Sue Galloway, who seemed to have worked there forever. They were in full scrub suits, but this somehow contrived to make the pathologist even younger looking, like an adolescent dressing up.

Few coppers relished attending post mortems, not least because of the grisly sights and dreadful smells as the body was dissected and organs removed. But Quarrel always found it a depressing experience from the very start. There was something about being stretched out on a stainless steel mortuary table under harsh lighting that somehow diminished the deceased even more than death itself had managed to do. Alastair Murdoch was no exception.

Stoddart wore a microphone so that he could dictate the basics of his report as he worked. He began with what Quarrel recognised as a fairly standard introduction: the subject was the body of a well-nourished white male, aged approximately forty-nine years. As he got down to work, any lingering reservations Quarrel might have had about his competence evaporated. He oozed efficiency and professionalism.

He rolled back the eyelids. "Petechial haemorrhages are present in the eyeballs. These typically occur when blood leaks from tiny capillaries in the eyes, which can rupture due to pressure on the veins in the head. This suggests that the subject's airways were obstructed. However, there is no sign of facial congestion, nor any kind of bruising to the throat. This indicates that, if the cause of death *was* asphyxia, then it is unlikely to have been through strangulation."

He waited while Sue Galloway took some photographs. "So what obstructed the airways in this subject? The lips had been sealed with duct tape, which I shall remove in a moment, but this was presumably to keep him from crying out, and is unlikely to have caused him to suffocate by itself. So were the nasal passages blocked?"

He took a small flashlight and shone it into each of the nasal cavities, then selected a pair of narrow tweezers. "There appears to be some foreign matter inside the nostrils." He deftly inserted the tweezers into the right nostril and withdrew what looked like some traces of white fibre. His assistant was ready with a metal pan, in which Stoddart deposited the fibres before repeating the process a couple of times, and then turning his attention to the left nostril. Soon he had a tiny pile of the fibres.

"Each nostril contained white fibres, possibly cotton or similar material," Stoddart dictated. "They will need to be sent for analysis, but it seems probable that they come from a pillow or cushion that was held over the face, preventing the subject from breathing. As he attempted to draw air into his lungs, he inhaled some fibres from the object that was suffocating him. We may learn more when I open him up, but at present the most likely cause of death is suffocation by smothering."

Dr Stoddart continued his examination, turning next to the tattoo. He concluded that the work was very recent, and that death had occurred soon after completion.

"There's some slight bruising and abrasion on either side of the head, by the temples," he continued. "It suggests that the head was restrained in some way. Sue, can you get some pictures and take some measurements?"

Whilst his assistant obliged, Stoddart stood back and studied the rest of the body. Quarrel had questions, but he preferred to hold off while the pathologist made his external examination and drew his initial conclusions.

"More bruising and abrasion across the arms, the torso and the legs," Stoddart observed. He glanced at his colleague.

"We'll need to measure and photograph that too, but the evenness of the marks is suggestive of some sort of strapping."

He paused and turned to Quarrel and Aliya. What with his scrub cap and mask, not much of his face was visible, but his disquiet was naked in his eyes.

"Well, Inspector. I've seen the results of some frenzied attacks in my time, but this isn't one of them. Quite the opposite. We'll need to do some toxicology screening, because, as yet, I'm not sure how our Mr Murdoch got into the situation he found himself in. No defensive wounds, nor any other sign that he was involved in any sort of struggle. I'll be checking the nails for any skin traces but, if I were a gambling man, I'd bet we won't find any."

"So what are you saying?" Quarrel asked.

"He was most likely drugged or something, taken to wherever the killer does his work, and strapped down with his head immobilised and his mouth taped. The killer sets about what looks like a meticulous and painstaking tattoo and, soon after it's finished, he smothers his victim with a pillow or similar. Finally, he places the body by the church in Tring. It all speaks to me of self-control, not frenzy."

"Me too," Quarrel agreed. "This took planning and utter ruthlessness."

"And it makes the tattoo even more significant," Aliya added.

"Go on," Quarrel prompted.

"Well," she said, "we already think the tattoo's personal in some way. Yet, whatever our killer felt about Mr Murdoch, there were any number of ways he could have killed him after he'd done it. He had him utterly in his power. He could have tortured him. Laid into him with a knife. God, even if asphyxiation was his chosen method, manual strangulation, or even a garrotte, would be a really intimate, personal touch. Looking into the victim's eyes until the light died."

"I worry about you sometimes," Quarrel murmured. "But you're right, Aliya. Stifling someone with a pillow? It's more like euthanasia than cold-blooded murder."

"I disagree, sir," Aliya said. "At least in this case. I think it's totally cold-blooded. Like I said, the tattoo's the thing. Once that was finished, the killer simply wanted to snuff out the victim's life. This was simple and not messy."

"She makes a good point," Stoddart concurred.

"She does," Quarrel said, pleased to see signs of the old Aliya returning. "And there's another thing. If the tattoo means something, so does the church. Why there, in particular?"

"As opposed to any other body dump?" Aliya said.

"Or even any other church? We're assuming he disposed of the body under cover of darkness, but he didn't just dispose of it. He propped it up against the wall of St Peter and St Paul. He chose the place. Why?"

"We know Murdoch didn't have an association with it. St John's in Aldbury was his church."

"Could you try and see the vicar, Aliya? See if any of this makes any obvious sense?"

"Sure."

Stoddart returned to the job in hand. The stage of organ removal was reached, and it was noted that, prior to his murder, Alastair Murdoch had been a pretty healthy human being.

Having removed the stomach, the pathologist emptied out the contents into a container.

"So what do we have?" he mused. "There are semi-digested food particles here. We know that the length of time it takes to empty the stomach varies, depending on the nature and consistency of the food, the environment, and emotional or psychological considerations. Still, even taking all that into account, we can make a working assumption that this chap probably died no less than six hours after his last meal."

"I'm not surprised," Quarrel admitted. "There's hours of tattooing work here. Factor in the time between him being taken and the work commencing…"

"It sort of tells us something, though," said Aliya. "In all probability, our killer didn't feed him after he abducted him."

"For all we know," Stoddart said, "the killer ate a sandwich in front of him, while his victim starved."

It was a cruel image, and one that depressed Quarrel. He remembered his conversation with Rob Murdoch. "He told his son he was having soup for lunch and going for his walk in the afternoon." A thought crossed his mind. "I'll be back in a moment."

He stepped out into the corridor, took out his phone and called Ricky James, whom he knew was retracing Murdoch's steps with Sophie Monahan. The DC answered on the third ring. He sounded as if he was eating.

"Where are you?" Quarrel asked.

There was a pause.

"Up near the monument, guv."

"The Brownlow?"

"Yeah," Ricky mumbled guiltily. Quarrel smiled, guessing that pause had been the DC hastily swallowing whatever was in his mouth.

The Brownlow was an open-air café next to the National Trust gift shop on the Ashridge Estate, a few hundred yards from the towering monument to the 3rd Earl of Bridgewater. On weekends and holidays, it was frantically busy, with long queues, and customers jostling for space on bench seats at wooden tables. Even at relatively quiet times, there was often a queue for service.

Quarrel and his partner, Laura, loved walking around Ashridge, 5,000 acres of woodland, chalk downlands and meadows with a variety of wildlife from deer to squirrels. Every season had something to offer: in the summer the sun streamed through the trees, dappling the footpaths, and Quarrel especially loved the reds and russets of autumn. He had a passion for the Brownlow's giant scones, served with strawberry jam and a coronary's worth of whipped cream. Laura bemoaned his ability to consume one and not gain an ounce on his tall, lanky frame.

He wondered if one of those scones had been Alastair Murdoch's last meal. Somehow, the thought of the man doing a walk he loved and stopping off for a sweet treat made him even sadder.

"That's good," Quarrel told Ricky. "Saves me sending you back there. You've got Alastair Murdoch's picture with you?"

"Yep."

"Show it to the staff. See if they remember him stopping off there yesterday. Did he have anyone with him? Did anyone sit with him and engage him in conversation? Or did they notice anyone watching him, maybe acting suspicious?"

"You think the killer might have been stalking him up here?"

"I think the killer may have studied his movements. Either he knew the best place to strike, or he was following him, biding his time."

"Broad daylight, on a Sunday? I'm really not convinced he was snatched from this walk, guv. Too risky."

"Maybe. But maybe the killer was patient, seeking an opportunity. If not yesterday, maybe today, or tomorrow. Yesterday was when he got lucky. Chat up the staff. In all probability, they were run off their feet and wouldn't have noticed a gorilla in a tutu, but it's worth asking."

He returned to the post mortem and Stoddart resumed his work. There was nothing else of note to be found. The exact time of death remained a working estimate, and they were no closer to knowing Murdoch's last movements before he met his killer. It was hopeful that the toxicology might reveal how the victim had been subdued during or prior to his abduction but, even then, there was no reason to suppose it would bring them any closer to identifying the killer.

Conjectures whirled in Quarrel's mind. He had a bad feeling about this. The killer had been on a mission, every aspect of his victim's death carrying some meaning for him. Quarrel sincerely hoped the mission related to Murdoch and Murdoch alone. If not, this could be only the beginning of a nightmare.

6

After his gloomy prediction that walking the route Alistair Murdoch would have taken the previous day would prove fruitless, Ricky James returned to the station with a sense of triumph. Quarrel was in the major incident room with Katie Gray, adding notes and images to the Wall when Ricky and Sophie Monahan walked in, excitement on both their faces.

"You two look pleased with yourselves," said Quarrel.

"We might just have something, guv," Ricky said.

Quarrel's stomach muscles tightened. "So tell us."

Ricky opened an app on his phone and showed him an Ordnance Survey map on the screen. Quarrel preferred a nice, big physical map, ideally laminated against wet weather. It was better, in his view, than squinting at a screen, and you could see more of an area at a time. But now was not the time for that debate.

"We started to think there was a particular area where Mr Murdoch might have been attacked," Ricky said. "Still risky, but if there was no one else about, you could pull it off."

"Where, exactly?"

"Well, see this fork here." Ricky stroked the screen. "There's actually two options. You could stay on the golf course, or you could turn right into this small wood."

Quarrel nodded. "Aldbury Nowers. It's managed by the local Wildlife Trust."

Ricky shrugged "Whatever. Anyhow, if he went that way, the path joins a trail, and he'd bear left, back toward Tring station. You come out of the woods, onto a bridleway, and from there you come down to the road leading back to the station. It's possible the killer was loitering somewhere on that stretch, lying in wait."

"Or that he followed our man," Sophie added. "Maybe he slipped something into Alastair's drink at the Brownlow—"

"He was there?" Katie checked.

"Yeah," Ricky said. "Good idea of the guv's to ask the staff. Turns out Mr Murdoch was a regular. So yes, they remembered him coming there yesterday, although they're utterly useless as regards the time.

"Always a granola bar and a tea, they said," Sophie added. "He really was a creature of habit."

"So you're thinking what?" Quarrel said. "The killer sits down with him? Maybe distracts him and drugs his tea? Then what?"

"Well," Ricky continued. "Say he does that? Whatever drug he used – and we know there are ways and means to get hold of most things – we thought he'd have somehow judged the dose, just enough to make our man a tad woozy. He comes up to him on the trail, when there's no one about. Asks if he's okay. Alastair says no, not really. He gives him support back to the road, maybe offers him a lift. He's left his car there already."

"Once in the car, he injects him with something, or uses a chemical-soaked cloth," added Sophie. "Anything to finish knocking him out."

"Not a bad theory," Quarrel acknowledged. "Maybe the cloth. The PM found no injection marks."

Ricky practically beamed at him. "It's more than a theory, guv. There are a couple of cottages opposite where you emerge onto the road. Me and Soph knocked on doors. Seems one of the occupants was tidying her front garden. She saw a couple of men come out onto the road, one supporting the other as if he was poorly. Helped him into a car, then drove off."

Quarrel's pulse quickened. "I don't suppose she could describe them?"

"Useless for that, I'm afraid. She thinks the ill man wore a black jacket, which could be our guy's Belstaff. Other guy might have had a blue anorak thing with the hood up. Car was dark, she thinks. Big, maybe. Not a clue about make and model."

"I'm guessing she didn't get the registration, then."

"Why would she?"

"But she was sure it was a man?"

"Fairly, guv. I did push her on that. Mind you, with the hood…"

"And what time was this?"

"Maybe four, four thirty."

"Get someone to check out CCTV footage in the area around that time. It's a long shot, but you never know. Did the café staff notice Alastair talking to anyone?"

"No. Too much to ask on a busy afternoon."

"Okay." Quarrel jotted a couple of notes on the board. "I don't suppose you got anywhere with that tattooist's register?"

"Not as such, no," said Ricky. "There isn't one. But I at least established that anyone offering body art services has to be licensed by the local authority. Registered premises and practitioners have to display a certificate showing that the premises and equipment have been inspected for cleanliness and safety and that the people doing the work are properly trained."

"So there's no national database?"

"No, but if we can get the lists from all the councils in a radius, we can start showing the tattoo around and see if anyone recognises the work. Assuming the killer's registered locally."

"Sophie, can you get on that?" Quarrel said.

"Of course." Monaghan scribbled a note in her notebook.

"It's a fair representation of The Fool from a particular Tarot deck – which one was it, Katie?"

"Rider Waite," Katie supplied.

"That's it. So I suspect any competent tattoo artist could copy the design. But there might be some technical quirks that an expert would notice."

"Are we any clearer what the tattoo means?" Ricky asked.

"Lots of possible interpretations," Katie said. "And it's possible that the killer would have stretched one of them to fit whatever point he was making."

"But surely," said Sophie, "if he wants to make a point, then he wants it understood?"

"You'd think. But maybe it's satisfying enough to have made the point. He might even think it makes him extra clever that it's all a bit cryptic."

"Or we're crediting him with too much cleverness," said Ricky. "Maybe all he's saying is that Murdoch's literally a fool."

"We might never know until we catch him and ask him," Quarrel said. But he was pleased with his team. "Good work, you two. But speaking of suspects, we have a potential suspect to check out." He smiled at Katie. "Come on, Katie. Let's see if we can chat to a rock god."

*

Jimmy Steele lived in an imposing Victorian pile in Little Gaddesden, not too far from the Ashridge Estate, where Alastair Murdoch had been spotted at the Brownlow, buying a granola bar and a cup of tea shortly before, it seemed, meeting his killer.

Jimmy Steele had grown up a posh Berkhamsted lad from a comfortably-off family and had settled just three miles from his roots. The village of Little Gaddesden lay within an area of outstanding natural beauty and a conservation area protected by the National Trust. The area's charms had attracted many a film crew, as well as a fair few celebrities looking for an idyllic place to call home.

The village fairly bristled with period properties of note, and Steele's mansion was one of them, all pointed roofs and tall chimneys. With dark clouds behind it, it reminded Quarrel of an old, dark house in a Hammer horror film.

"Spooky," Katie commented, evidently sharing his thoughts. "All it needs is a couple of gargoyles."

The house was set in substantial grounds backing onto open countryside. Their arrival was heralded by a sonorous *boom* in response to Katie yanking on the old-fashioned bell-pull, followed by the barking of what sounded like a large dog, When Steele himself opened the door, he was clutching the collar of a monstrous animal, still barking, which looked exactly like Quarrel's mental image of the Hound of the Baskervilles.

Jimmy Steele's public image was unsmiling, a study in seriousness, but the man who admitted them to his high-ceilinged hall was all smiles and professed willingness to help the police.

"Of course, of course," he said smoothly. "Come in, come in. Let me just shut Jasper away."

He led the still barking dog down the corridor, guided it into a room near the end and closed the door. It gave a couple more desultory barks, then fell silent.

"Come through," he said when he returned, and led them into a room you could probably hold a small ball in, with a large open fireplace, original-looking ceiling beams and well-matched antique furniture. It was an airy room, lightly decorated, and a contrast to the house's forbidding exterior.

Without his pale make-up and heavy eyeshadow, Jimmy Steele bore only a passing resemblance to the familiar figure of goth rock legend, although he still wore his trademark jet black hair – which surely came out of a bottle these days – shoulder-length. He had teamed a black waistcoat with faded denims and a crisp white shirt.

"Well, this is exciting," he said. "I take it this isn't a drugs bust? Only we haven't had one of those for years, and neither Anthea nor me touch the stuff these days. We won't knowingly let it in the house, either." Anthea Swallow was his third wife, a former fashion model, maybe twenty years his junior.

Quarrel was still taking in the room. Framed gold and platinum albums shared wall space with what were almost certainly genuine old masters plus, slightly incongruously, a Picasso and an Andy Warhol.

"It's not about drugs, Mr Steele," he said. "It's about your former accountant, Mr Alastair Murdoch."

"Yeah? I really can't imagine why. Alistair and I parted the ways months ago. Hey, what's he been accusing me of? My investments are totally legit—"

Quarrel held up a palm. "Let me stop you there, Mr Steele. We're not the tax police and it's not about your investments. Not directly, at least."

"What does that mean?"

"Mr Murdoch was murdered sometime last night."

Steele's mouth fell open. "No way! Seriously? Christ, what happened?"

"We can't say much for the moment, but we'd appreciate it if you'd outline your movements yesterday."

His face darkened. "Outline my what? Jesus, am I a suspect?"

"If you'd just answer the question."

"No way." He pulled a phone out of his jeans pocket. "I'm phoning my lawyer."

Quarrel attempted a reassuring smile, but also injected a little iron into his tone. "Of course, sir. That's your right, if you'd prefer to help us with our enquiries at a formal interview down at the station. But no one's accusing you of anything right now. This is just an informal chat, one of many we'll be having with different people."

Steele stood there looking indecisive, the phone still in his hand. "Yeah, but why me? I mean, yeah, I suppose someone told you our last get together wasn't exactly cordial, but come on. I'm not going to murder him over that."

"Over what, sir?" Katie said.

He stared at the phone as if he thought he might find the answers there, then pushed it back in his pocket.

"Look, you'd best sit down." He gestured at a sofa. Quarrel and Katie sat.

"Look," he said again, "you've got this all wrong. I mean, yeah – I fell out with Alastair a bit. See, someone came up to me with these great investment opportunities. Great return, no tax."

"Tax evasion," Quarrel suggested.

"No, no, Inspector. Tax *avoidance*. And yeah, yeah, I know it's fashionable to knock that, say it's wriggling out of our civic duty. But I've never seen a headstone saying 'He wished he'd paid more tax'. Anyone who can pay less is gonna do so, am I right? If something's a loophole, then close it. Don't knock guys who exploit something perfectly legal."

"Except ordinary people aren't able to invest in these fabulous schemes, are they?" Katie pointed out.

Steele shook his head pityingly. "You have to see the big picture. Taxes get spent on loads of things no one wants. If I can save a few grand, I can donate it to causes that really matter."

Katie opened her mouth to argue, but Quarrel forestalled her with a touch on the arm.

"But Mr Murdoch didn't support your philosophy, did he?" Quarrel said.

"It's true. He got quite pompous. Said it wasn't the sort of thing Piper Murdoch could condone. I suppose I got a bit excitable and shouty. Said I was taking my business elsewhere and went off in a huff."

"I believe you also told him he'd better watch his step. What did you mean by that?"

Steele blinked. "Did I say that? I honestly can't remember. It was months ago. It sounds the sort of thing I might say, though."

"It sounds like a threat."

"No, no, no. It's just a stupid, stroppy thing to say. Look, the truth is, Anthea gave me a right bollocking when I told her. Said Alastair knew what he was talking about and I should listen to him. Made me drop the investment idea and said I should apologise to Alastair. I dropped the scheme, but I was too pig headed – maybe embarrassed, too – to go back to him. I just found a new accountant and moved on."

"And your movements yesterday?" Quarrel asked again.

He sighed. "Let's see. I got up late, made myself some brunch about 11am. Some of the guys who are playing on my new album came over about noon and we spent some time in the studio. We broke up, it must have been gone five. I had a bite up the road at the Bridgewater Arms around six. I've got three musicians who can vouch for me most of the afternoon, and the staff at the pub know me and will confirm I was there in the evening. I've no one who can vouch for me in the morning, though. Anthea's on a girlie weekend in Paris."

It sounded plausible, but then Quarrel thought that, if Steele had wanted to arrange Murdoch's abduction and all that had followed, he probably had deep enough pockets not to get his own hands dirty.

"I seem to recall there was a bit of mysticism in your act, and your lyrics," he said.

"Still is. It's just an act, mind."

"Has it ever included anything to do with Tarot, though?"

"Tarot? No, not really. There's a song about a Ouija board on my third album, *Face Your Fears*. Tarot's a bit tame. Anthea's had a couple of readings done, I think. She didn't take it seriously. But what's that got to do with anything?"

Quarrel ignored the question. "I know you've got some impressive tattoos. Have you had any new ones recently? Are you still in touch with the tattooist?"

"No. That was all years ago. This is all getting a tad surreal, Inspector."

Quarrel stood up. "You've been helpful, Mr Steele. If you could just give us contact details for the band members who were here yesterday?"

"I'll get them for you."

Steele left them alone. Katie wandered around the room, looking at the artwork, and then studying the albums.

"I used to love this one," she said, standing in front of a gold disc.

"Which one's that?" Steele said, coming back into the room with a piece of paper that looked as if it had been ripped from a notebook.

"*Night Wind*," she said.

He handed the paper to Quarrel. "Names and mobile numbers." He went and stood beside Katie. "Are you a fan? You look too young."

Quarrel saw her blushing. "I was sort of a 21st century goth, although, to be honest, it was always more about the clothes and the music than anything else. Me and my mates saw one of your gigs at the O2, though."

"I'll have to send you a signed photo. Oh, and I'm playing the Birmingham Arena in the summer. I could get you tickets." He looked Quarrel's way. "Or would that be bribery and corruption?"

"Probably not a good idea," Quarrel said. It wasn't, but he saw disappointment flash across her face.

"Well, as I say. Always happy to help the police." He shook both their hands, holding Katie's perhaps a little too long.

"We'll check out your alibis," Quarrel said. "I'm sure it's just a formality."

"By the way, Inspector," Steele said at the door, "is that a hint of Yorkshire I detect in your accent?"

Quarrel felt himself stiffening. "Maybe. I lived there for a while as a kid. But that was a long time ago."

"I knew it. I'm good at accents. Got an ear for it."

"You should write a rock version of *My Fair Lady*," Katie said. "You could be a goth Henry Higgins."

Steele laughed. "Great idea. I'll give you a percentage of the profits if I do."

Back in Quarrel's Volvo, he asked Katie for her impressions.

"If you believe him," she said, "that row sounds just a storm in a teacup, doesn't it? And not exactly a powerful motive for murder."

"I suspect he's a man used to having his way."

"Even so. One thing struck me, though."

"Which was?"

"He seemed shocked to hear Alastair had been murdered. But he didn't seem sorry."

7

The team were assembled for the end of day briefing. Katie had caught them up on her discussions about Tarot with Lucy Andrews, and Quarrel had filled them in on the visit to Jimmy Steele. Now Ricky James was winding up his report back from his and Sophie Monahan's circular walk from Alastair Murdoch's home, and the possible sighting of him being helped into a car – or abducted.

"No CCTV at that spot," he concluded. "Wouldn't you know it? The killer either got lucky, or he knew there wasn't a camera."

"The homework he did, making sure he knew his victim's movements, I wouldn't be surprised if he knew," Katie commented.

"I suppose we could get the nearest cameras checked out," Quarrel said. "Work out a window in time and look out for dark cars, uncertain colour and unknown make or model, with two men in. See if we can spot Alastair."

"Shall I get the specialists on it?" Ricky asked.

"Please," Quarrel said. Ricky sat down. Quarrel turned to Sophie. "Sophie, you were going to talk to local councils about lists of registered tattooists?"

"Still working on that, guv. Getting through to the right number's often a struggle, then half the time it goes to voicemail. Those I got through to are going to call me back."

"Let me know if you get too messed about," DCI Sharp said. "I'm not above kicking chief executives' arses."

"Thanks, boss," Quarrel said. "Aliya," he said to Nazir, "did you speak to the vicar at St Peter and St Paul?"

"I did. He's pretty upset that someone chose his church as a body dump, and hasn't a clue why it was chosen. He'd never heard of Alastair Murdoch."

"Did you show him a photo?"

"Yep. He didn't recognise him. Had no idea what The Fool might be about, either."

"Okay for now. But I still think the location has some significance for the killer."

"Anyway, guv," Aliya said, "I thought, since I was speaking to vicars, I'd go see the one at St John's in Aldbury, where Alastair worshipped."

"Good thinking," Quarrel said approvingly. "Anything useful?"

"He was well liked, rarely missed a service, couldn't do enough for the church. Seemed to find some comfort there after his wife's death. I asked if the vicar knew anyone who might have it in for him. No one she could think of. I also asked about Tarot, but I drew a blank there too. Or so I thought at first," she added with a smile.

"You've got something?"

"The vicar rang me back just before I came into the briefing," she said. "Sorry – I didn't get a chance to tell you. Seems she thought it over after I'd gone, and remembered that a woman Alastair worked closely with on some fundraising projects had had some Tarot readings done. The vicar wasn't sure how seriously she'd taken it, but thought I ought to know."

"And does this woman have a name?"

Aliya grinned again. "She does. Anthea Swallow."

Quarrel stared at her. "As in Jimmy Steele's wife?"

"The same. Seems she's originally an Aldbury girl, and her family used to worship at St John's. She went on to be a bit of a wild child, as you probably know – quite literally sex, drugs and rock 'n' roll. But she's calmed down more recently, and she returned to the fold a year or so ago, not just attending services, but wanting to help."

"And she worked with Alastair?" Quarrel pursed his lips. "I can't believe she never mentioned it to her husband. So why didn't he say anything to us?

*

"Why?" Steele's grin was insolent. "How about, you never asked?"

As soon as the briefing had broken up. Quarrel and Katie had headed back to Little Gaddesden. Steele hadn't looked exactly delighted to see them – had looked half-inclined to turn Jasper the Baskerville Hound loose on them, and had admitted them with none of the bonhomie that had accompanied their previous visit.

Quarrel knew he shouldn't let the man's attitude needle him, but it had been a long day.

"You think this is funny? We had to *ask* you whether your wife knew Alastair Murdoch? Whether she was, in fact, a member of the same church congregation as him, and had been working with him on fundraising projects?" Quarrel folded his arms. "How on earth would we know to ask that, Mr Steele? You knew we were investigating Mr Murdoch's murder, we specifically asked you about Tarot, and you admitted that Anthea had dabbled in some readings. But you deliberately chose not to mention that she was seeing Alastair. I'm wondering why."

"Maybe I didn't know." Jimmy Steele walked over to a platinum disc and straightened the frame. "Maybe she hadn't told me. We don't live in each other's pockets, Inspector. She did know Alistair and I had parted badly and that I was too embarrassed to go back and apologise. So maybe, when they started working together, she decided it was best not to tell me."

Quarrel cocked a sceptical eyebrow. "Is that your story? That you had no idea?"

"I'll give you Anthea's mobile number. As I told you before, she's in Paris. You can ask her if she told me."

"And how do we know you didn't ring her as soon as you closed the door on us this afternoon?" Katie said. "How do we know you haven't told her what to say?"

"Plus," Quarrel added, "the notion that she was keeping her relationship from you makes it worse, if anything."

"Relationship?" Steele guffawed. "Those two? Do me a fucking favour."

"Really?" Katie said. "Let's look at that for a moment. Mr Murdoch loses his wife and finds some solace in the church. Then your wife returns to the same church, presumably looking for something spiritual. They start working together. Closely, according to the vicar. And now you say she kept that from you?"

He sat down. "So what?"

"Well," Katie continued, "maybe you found out, and you didn't like it. Because she chose not to tell you, you read more into it than perhaps was there. Or maybe there *was* something. He was closer to her age than you are. Maybe you got jealous and decided to punish Mr Murdoch. You must have plenty of connections, or connections with connections."

"This is bullshit," Steele said. "I'm definitely phoning my lawyer."

"Do that," Quarrel said. "You might need them. For now, though, give us your wife's number and we'll talk to her. We'll also have another little chat with those convenient alibis of yours from yesterday. If we're not satisfied, our next conversation will be at the station, under caution."

"This is harassment," Steele protested. "The media will be interested in this."

"So call them," Quarrel said. "Tell them how you withheld information relevant to a murder enquiry. I'm sure that'll read well."

"Get out of my house."

"As soon as you give us that number."

Steele rose, crossed to a paper-strewn table under a window, and scribbled a number on the back of a used envelope. He practically thrust it into Quarrel's hand.

"We'll be in touch," Quarrel said. "We'll see ourselves out."

*

Calling Anthea Swallow was the last job on Quarrel's list today, so he decided to do it from home, rather than go back to the station.

Quarrel and Laura lived in a three-storey terraced house by the canal. When they'd first decided to try living together, she'd moved into his home in the neighbouring village of Northchurch. After a year together, they'd committed to selling both their houses and sinking the proceeds into this place.

The house in Dudswell was a light and spacious property with high ceilings. There were two double bedrooms and a bathroom at ground level, whilst the living accommodation and kitchen lay on the first floor. The layout suited them, and Quarrel enjoyed the views of the canal from here, often relaxing – insomuch as he ever relaxed – while watching the local wildlife and the narrow boats going by. He used the top floor bedroom as an office.

Laura's watch worked a four day on, four day off, shift rota, consisting of two day shifts and two night shifts, with some weekend work. She and Quarrel were often like ships in the night, and she was already at night shift by the time he got in.

The arrangement didn't bother either of them. Since moving out of his paternal grandparents' home, Quarrel hadn't lived with anyone, until three years ago when Laura had moved in with him. She had also lived alone since splitting with the man she'd married at nineteen. The marriage had crashed and burned in less than three years, and she was now thirty-nine, so both of them were used to their own space. Both were accomplished cooks, so they shared cooking duties when they were together and were happy to look after themselves when work separated them.

They also had a well-organised household, with the week's meals planned out in advance. Quarrel consulted the list and saw that both were having salmon fillet with salad today. Laura had cooked both the fillets and eaten hers before she left for work, so Quarrel didn't have much to do to feed himself tonight. He'd deal with that after this call.

He got the kettle going and threw a teabag in a mug. While he waited for the water to boil, he powered up his laptop and, seated at the kitchen table, ran an Internet search on Anthea Swallow. Her grandparents on her mother's side had been Danes, which might explain her Ice Maiden good looks and her height, apparently an inch taller than her husband. The grandparents had moved to England, where her mother had been born and had married Roger Swallow, a property developer. The couple had settled in Aldbury and produced Anthea and a son, Freddie.

Anthea had been spotted by a modelling agency at sixteen, married an artist at eighteen, divorced at nineteen. By the age of twenty, she was running around with actors and rock musicians and was all over the gossip magazines for her excessive lifestyle. Then, thirteen years ago, she'd met and married Jimmy Steele, who'd professed to be tiring of the clichéd rock star life and now wanted to settle down and just make music.

As far as Quarrel could see, the newlywed Anthea had been a mess of drug and alcohol dependency at first, but her husband had stood by her, helping her through rehab and therapy. She still enjoyed a good time, but, in a recent interview, had claimed to be 'high on life' and 'resolutely on the wagon'. He noted her assertion that 'Jimmy and my faith' had helped see her through the bad times. It chimed with her return to the church of her childhood.

He made his tea and dialled the number Steele had given him. He was just expecting the call to go to voicemail when it was finally picked up and a throaty female voice purred hello.

Quarrel introduced himself, confirmed he was speaking to Anthea Swallow, and explained that he was investigating Alastair Murdoch's death.

"I heard," she said. "Jimmy told me. I can't believe it. And you think it's murder? I can't imagine who'd want to hurt poor Alastair. Such a good guy."

"You say Jimmy called you?"

"That's right. Perhaps half an hour ago, after your second visit."

"He didn't call you after our first visit?"

"No. He only called this time to warn me you might be in touch."

I bet he did, thought Quarrel.

"We understand you did some fundraising work with Mr Murdoch?"

"That's right. Putting together events. I was using my connections to get celebrities to open them, take part, whatever. He did the organisation. We made a good team." She paused for a heartbeat. "He was a sweet man."

"And your husband claimed you never told him you were working with Mr Murdoch?"

"Also right. He only found out when you told him."

Quarrel took a quick sip of tea. "Why was that?"

"Why? I don't know, really. I mean, it's true that their professional relationship ended in tears. Jimmy had done some stupid investments – but I suppose you know all that?"

"I know what Mr Steele told me."

"Well, I didn't like the sound of it, and clearly Alastair didn't either. Jimmy doesn't like not getting his own way, and he doesn't like backing down, even when he's wrong. He actually dropped that dodgy portfolio soon afterwards, losing a bit of money in the process, but he couldn't bring himself to go back to Alastair, apologise and carry on being his client. My husband can be such a child, Inspector."

"So... when you found yourself working with Mr Murdoch...?"

"I knew Jimmy wouldn't like it. The whole thing was something he'd rather forget. So the easiest thing was not to tell him."

"And now he knows. How was he about that?"

"Cross. He likes to think he knows everything about me. He thought my work for the church was a harmless little hobby that he let me do—"

"*Let* you do?"

"Honestly? He thinks everything I do for myself is something he *lets* me do. He imagines this Paris break with my girl friends is only happening because he *allowed* it."

Alarm bells were ringing. "Sounds a bit controlling, if I may say so."

Her laugh was husky. "You may say so. But it isn't really. Believe me, I've been with controlling men. Jimmy isn't like that. You have to understand the state I was in when I met him. He literally saved my life. I'm clean now, and he sees it as his personal mission to help me stay that way. So yes, he likes to know where I am, what I'm doing, and who I'm with. Okay, he's probably got this self-image of himself wearing the trousers in our house, but I stand up to him, and he usually sees reason. No, he was cross that I'd been deliberately vague about who I was working with at the church and kept Alastair a secret from him."

"Would you say he was jealous that you were keeping a secret?"

"Perhaps a little. There was no need. Alastair did become a friend – but nothing more."

"But what if he'd actually found out before now? Discovered you were going behind his back? How 'cross' might he have been?"

She burst out laughing. "As in, would he have killed Alastair? Or had him killed? That's not my Jimmy, even though he does have a temper. Violence isn't his thing."

"You're sure about that?"

"As far as anyone knows anyone, yes. Shouting and jabbing his finger at you is as violent as it gets. I don't think he ever got into actual fights, even in his hell-raising days."

Quarrel thought he might poke around a bit more on that.

"I gather you've dabbled a bit in Tarot readings?"

"What's that got to do with anything?"

"But did you?"

"Couple of times. One of my friends I'm over here with was interested, and we all got a couple of readings. I thought it was quite fascinating. Read up on it, bought a few decks. Bored Jimmy on the subject. In the end, it was a five minute wonder."

"And one of those decks – is it Rider Waite, by any chance?"

"That's the one with the really pretty pictures, right?"

"It depicts the fool on a cliff-edge with a dog, for example."

"Yes, I got that one. My, Inspector, you seem to know a lot about it yourself."

"One more thing," he said, dismissing the comment. "Your husband's got a few tattoos – are you into them?"

"Not so much. I've got a humming bird on my ankle from way back, and Jimmy got me one for my last birthday – my fortieth. That's the lot, though. I didn't especially want the birthday one, to be honest."

"May I ask what it is?"

"It's a pink unicorn on my shoulder. I quite like it, I must admit."

"Where did you get it done?"

"Conor's Body Images. Just off Tring High Street. Very discreet."

Quarrel noted the name. "Coming back to Alastair Murdoch. When you last saw him, how did he seem? Worried? Frightened?"

"Nothing like that. He was his usual self. A bit dull and turned in on himself, but friendly enough, and enthusiastic about what we were doing. Like I said, I really can't imagine who'd want to hurt him.

"How long are you away for?"

"A couple more days."

"Back on Wednesday?"

"Thursday."

"I might come and see you, if we have more questions."

"Of course. Anything to catch whoever killed Alastair. He didn't deserve that."

Quarrel terminated the call, finished his tea, then put his salmon salad together and poured himself a glass of white wine. As he ate, he played back the events of the day.

At this stage, theories and suspects weren't exactly thick on the ground. But Jimmy Steele and Anthea Swallow were an interesting couple. A man who, despite his wife's protestations, did sound a little controlling, and a woman who'd kept her working relationship with Murdoch from her husband. How much had they both underplayed Anthea's interest in Tarot? And how well did Steele know the people at Conor's Body Images?

Anthea had a Rider Waite deck. How easy to slip The Fool out of the deck and pay someone to tattoo the image onto a person's face? Some people would do some pretty bad things if the price was right, and Jimmy Steele seemingly had the resources to pay a high price indeed.

He wondered how Sophie Monahan was getting on with those lists of tattooists. Presumably Conor's would be on it. Tomorrow he'd pay them a visit.

8

For the umpteenth time, PC Isabel Cole glanced at the digits on her alarm clock, glowing ghostly green in the darkness. She'd gone to sleep with a dead man and a Tarot tattoo on her mind, woken from a half-forgotten nightmare just before 4am, and her brain had been buzzing ever since. She knew she might as well get up and make herself some hot chocolate, but Matt had stayed over last night. He lay beside her, snoring happily, and she didn't want to risk waking him.

Most of yesterday, the murder of Alastair Murdoch had dominated her thoughts, and again since she'd woken this morning. Her feelings were muddled: mostly horror at what had been done to the man, and pity for him and his family; but also, she couldn't deny, more than a frisson of excitement that she had a case like this on her doorstep.

She'd joined the force a couple of years ago, not long after uni. She'd tried a fast track corporate career, putting on a dark suit, watching the grown-ups playing hardball, trying to imagine herself doing the same in a few years' time, and she hadn't lasted six months. It just wasn't for her. Power plays and ruthlessness, the way her colleagues scented blood like sharks and went in for the kill…

She still wasn't sure whether the suicide of a business rival – who'd come into a meeting sweating, pop-eyed and visibly under unbearable pressure, his weakness exploited to the full, and who'd gone on to jump off a railway bridge that same evening – had been the wake-up call she'd needed. But she'd decided she didn't need to commit her future to hurting people in the name of profit. Helping, maybe making the occasional positive difference, felt more the sort of life Izzy Cole would enjoy.

She knew the police didn't always get the best of press, but she also knew that trying to make the world a safer place wasn't a bad motivation for getting up in the morning.

Still, she was only human. Tring was just about as far as you could get from a hotbed of crime. It didn't mean bad things didn't happen here. She'd seen her share of misery and blood and, yes, death too.

Even so. She didn't want to spend the rest of her career as a small-town bobby. She had ambitions to rise through the ranks, and she wanted to be a detective, putting the analytical skills she'd gained at university to practical use. Watching those two detectives this morning, outside the church, had only strengthened those ambitions. She wished she could have been right alongside them, hearing their talk, making contributions perhaps.

It didn't take a genius to recognise what had been done to the dead man as something calculated, personal and symbolic. The detectives had been guarded in what they'd said to her as they left the scene – although DI Quarrel had made a point of thanking her for her help. But she wouldn't be surprised if a thing like this was only the beginning. If there was someone evil out there, maybe right in the heart of her community, someone who needed to be stopped, then Izzy wished she could play at least a small part in stopping them.

She scolded herself. She needed to stop this and try to get a little more sleep. These thoughts of a serial killer were likely the product of her nightmare, her tiredness, and an over-active imagination. No doubt the Murdoch case would turn out to be something sad and small, the tattoo mere novelty.

Sighing, she turned over and closed her eyes.

That was when her phone started to shrill.

*

For Quarrel too, it was the second bone-crushingly early start in as many days. The call came just before 6am. Laura's shift didn't end until 8am, so Quarrel left her a note before phoning Katie, breaking the bad news to her, and setting off to meet her.

It was chilly by the canal. Quarrel knew this stretch fairly well. Little Tring Bridge No.3 was part of the Wendover Arm of the Grand Union Canal, some 6.5 miles long and leaving the main canal at Bulbourne Junction to run through to the small Buckinghamshire town of Wendover. Quarrel had paid a few visits to nearby Bulbourne Yard, a historic complex of former lock gate construction workshops, although many of those workshops were now disused.

The towpath was slick with moisture and there was damp in the air. The body was propped up, in similar fashion to Alastair Murdoch's, under the bridge. A man in a dark suit, blue and white striped shirt, sober blue tie. The local uniforms had again moved speedily to secure the scene, and Quarrel was pleased to see the efficient PC Cole on duty again, nearest to the body this time.

"This is getting to be a habit," he told her. "I suppose we should be grateful the jogger who found him was such an early riser."

"You can say that again," she said. "This stretch gets busy quite early on, and we could have had all manner of trampling in the vicinity before someone spotted him. This guy called it in about 5am."

"Do we know what he was doing out so early?" Katie asked.

"We're doubly lucky," said Cole. "He's actually between jobs, but his last job used to be quite an early start. Plus he's a running fanatic – so he's got into doing a silly o'clock run before breakfast, and he's not been able to break the habit. He's in a squad car up by the bridge. Pretty shaken, I think."

Quarrel bent down to study the dead man's face. "Not much doubt this is the same killer."

The man was probably of a similar age to Alastair Murdoch, perhaps a few years older, with a full head of salt and pepper hair and aquiline features. But these were details compared to the tape across his mouth. And the tattoo.

A coldness that had nothing to do with the weather settled upon Quarrel. He'd been trying to convince himself that, for all its bizarreness, Alastair Murdoch's murder had been a one-off. That, whatever the significance of the blackwork tattoo on his face, it was a message that had applied directly to the accountant, and only to him.

Now it was evident that, whatever point the killer had been making, he wasn't done making it.

"What do you think, Katie? Does it look like another Rider Waite to you?" The figure was female, crowned, and seated on a chair or throne. "She looks like a queen."

She already had her phone out and was busy with her thumbs. "Certainly looks a similar style. Just give me a mo."

"Rider what?" Cole asked.

Quarrel debated what to tell her. The more of the killer's modus operandi that could be kept out of the public arena for now, the better he would like it. Yet there was something about Cole that inspired trust.

He lowered his voice. "Rider Waite," he said. "It's a particular deck of Tarot cards, and it would appear that our tattooist is copying them. But I'd really appreciate it if you'd keep that to yourself – don't even share it with your colleagues."

"Understood. Tarot tattoos, though. That's more than a little weird, isn't it?"

"It's a first for me," he agreed.

"Here we are," Katie said, "and yep, it's Rider Waite all right. Not a queen, though. Justice Reversed. The Justice card symbolises truth, fairness, and law. See the square on her crown? Apparently it symbolises the clarity of thought needed to dispense justice. Those scales in her left hand represent a balance to be struck between intuition and logic, and the double-edged sword in her right hand signifies impartiality."

"But this is upside down again," Quarrel observed. "So those meanings are reversed?"

"Yup. The upright card is a reminder that our decisions have long-term effects for ourselves and others, and we will be fairly judged on those decisions. If, for example, your actions have caused pain to others, this card serves as a warning that there will be consequences. But Justice Reversed… let's see. Here we go."

She paused, reading, then smiled without humour. "I'm getting the hang of these cards now. Nothing's simple. As always, this could have various meanings. It could suggest you're living in denial and not prepared to accept the consequences of your actions. Effectively, you're running from your guilt. You need to make up for your wrongdoing in order to change and stop judging yourself."

"So it's a punishment?" Cole suggested. "This guy did someone wrong?"

"Perhaps. Or it could be more subtle than that," Katie said. "I should talk to my Tarot expert."

The PC's eyes widened. "You've got a Tarot expert?"

"Oh, yeah. You'd be surprised what we've got." She flashed a grin. "It's just someone I sort of know."

Cole was looking at the tattooed face again. "So have we got a serial killer?"

"Too early to say that," Quarrel said, "and, for Christ's sake, don't encourage people to start thinking that way. The usual definition of a serial killer is someone who murders three or more people, with the murders taking place over more than a month."

"Well," Cole pointed out, "we've got two in as many days. Maybe there's a third body we haven't found yet."

"Maybe," Quarrel conceded, "but I'd say the killer is choosing places to pretty much display the bodies. He *wants* them to be found, and quickly. But there's normally a significant period of time between victims, with the violence escalating and the gap between killings getting progressively shorter as the killer grows in confidence. Here we have, as you say, two in two days. That's quick, arguably too quick."

The young PC still wasn't satisfied. "Isn't there usually some sexual element?"

"Well, a serial killer's crimes do usually serve some abnormal psychological gratification. Often sexual, but not necessarily so. Right now, we're miles from establishing motive." He looked Cole in the eye. "Do *not*, whatever you do, start putting it around that this is anything other than the second of two murders that bear certain similarities."

"Don't worry," she said. "I'll use exactly the arguments you've just deployed with me, if anyone starts talking serial killers. Because they will, whether I say anything or not. I get it. You won't be able to move for reporters, people will start to panic…"

"You get the picture," he said. "Okay, no sign of the CSIs or pathologist yet. You said the guy who found the body was around?"

"I'll take you to him."

They found their witness up on the bridge, still in jogging gear, with a car blanket around his shoulders. He was leaning against a squad car, drinking coffee from a thermos mug. His name was Harry Baker. He was average height, but toned and muscled, as befitted a man who went running at five in the morning.

"How are you doing?" Quarrel asked as Cole left them to it.

"Okay, I suppose. Although Christ knows what dreams I'll have tonight. His face…"

"Do you always run the same circuit?"

"I try to vary it, but I come this way at least once most weeks." Harry Baker stared into his cup. "It'll be a long time before I come here again, I reckon."

"So walk us through it. Where did you start?"

"For this run, I start at Startop's End car park, in Marsworth. Then I follow the towpath, past Heygates Flour Mill and Tringford pumping station, under Little Tring Bridge here, then past Wilstone Reservoir to finish up at the car park again. It's six or seven miles altogether. You don't see too many people at that time of the morning. It's just you and your thoughts."

Quarrel was no runner, but he could vaguely envisage the route. He and Laura sometimes took a stroll around Tring reservoirs in the better weather, and might call in at the Bluebells Tearooms at Startops.

"But did you see anyone?" Quarrel pressed him. "Maybe someone out of place, acting a bit suspicious? A car going a bit too fast, or maybe unusually slowly, like the driver didn't want to attract attention?"

Baker shook his head. "Nothing like that." He frowned. "Actually, though, as I was driving to the car park, there was a white van belting in the opposite direction. He'd just come over the bridge by the White Lion – the pub that's closed? He was all over the road. For a moment, I thought he was going to take me out."

"So which way was he headed?"

"Towards Aston Clinton, I suppose."

"Can you describe the driver?"

"I really didn't notice. Sorry. That man was murdered, wasn't he?" Baker grimaced. "I mean, that tape on his mouth…"

"We'll be treating it as suspicious, certainly. We'd like not to release too many details at the moment, so if you could—"

He half-smiled. "Understood."

"Thanks. Now, let's get back to this van," Quarrel said. "You're sure it was white?"

"Fairly sure."

"A big one?"

"Bigger than an estate car. A fair size."

"I don't suppose you got the registration?"

"Sorry." He hesitated. "I've got a funny feeling it was a 59 plate."

"Good," Quarrel encouraged. "You're doing really well. Was there any writing on the side, or any other markings?"

"I don't think so. It was just a white van."

While they were talking, Quarrel saw the CSI van pull up and Debbie Brown and her team getting out. A few minutes later, the pathologist, Jordan Stoddart, arrived.

There wasn't much more that could be obtained from Baker for now. Quarrel thanked him, asked him to make a formal statement at the station later, and handed him a card. As they walked back to the towpath, Quarrel asked Katie for her thoughts.

"He likes his early morning body dumps, doesn't he?" she said.

"What do you make of this van?"

"Interesting. Could just be some fool going too fast because he assumed there was no one else on the road. We should check out local CCTV."

"That man, apparently answering Alistair Murdoch's description, was seen being helped into a dark car on Sunday. Not a white van."

"Doesn't mean it's not the same driver. A dark car for leisure, a white van for work. Maybe the car would be easier to persuade a victim into. The van's more convenient for transporting a corpse."

He nodded his agreement. "We need to identify this victim and see if there's a connection to Murdoch. Maybe to Jimmy Steele, too."

Katie stopped and looked at him. "How much do you fancy Steele for this?"

"Honestly?" He shook his head. "I really don't know. It would be good if this one pointed to him, wouldn't it, or at least we found some sort of connection. The last thing we need is some nut job running over the region doing this stuff at random."

"Middle aged males. There's at least a common victimology there."

"The suit suggests he might have been some sort of professional too. Maybe even another accountant?"

"Could be they knew each other."

"That would be useful." He started walking again. "Come on. Let's see how Debbie and the doc are doing. With any luck, we've at least got a name."

Debbie Brown had already bagged a wallet, a phone and two sets of keys – one for a house, one for a Jaguar car – when they reached her.

"Business cards again," she said. "And credit cards with the same name on. It would appear this was Michael Woodley, QC."

"A lawyer?" Quarrel stared at the tattoo. *Justice Reversed.*

Debbie nodded. "Practice based in London. Nothing to indicate his home address. Cash in his wallet, like our other tattooed man. Like our Mr Murdoch, no signs of violence, either."

"We don't even know if he was local, then," Katie said.

"Anything *you* can tell us yet, doc?" Quarrel asked Stoddart.

"Well, he's definitely dead," the pathologist said. Quarrel said nothing, but tapped his foot impatiently. "Right," Stoddart cleared his throat. "These outdoor corpses are always hard to put a time on but, as an initial assessment, I'm thinking he died quite a bit later than Mr Murdoch – between around midnight and 2am. But, as always, that's subject to a proper examination."

"Let me know when that is."

"Will do. Oh, by the way, Inspector, those marks on the sides of Mr Murdoch's head. We've done some measuring and made a couple of phone calls. It's possible – likely, even – that his head was held in a vice, presumably to keep it still while our tattooist did his artwork. There are similar marks on this one. With the restraint marks, it's possible he was strapped to some sort of work bench, head in a vice..." He shuddered at the picture he had painted. "Not nice."

"Thanks, doc. Something else to think about. First things first, though. Unless he lived alone, like Alastair, someone must have missed him," Quarrel mused. "Otherwise we'll need to start with his firm."

"Two professional middle-aged males, both bodies looking posed," Katie said. "Two Tarot tattoos."

Quarrel knew where this was leading. No matter how hard he tried to stop everyone jumping to serial killer conclusions, they kept coming back to it, and he could hardly blame them.

"Look," he said. "We all know what we're thinking, but let's take this one step at a time. It could still be that someone had a grudge against these two men, had a particular point to make, and has made it. Let's work the cases in front of us for now. Although it wouldn't go amiss to see if anything similar's happened elsewhere."

9

Michael Woodley's home was in Harpenden, so was strictly outside Quarrel's patch, but still in Hertfordshire. The lawyer had been reported missing by his wife, Clare, around 11pm last night. He often worked late, but as time ticked on, she had begun to wonder where he was. She'd tried his phone several times, then started on colleagues and friends. Finally, still half-expecting him to walk through the door at any second with a reasonable excuse, she had contacted the police.

The notion that police often wouldn't do anything until the person had been missing for at least twenty-four hours was something of a myth. It was true that the majority of missing persons enquiries were quickly resolved, with the person returning soon after their disappearance. But it was also recognised that any missing person report could be the start of a major crime enquiry. It was far easier to row back than to attempt to recover from missed opportunities later.

Quarrel and Aliya Nazir knew all this, but DS Lewis Appleby, from the local CID branch, had explained it to them anyway, in painful detail, on the way here from St Albans police station. Aliya had only rolled her eyes once. She was with Quarrel while Katie consulted Lucy Andrews about the latest tattoo.

"We did a risk assessment," Appleby said. "It was obviously quite out of character for Mr Woodley to be so late. So, although we didn't view him as a vulnerable person, as such, we did think he might be at risk. So we spoke again to family, friends, colleagues, anyone he might have been in touch with. We also checked the car park at Harpenden station, and his Jag was still there."

"So he must have been abducted somewhere between his office in London and the car park?" Quarrel suggested as he slowed down for a sharp bend.

"There were still clerks in his chambers when he left about 6.45pm. We've also tried to locate his mobile phone, but that's switched off. Just before 8pm, though, it pinged a mast near Harpenden. So, for purposes of a timeline, he – or someone else – turned off his phone either at the station, or still on the train."

"So it's theoretically possible he didn't get off?"

"Doesn't seem likely though, does it?"

"I don't know," Quarrel said. "That's why I'm asking." He was thinking of Alastair Murdoch being possibly drugged at the Brownlow café. "Do you know if he was in the habit of buying a coffee for his train journey?"

"No," Appleby admitted.

"Well, if our first victim's anything to go by, we think our killer is a meticulous planner who learns their routines and identifies moments of opportunity. Say he had a coffee? The killer somehow drugs it. Our Michael goes woozy, falls asleep, whatever, misses his stop. What's the next stop?"

"Luton Airport Parkway, then Luton, Leagrave—"

"The killer gives him a shake further down the line. Michael's still woozy, realises he's missed his stop. But the guy who's woken him seems like a Good Samaritan."

"*'I'm getting off next stop,'* he says," said Aliya. "*'I've got my car there. You don't look too good. Let me run you home'.*"

"But he stops the car somewhere secluded and properly incapacitates his victim," Quarrel said. "Then he takes him to wherever it is he does his work. We need to check out CCTV at every station along the line."

"We've already pulled the footage from Harpenden," Appleby said. "Don't we need to check whether he'd have bought that coffee before we widen it?"

Quarrel was pulling the Volvo up on the Woodleys' drive. "We can ask his wife."

With a population of just over 30,000, Harpenden was a short distance from both Luton to the north and St Albans to the south. A commuter town, with a direct rail connection into

Central London, its property prices were well over double the national average. Looking at the imposing detached house in Roundwood Park, where the QC had lived, Quarrel guessed it had cost the Woodleys a formidable chunk of change.

As well as Appleby, Carol Nugent, a St Albans-based family liaison officer, had also come with them. The four got out of the car and walked up to the front door. It was opened by a man in his early to mid-twenties with long, dark hair tied back in a ponytail. Quarrel surmised that this was Michael Woodley's son, Luke, who'd been supporting his mother overnight.

"Any news?" Luke said, taking in Nugent's uniform. This was the moment when loved ones often realised, before even being told, that the hope they'd been clinging to had died. His shoulders sagged, and Quarrel read the fear in his eyes. "You'd better come in."

They followed him into a state-of-the-art kitchen, all glossy white and gleaming chrome. Clare Woodley, blonde, freckled and probably in her fifties, sat on a stool at a breakfast bar with a full cup of black coffee in front of her. No steam rose from the cup, and Quarrel wondered how long it had been cold.

"Mum, it's the police," Luke said. His voice shook.

He moved to his mother and took her hand. She winced, as if he was squeezing too tight. But she wouldn't meet any of the officers' eyes.

"Have you found him?" she whispered. "Have you found Michael?"

"I'm afraid we've found a body," Quarrel said. "He'll need to be identified, but we believe it's Michael."

"Oh, God." Luke doubled over, and suddenly it was Clare who was being the strong one, rubbing his back, and finally looking at Quarrel.

"Where was he?" she asked.

"Near Tring. On a canal towpath."

"Tring?" She shook her head. "That can't be right. Why would he be there? Are you sure it's Michael?"

"Fairly sure, yes. As to how he came to be there, it's obviously early days in our investigation. We're all so sorry for your loss."

"Yes, but that's just something you say, isn't it?" she said, tonelessly. Then her face crumpled. "I'm sorry, that was rude."

"Why doesn't PC Nugent here make us all a hot drink?" Quarrel suggested. "We need to ask you some questions."

"What—" Luke began. He swallowed and tried again. "What happened to Dad?"

"It's early days," Aliya said, "but we're treating his death as suspicious."

"Murder?" The younger man looked in danger of being sick. "What happened? A mugging? But what was he doing in Tring?"

Nugent had got the kettle going. It was a noisy one. They irritated Quarrel like few things did. The theory was that they boiled faster. He wasn't convinced. He reckoned you put up with all that racket, drowning out the radio or conversation, for marginal gain at best.

"When we know more, so will you," he said. "As DC Nazir says, the investigation is just getting started. And there are things we can't go into too much detail about yet."

"I need to see the body," Clare said. "I'll get my coat."

"I'm afraid there will have to be a post mortem first. I'm sorry."

"Ask your questions, Inspector," Luke said, seemingly rallying a little.

"Thank you. First of all, can you tell us how Michael has seemed lately? Was he anxious, worried, anything like that?"

"He always was," Luke said. "He was a defence lawyer. It was his job to get people off criminal charges. If he failed, it often meant prison for his clients. So he tried very hard not to fail. And he rarely did," he added proudly.

Quarrel understood and related to that. It was the flip side of what he did in a way. Quarrel's job was to get bad people *off* the streets.

"What sort of cases did he cover?"

"All sorts. He did a lot of sexual assaults."

"But did he seem any different to usual?"

"I don't live here any more," Luke said. "I've got my own place in St Albans, with my girlfriend. But he'd seemed the same as always to me, I suppose. Mum?" He looked at his mother.

"What?" She blinked. "Oh, no, no, nothing different."

"He didn't seem frightened?" Aliya asked.

"Not at all," Clare said. "Of what?"

"Was there anyone who'd wish him harm?" Quarrel probed. "A client who'd lost his case and blamed Michael? A victim who maybe thought a client had unfairly escaped justice?"

"Inspector," Luke said, "he dealt with some nasty cases, and there were always winners and losers. The losers are always going to be sore and looking for someone to blame. That was what he often said. But that's a long way from killing him, surely."

"Did any of his cases involve Jimmy Steele in any way? The rock star," he clarified as Luke looked blank.

"I'm not sure I've heard of him. Mum?"

"Jimmy Steele, yes," she said. "I never really liked his stuff though."

This was like pulling teeth. "But did Michael have anything to do with him? Or his wife, Anthea Swallow?"

"I don't think so. Although he didn't say a lot about his cases. Didn't like bringing his work home. That was why he often stayed late in the office. So he could leave all the filth he dealt with behind him."

Quarrel looked at Clare sharply. "Was that how he thought of his clients? Filth?"

"No," Luke answered for her, "but a lot of his cases were bleak and grubby, especially the sex ones. He said he always had to believe in his client's innocence, but he often needed a long shower after some of the things he heard, and questions he had to ask."

Quarrel sidelined his natural cynicism. He thought the questions defence lawyers 'had to ask' in rape or sexual assault cases often amounted to putting the alleged victim on trial. But, in fairness, there had been several such cases that had collapsed only after the accused's life and reputation had been ruined.

The kettle had fallen silent. Nugent asked who wanted teas and coffees and got to work making them

Quarrel thought it was a good point at which to change tack. "We were wondering if he was in the habit of buying a coffee or some other drink for his train journey?"

Clare smiled. "How did you know that? Yes, if he had time before the train, a cappuccino. I check the credit card bill, and I'm always telling him off about the number of times Café Nero appears."

Quarrel glanced at Aliya, then back at mother and son. "And did he have anything to do with Tarot cards, Tarot readings, anything like that?"

Luke laughed. "He didn't believe in fortune telling. He said the only sort of future he wanted to know was who was going to win the Grand National and what the winning lottery numbers would be."

Standing in this expensive house, in an expensive and affluent town, it was hard to imagine an eminent barrister being interested in winning more money. But then, 'money goes to money' had been one of Quarrel's grandmother's maxims.

"What about tattoos? Any significance there?"

"He detested them. Said they were a form of self-mutilation." Michael's son made a face. "This is turning out to be a bloody awful year, isn't it, Mum?"

"In what way?" Appleby asked quickly. He'd left Quarrel and Aliya to it thus far.

"It doesn't matter." Luke dismissed the subject.

"You're sure?" Quarrel pressed.

"We all have bad years, Inspector," Clare said. "Although having your husband murdered doesn't usually feature." She made a noise halfway between sob and giggle and buried her face in her son's shoulder.

"Tell us a bit about him," Aliya said gently. "What kind of man was he?"

"He couldn't do enough for people he cared about," Luke said. "He was stubborn, but not inflexible. He said life was like the law – there were shades of grey but, once he'd made up his mind about something, it'd take a lot to shift him."

"He could be incredibly pompous," Clare ventured. "But he knew it, and he was capable of laughing at himself. He was fabulous at what he did," she added proudly. "He was destined for even greater things." Tears streamed down her face. "I don't understand. You seem to be saying he was picked out to be murdered. Not a mugging or something. And I still don't see what he was doing in Tring."

"Have you heard of a man called Alastair Murdoch? An accountant?"

Clare and Luke looked at each other, clearly puzzled.

"Not me," Clare said.

"Me neither," said Luke. "Is he a suspect?"

"His name's been on the news." There was no point in dancing around. "He was murdered on Sunday night."

"What?" Luke Woodley's eyes were wide. "And you think there's a connection? What had Dad got himself mixed up in?"

"Please don't jump to conclusions," Quarrel said. "But there are similarities." He knew what an understatement that was. "Is there anything else you think we should know?"

"My father was in the justice business," Luke said. "I hope you're going to get justice for him."

"That's the plan," said Quarrel.

10

The day was getting on. Once again, Quarrel stood in front of the Wall. With Michael Woodley's murder, and the results of further enquiries into the Murdoch killing, the board was looking a little less barren now, but what was there amounted to many questions and few answers.

"First of all, these tattoos," he said. "Katie, did your friendly Tarot reader have anything to add that we don't already know?"

"Honestly?" Katie shrugged. "Not really, Nate. Basically, all the cards have wide interpretations. It can depend on the subject and what's going on with them, the instincts of the individual reader... and that assumes the tattooist, or whoever's paying him or her, even knows that much about Tarot. I think it was Ricky who said that the first tattoo could simply have been saying Alastair was a fool."

"Yeah," Ricky James said, looking pleased with himself, "that was me."

"So," Katie continued, "this new one is definitely about justice and judgement, and Michael Woodley worked in the justice system. A reversed card reverses its meaning. Maybe the killer thought Michael had been unjust. At work, or elsewhere in his life."

"Did you ask what The Fool Reversed and Justice Reversed might mean in combination?" Quarrel asked.

"I did. Possibly an unwilling participant in a dishonest legal case." She frowned. "We also talked about an Order of the Golden Dawn and Chaos magicians."

"What?" Ricky guffawed. "Does she believe in elves too?"

"Thank you, Ricky," Quarrel gave the DC a hard look. "What about them, Katie?"

She shrugged. "Lucy mentioned them before, but I didn't think much of it when we were only looking at one murder.

Now we've got two of a kind, I don't think we should rule them out. Basically, they're different wings of the Tarot community. Lucy's going to let me have a list of Golden Dawn organisations and ask around to see if there are any Chaos magicians locally."

"Push her for that, although I'd prefer it not to be some sort of occult nutcase with an agenda. A dishonest legal case, though… that sounds like the beginnings of a motive for murder."

"Shall I ask Michael's firm if any of his cases are to do with the Tring area?" Aliya suggested.

"Yes please," Quarrel said. "Although they'll be cagey about their clients. Legal privilege and all that." He turned to Libby Statham. "Libby, you've been in touch with Alastair's son, Rob. Any connection with Michael Woodley they're aware of?"

"I didn't push them hard, guv," Libby said, "but I drew a blank. Or at least, I think I did."

"Explain."

"I don't know. There was something in Rob's eyes for a moment, like the name might ring a bell. But then he seemed certain it didn't. He was probably just dredging his memory to make sure he wasn't overlooking anything."

"Probably." He might get someone to ask again later. Vague memories sometimes solidified with the passing of some time. And sometimes not, he reminded himself. "Did you also talk to the FLO in Derbyshire, who's liaising with the daughter?"

"Yes. She raised the name with her. Nothing."

"Okay. Now, Sophie," he turned to Monahan. "I gather we've got quite a list of tat shops together?"

"Yes, guv," the PC said. "Ricky and I have officers out showing the Tarot designs around. It's not so simple as you might hope. It seems any number of professional tattooists could probably do a decent reproduction of those cards and, indeed, it's not an uncommon request. And, while a tattoo right across the face isn't exactly common, that's not unheard of, either."

Quarrel nodded. He'd done some online reading about tattoos last night. There was a man whose mission in life was to cover his entire body with tattoos. His face had been transformed into a skull. Another man had tattooed his entire body, including his eyeballs, black.

"At least I cleared up one thing that I was curious about," Sophie said. "I wondered why our killer does the tats in monochrome, and not full colour."

"I'd just assumed it was quicker," Quarrel said.

"It probably is, but it's also nigh on impossible to reproduce the level of detail on the cards in a tattoo, so the artist will stick with black and use dotting, hatching and fine lines to achieve different effects."

"Thanks," he acknowledged. "It's all useful detail. I take it you made sure no one rattled the cage at Conor's Body Images?"

"Absolutely. I know you want to pay them a visit yourself."

"Good, thanks. Next," he moved on again. "CCTV. Ricky, anything useful from around where we think Alastair was abducted?"

"The experts are still reviewing footage," Ricky said, "Lots of dark cars, though. Too many. And, even when there are two occupants, it's not always clear whether either of them is male. We can question every owner, but it would be good to at least narrow down the make, if not the model."

"We won't do that for now," Quarrel said. "St Albans are getting footage from Harpenden and other stations along the line. With any luck we'll see our Mr Woodley being helped into a car, or at least a dark car with two people in it, being driven away at about the right time. All we need is a match between one of those and one on your Tring list and we might have ourselves a bullseye."

He scrawled 'Tring/train station car connection?' on the Wall. "Any luck with the white van our witness saw near Startops?"

"Not at the time reported, guv, no. But a couple of cameras in the vicinity were out – not working or no film. In any case, it's a fair distance from our body dump. Probably a red herring, to be honest. I'm not even sure you'd be traveling in that direction if you'd come from Little Tring bridge."

"You could go either way," one of the uniformed PCs, Tom Roberts, opined.

Quarrel winced. "Let's not get into a debate about routes. That van could be important. If it was coming away from the body dump, it's possible that our Mr Baker missed seeing the killer by a matter of minutes. I'd like to trace it. Can we widen the trawl area? And let's check CCTV around Tring yesterday morning. If we spot the same van anywhere near both body dumps, that could be a significant lead."

"On it," Ricky said.

"There's something else, for what it's worth," Quarrel said. "We're already thinking the two body dumps – the church and the bridge – might have significance. But it strikes me there might be a specific reason why he chooses Tring locations."

"He lives locally?" Katie suggested.

"That's my thinking. He's either got a tat shop in the area or, more likely, he's taking his victims home to work on and then wants to dump them quickly and get back to his lair."

"It's certainly not uncommon for serial killers to stick close to home," Aliya pointed out.

"True," Quarrel agreed, "but I'd wager a great deal that these victims are being hand-picked. There's nothing random about spiriting Michael Woodley away during his journey from London to Harpenden. But yes, it's possible our killer doesn't live a million miles from Tring."

He surveyed the room. "I'll be questioning Jimmy Steele and his wife about any connection to Michael Woodley. Is there anything else?"

"I'm worried about the press," DCI Sharp said. "We can't not put something out but, even if we stay silent on the tattoos and any possible connection between the victims, two bodies turning up in two days, in a place where basically nothing ever happens, will be news in itself. By tomorrow, we could be knee-deep in cameras and microphones."

"Wonderful," Quarrel groaned. "I don't suppose we can hold off on a statement for twenty-four hours?"

"You know better than that, Nathan. Besides, Superintendent Taylor is pushing for it. And what if there's a third body tomorrow and we've kept today's quiet? It could be very awkward."

He sighed. "I suppose so, ma'am. But a third body? I do hope not."

Sharp came up to him as the briefing was breaking up. "I think I need to find you a couple more people, don't I, Nathan? I doubt another detective can be spared, but maybe a couple of uniforms?"

"That'd be great, boss." He was conscious that his little team was being loaded up with work, and things that needed doing were already queuing for attention. "Actually," he said, a thought crossing his mind, "I've been impressed with an officer from Tring who was at both our crime scenes – a PC Cole?"

"I'll ask," the DCI promised. "No guarantees, of course."

Back in the office, Quarrel asked Katie to accompany him to Conor's Body Images. He decided to visit the gents' before departing. On his way back, he passed PC Michelle McGrath in the corridor.

"What on earth is going on in Tring?" she demanded. "It can't have seen this much excitement since The Fox."

She was referring to a one-man crime wave in the summer of 1984, when a series of armed burglaries, rapes and indecent assaults had been committed around Leighton Buzzard, Dunstable and Tring. Both Quarrel and Michelle were too young to personally remember those times, but the case was ingrained in the local force's collective memory. Terrified residents had barred their windows and formed vigilante groups, and the police had drafted in officers from different force areas, even from Miners' Strike picket lines. In the end, the man who became known as The Fox had only been apprehended as a result of a routine but thorough police line of enquiry.

"You can say that again," he acknowledged. "I suppose your team are sitting around with your feet up, drinking gin."

"Too right, mate," she beamed. Then her face clouded. "I wish. Nasty sexual assault in Grovehill last night."

Michelle was one of the local go-to officers for rape and sexual assault cases. As a Sexual Offence Investigative Technique Officer, she was specially trained to provide victims with the help and support they needed throughout the investigation and any subsequent judicial process. Her dark hair, cut in a bob, had grey streaks that she didn't seem inclined to colour out. Quarrel knew she was only forty-one – he still remembered her fortieth birthday drinks – but, like him, she looked older than she was.

"Do you think you'll catch the guy?" he asked.

"Hope so. There's DNA. But, of course, if he's not on the database…"

"Fingers crossed." A thought flashed through his mind. "A lot of your cases go to court, don't they?"

"Whenever we can convince the CPS, yes."

"Have you come across a QC, name of Michael Woodley?"

She made a face. "Woodley? Oh, yes."

"Well, he's our latest victim."

Her eyes widened. "Really? Bloody hell."

"What do you think of him?"

She folded her arms. "You want the truth?"

"Always."

She sighed. "I really don't like to speak ill of the dead, and I know he was only doing his job, but frankly he was a shit. He made it his mission to demolish vulnerable victims, who often showed amazing courage in reporting their assault and giving evidence in court. He really did put them on trial and make them out to be nymphomaniacs and pathological liars. He was bloody successful, too. Rapists he's defended have been acquitted and gone on to rape again. One in London went back and killed his victim within a week of walking free."

He hadn't expected his simple question to unleash such vitriol. Her face was contorted with loathing. "After one of the cases I prosecuted collapsed, the victim killed herself. Another is still self-harming, three years on. She was thirteen when she was abducted and repeatedly raped, and still Woodley painted her as a fantasist and the provocateur of her own assault. The fucking jury believed him."

"Christ," he said soberly. "It sounds like there's a queue of people who would have happily taken him out. And you're in it."

"And they're just the ones that got to court. Where his clients' pockets are deep enough, some cases simply go away. I suspect he or his team persuade the victims' families that a big payout and a non-disclosure agreement is better all round than a sordid court case."

"Does our other victim, Alastair Murdoch, mean anything to you?"

"Sorry, not a thing."

"What about Jimmy Steele, the rock star? I don't suppose he's crossed your radar?"

"No, although so many celebrities are being fingered by the 'me too' movement, it's hard to keep track. But we've received no allegations about him.

"Look," Michelle continued, "this job. It changes you. I try to make sure I'm professional and detached, but sometimes..." She shook her head. "Sorry about the rant. I'm not pleased Woodley's dead, but..." She gave him a mirthless smile. "I'll just shut up."

Quarrel watched her walk back towards her office. Clearly Michael Woodley had made a number of potential enemies, and the Justice Reversed Tarot card chimed with a lot of what Michelle had just said. But would any of those enemies want to kill him?

And, if so, how did Alastair Murdoch fit in?

11

Conor's Body Images was housed in a discreet-looking white-fronted premises in a road just off Tring High Street, where it was quieter than the main drag. The front windows were dark-tinted and, inside, the walls were white and clean, adorned with funky artwork. Medical-looking beds with plastic coverings were positioned a respectable distance from their neighbours.

What Quarrel thought of as 'Celtic spiritual' music, with flutes or recorders, played low in the background while two tattooists – one male, one female – worked on clients. The female was adorning a woman's arm with an elaborate sleeve, featuring intertwining patterns. The client already had something similar on her other arm. The male seemed to be putting the finishing touches to a majestic bird in flight on a young man's upper arm. Quarrel thought it looked like a red kite.

The tattooing machines hummed, their sound somehow blending with the music. Quarrel glanced at Katie, realising too late that perhaps she hadn't been the best choice to accompany him here. She'd gone a few shades paler and was looking anywhere but at the work in progress.

A third member of staff, a woman of indeterminate age with pink hair, flinty eyes and a weasel-ish look about her, turned her nose up at their warrant cards. A name badge, identifying her as Tabitha, hung on a lanyard along with a key.

"We run a clean, respectable business here," she said, her voice a rasp. "I dunno what you're expecting to find. Haven't you got any criminals to catch?" She wore a white singlet, her sleeves and neck a riot of steampunk-style tattoos. There was a gold ring in her left nostril.

"We have," Quarrel agreed, "which is why we're here. But it doesn't follow that anyone here's being accused of anything."

"Sure," she sniffed, radiating disbelief. She jabbed a thumb in the direction of the male tattooist. "Well, that's Conor over there. He's the boss. You'll have to wait. Looks like he won't be long. I suppose you might as well sit down."

They eased themselves into seats, Katie's knuckles whitening as she gripped the chair arms. The pink-haired woman wandered over to her employer and whispered in his ear. He glanced the detectives' way, frowned, and resumed his work.

"Warm welcome," Quarrel murmured.

"Christ knows what the appeal is," Katie hissed back. "I mean, that's beautiful work they're doing, but it's still someone's skin, being changed forever. And as for the blood…" She shuddered.

"Well, they can actually remove them with lasers these days," Quarrel told her, "but I know what you mean. A little motif maybe, but I'm not a fan of the big designs."

She smirked. "You'd consider a little motif? Or perhaps you've already got one, that only Laura has seen?"

"I wouldn't tell you if I had."

They waited over ten minutes for Conor to complete his work. Quarrel watched fascinated, while Katie buried her face in a magazine from the pile on a low table. When the kite design was finished, the tattooist carefully cleaned the area with what he told the client was an antibacterial soap, then bandaged the tattoo.

"This is for protection against bacteria until you get home," he explained. "You should keep the bandage on for twenty-four hours. Where I've injected the ink is now basically an open wound, and your skin is already producing plasma to start the clotting and scabbing process. When you take the bandage off, it's most likely the tattooed area will be weeping and oozing. Don't worry. It's just the body's way of repairing itself."

Quarrel stole a glance at Katie, whose nose was even deeper into her magazine. If anything, she'd turned a shade or two paler.

Connor went on to advise the young man on hygiene and the healing process, and the tell-tale signs of infection, before directing him over to pink-haired Tabitha, to settle his bill and talk about after-care products. He then proceeded to wash his hands fastidiously before coming over to Quarrel and a shaky-looking Katie.

"Sorry about the wait," he said. "You can't really stop in mid-tattoo, and you can't mess around with a client's health." He held out a hand. "Conor Burke."

He had thick, black hair, shaved at the sides, a goatee beard and a gold earring. Quarrel, then Katie, showed their ID, then shook his hand.

"Come into the office," he said.

The small office out back was a contrast to the pristine efficiency of the shop area. It looked like it hadn't seen a lick of paint for decades. An aged partner desk groaned under the weight of paperwork that looked an utter shambles but which, Quarrel half-suspected, might belie some sort of system. Unmatched desk chairs that looked as if they had seen much better days sat either side of it. A battered metal filing cabinet stood in a corner, with more paperwork piled on top.

There was a small, sagging two-seater sofa just inside the door, which Burke gestured them to. They sat and he swept some papers aside to perch on the desk.

"So how can I help you?"

Katie produced printouts of the Rider Waite cards that had been reproduced on two dead men's faces.

"Ever seen these?"

"They're Tarot cards," he said without hesitation. Quarrel was watching him closely for signs of tension or anxiety, but saw none.

"You're familiar with them?" Katie asked.

"An ex-girlfriend was a Tarot reader. She had a few decks, including this one." He smiled a little sadly. "It was her favourite. Why?"

Katie tapped The Fool. "Do you know what this particular deck's called?"

"Sorry, no. Why are you asking me?" He looked puzzled now.

Katie continued to ignore his questions.

"Have you ever done a tattoo like either of these?"

He shook his head. "No."

"But could you?"

He studied the two images for a moment.

"Sure. I could create a template, or you can most likely buy them. If you're a trained tattoo artist, you can do a lovely tattoo based on either of these. But we've had no demand for it in here. Why are you asking all this?"

"Just some research relating to a case," Quarrel said lightly. "By the way, I gather you did a tattoo for Anthea Swallow? The model?"

Conor Burke blinked. "I can't discuss our clients."

"This is police business, Mr Burke. There are ways I can get to see your records, but they'll be time consuming for me and more inconvenient for you. Plus, trust me, Ms Swallow has already confirmed that she came to you. A gift from her husband, apparently."

Burke shrugged, evidently unwilling to resist further. "Since you already know, why are you asking, Inspector?"

"Have you done any other work for her husband, Mr Steele? Any other commissions for third parties?"

"Nope, just that one."

"Have you or your colleagues ever tattooed a whole face?"

He stared at them "What?"

"Just answer the question, please."

"Not here, certainly. Tabby and Jane have worked in other tat shops before they came here, so I can't be sure what they've done in the past. But they haven't said so. You'd have to ask them."

"We will," Katie said.

"Does the name Alastair Murdoch mean anything to you?" Quarrel said.

Burke blinked again. "Wasn't he on the news? The guy who was found dead down at the church? Is that what this is about?"

"Have you come across him before he was on the news?"

"No."

"What about Michael Woodley?"

"Who?"

Quarrel repeated the name.

"I don't think so." Burke stood up. "Look, what's going on?"

"Don't worry," Katie said smoothly. "We're talking to all the tat shops in the area. Asking more or less the same questions."

"But not about Anthea Swallow, right? Where does she come in?"

"You're doing fine," Katie soothed, "and being really helpful."

"Can you take us through your movements on Sunday and after say 6pm last night?" Quarrel asked.

Burke shrugged and perched again. "All right. Let's see. Not a lot. Both nights I was in, watching telly. I usually go to bed around eleven."

"Where's home?"

"I live over the shop."

Quarrel thought this sounded convenient, if Conor Burke was the face tattooist.

"Was anyone with you?"

Burke half-smiled. "I sometimes think this place is haunted, but I don't suppose you'll want to ask the ghost."

"And Sunday afternoon?"

"A long lunch with a few friends at Lussmanns in Tring. They had to throw us out at half three, when they were wanting to close. Then we all came back here. Jane and Tabby were with us. Jane was last to leave, around seven." He looked at Quarrel sharply. "It sounds like I need an alibi. What do you suspect me of? Not murder, I hope?"

"All just routine, sir," Quarrel assured him.

Assuming his friends backed him up about the lunch – and someone could check with the restaurant, for good measure – then Burke wasn't the one who'd abducted Alastair Murdoch nor, in all probability, Michael Woodley. It didn't rule out someone else having done that and then bringing the victims to him. But who?

"How do you become a professional tattoo artist?" Quarrel asked.

"Well, it's best to do an apprenticeship, or at least a tattoo course, and you need a tattoo, piercing and electrolysis licence to work in the business full-time. There's no set national tattoo qualification standard, and there are training courses all over the country, from a one-day introduction through to something a lot longer. For me, though, an apprenticeship is best, if you can find one."

"Learning on the job?"

"Well, to start with, you're watching and learning while you help out round the studio. Sweeping up, putting things back where they belong, making sure the clients are comfortable. It's grunt work, but you get to understand how a studio operates. You get into the right habits, like regular hand washing. You'll only get the chance to actually use the needles when your mentor is sure you're up to it. Reputation can take a lifetime to build up, and just one bad tattoo can ruin it in a heartbeat."

"So what does it take to be ready?"

"There's the health and safety aspects – equipment needs to be cleaned and sterilised, you need a cross-contamination regime, and the machinery needs ongoing maintenance. There's the actual artworking, of course. Then outline theory, shade theory, needle configuration... There's no official, formal structure for a tattoo apprenticeship, and no set time. In a sense, you never stop learning – even old hands like me. But I'd say a decent apprenticeship can take at least two or three years. It depends on the person."

Quarrel made a note. "And how painful is the process?"

Conor smiled. "You'd be surprised how many clients ask that. And there's not a one-size-fits-all answer. The fact is, no matter where you get tattooed, it's going to be uncomfortable, at least to start with. Most people find it goes a bit numb after a bit – maybe their perception of pain reduces as the tattoo proceeds. But how numb, and how soon, depends on your individual pain threshold and where you're getting tattooed."

"So where are the worst places?"

"Well, if you wanted to minimise the pain, you'd have your tattoo on one of the plumper parts of your body – more cushioning to absorb the impact of the needles, see? Places like the outer tops of your thighs, or the meat of your calves, your outer arms. Your bum. On the other hand, the armpit and back of the knees are the most painful places to get a tattoo. After that, it's the soles of your feet. Then the boniest parts of your body. The ribcage is one of the worst. There's not much skin, muscle or fat to provide padding, and every time you breathe, your ribcage expands and contracts. Movement and lack of cushioning are a real recipe for pain."

"The face?"

"Not good news either. However chubby your cheeks might be, there's very little fat on most of the head and face, so the reality is that the needles are bound to hit quite a bit of bone. Just to make it even worse, the head contains no fewer than twelve pairs of major cranial nerves. The eyes, ears, nose, and taste buds all use these nerves to send sensory details to the brain, so tattooing can trigger any number of those to send pain signals there."

"So not pleasant?" Quarrel wasn't surprised.

"A topical anaesthetic, applied about three quarters of an hour before the tattooing starts will help a bit and, as I say, it's all down to individual pain thresholds. But no, I wouldn't fancy it."

"That's helpful, thanks. We'd like a quick word with your staff before we get out of your hair."

Jane Dorcas was still working on her client, so they spoke to Tabitha Hunt next. Hostility came off her in waves as she sprawled in one of the desk chairs, chewing gum.

"How am I supposed to remember every tattoo I've ever done?" she demanded when they showed her the Tarot designs. "I've been doing this for years."

"Surely you'd remember something this elaborate?" Katie suggested.

"You think I don't do classy shit like this all the time?" She looked at the pictures again. "Anyhow, no, I haven't done them designs."

She confirmed the Sunday lunch at Lussmanns, said she'd been to the cinema in Hemel Hempstead with a girl friend on Saturday evening, and claimed a bath, TV and an early night on

Sunday. Jane was free by the time they'd dragged answers out of the recalcitrant Tabitha.

"What can I say?" she said, smiling. "Apart from Sunday lunch, I've no alibis. My partner's working abroad for a couple of weeks, so it's been just me and the cat. I mean, you could try asking Bugsy—"

"Bugsy?" Katie repeated.

"My cat. But he never tells me anything, so good luck with that."

*

"Well, that was actually useful," Quarrel said as they got back in the car. "I mean, we both know there's no real reason to suspect those tattooists, as opposed to any other, of involvement in the case, other than they've done work for Jimmy Steele. And Steele himself is less than a suspect at the moment. At least I've got a bit more of an idea how the business works. Whoever did those tattoos must have put in at least a couple of years training."

"All we need to do now is find them," said Katie.

Quarrel's phone rang. It was Aliya Nazir.

"When do you think you'll be back at the station?"

"Just leaving Tring now, so maybe twenty minutes?"

"Good."

"What's up?"

"I think we might just have a new line of enquiry."

12

"You asked me to see if I could find any hint of a connection between the two victims," Aliya Nazir said. "I spoke to both their workplaces and drew a blank, and then I thought I might as well put both the names into a search engine, just to see if anything came up."

Quarrel, Katie and Aliya were gathered in the incident room.

"And did it?" Quarrel asked her.

"Not specifically, no. Nothing with an actual Alastair Murdoch and Michael Woodley mentioned in the same result. Oh, you know, a few with one of the names plus the first or second name of the other. More than one person with the same name who obviously wasn't them. But not our guys." She gave her head a little shake. "I almost missed it. There was a bit from one of the St Albans local papers to do with a hit and run a few months ago. It mentions a Robert Murdoch and a Luke Woodley.

Quarrel looked at her. "Not the victims' sons?" He snapped his fingers. "Rob Murdoch's best mate was killed by a hit and run driver recently. I remember being told his father's death, on top of that, would be doubly devastating."

Aliya nodded. "This must be the same incident. It seems this guy, Ed Barnes, was drinking with Rob in Marshalswick, St Albans. He had a drop or two more to drink than he should, and had the good sense not to get behind the wheel. He refused a lift home from Rob, took a short cut, and was struck by a car on a dark country lane. Driver never stopped."

"And where does Luke Woodley come in?"

"Ah." Aliya looked pleased with herself. "That's the thing. A witness saw a black Vauxhall Corsa driving away from the spot where Ed was killed around the time the accident's thought to have happened. CCTV picked up Luke's Corsa. He was questioned but released."

"Was he the only motorist questioned?"

"No. But it somehow leaked that Luke's vehicle had a dent in the front nearside wing. His story was that he'd been clipped in a car park earlier in the day.'

"How on earth did details like that even get out?" Quarrel was incredulous. "I take it there was no compelling evidence other than the dent and where he was?"

"Correct. As to how it leaked, though, maybe it had something to do with who Ed Barnes's father is?"

"Go on."

"His name's Jacko Barnes. I made some calls. Bit of an allegedly reformed local bad boy. Nothing big, mind you. A bit of receiving stolen goods, some minor drugs stuff, one small-time burglary. Somewhere along the road, he befriended a few coppers."

"As in bent coppers? He doesn't sound the ideal person for a police officer to be mates with."

"He doesn't," Aliya agreed. "But there doesn't seem to be any suggestion of corruption as such. Nevertheless, he drinks with a couple of local cops. His son's killed in a hit and run and, next thing you know, he's in the paper, the devastated father wanting justice for his son. Someone must have spoken out of turn."

"And he came right out and accused Luke of being the driver? Libel suits have been mounted on less."

"He's too clever for that. Stuck to the facts, demanded answers, and implied that the police hadn't asked enough questions. Didn't mention Michael Woodley by name, but named Luke and accused the police of going soft on a lad born with a silver spoon."

"Okay," Quarrel said. "So he's got a grudge against Luke. Not Rob, presumably, though?"

"You might think that. But in this interview, Jacko said a lot of blame lay with a 'so-called friend' who allowed his mate to walk home half-drunk on a dangerous road in the dark."

Katie frowned. "That's a bit harsh, surely? Ed Barnes was an adult, and you say Rob did offer him a lift. It was Ed's decision to turn it down."

"Jacko talked about him 'claiming' to have offered a lift." She made quote marks with her fingers. "He also said he should have tried harder to make him accept."

"Let's just take a step back," Quarrel said. "We've got a grieving dad, angry, wanting someone to blame – with some justification – and hitting out. But even if he's angry enough to kill, it's Rob Murdoch and Luke Woodley he seems to be blaming. Why wouldn't he target them? Why go after the fathers?"

Aliya grinned at him. "I'm glad you asked that question. It so happens Jacko also said – and I quote – 'I only hope the people responsible will go through what I'm going through one day'."

"He's lost a son…" Katie said.

"So he punishes the men he sees as responsible by taking their fathers away?" Quarrel mused. "It's not a bad shout, is it? Although, why tattoo Tarot cards on their faces? And why those cards?"

"As to the choice of cards," Aliya said, "we're back to what Ricky said. Maybe we're setting too much store by the more esoteric interpretation of the cards. It could be cruder. Rob was a fool to let Ed walk home. Luke has cheated justice."

"We're still stuck on what would make him choose Tarot, or tattoos. I mean, if they really are a message about young Ed Barnes, it's worked, hasn't it? And it's cast suspicion on his dad."

"It does seem stupid," Katie said. "He might as well have pinned a handwritten note to their chests."

"And I still don't see where Tring church or Little Tring Bridge come into it," Aliya admitted. "It's a fair way from St Albans."

"We need to talk again to Rob and Luke and, especially, to Jacko Barnes," said Quarrel. He checked his watch. "I need to get to the post mortem soon. Aliya, you're with me. Katie, can you get hold of Libby and go see Rob and Luke? Then you and I will tackle Mr Barnes."

Katie nodded her agreement. "There's one thing," she said. "If this is really what those murders are about, then maybe Michael Woodley is the end of it, and we can stop worrying that there will be more."

"Then let's hope so," said Quarrel.

*

It was no surprise to Katie that Rob Murdoch was taking some time off work. At this stage, it was far too soon to know when his father's body could be released for a funeral, but the dead man's son was taking the death badly. His sister was sorting a few things out in Derbyshire and then would be coming down for a couple of days.

"We agreed there's not much she can usefully do in Hertfordshire right now," Rob had admitted on the phone, "but we need a bit of time together. Whether it'll help or not? We'll see."

Now they were in his smart flat in Prospect Road, just to the south of St Albans City Centre. The living room was a decent size – larger, Katie thought, than the one in her terraced house in Berkhamsted – and nicely enough furnished, with a fair bit of what was probably Ikea in evidence. But if Rob normally kept it at least vaguely tidy, that had gone out of the window. Katie counted five half-full mugs of either tea or white coffee on various surfaces, and post appeared to have been opened and tossed aside on the black leather sofa. A couple of newspapers and a TV guide had been chucked on the floor.

"Sorry about the mess," he'd said as they followed him in. "I can't seem to..." He made a helpless gesture.

"You should see my place," Katie lied. She kept her own home in impeccable order, to the point of obsession. Anything out of place, she couldn't help correcting. She itched to tidy up this room.

He swept up the post and dumped it on a coffee table, offering them the sofa to sit on.

"Tell you what," Libby Statham said. "Why don't I make us all a cuppa? I can rinse these mugs while the kettle's boiling."

"Libby's very good," he said, as she gathered the mugs. "She keeps in touch, has dropped by a couple of times."

Libby smiled. "Just doing my job, Rob."

He nodded absently, then regarded Katie. "But I'm guessing this isn't just a liaison visit, Sergeant. Is there news?"

"Not very much," she admitted. "It's still very early days."

"I heard on the news you had another suspicious death in the area," he said. "You must be busy."

"Early days for that one, too," she said. "But I'd like to ask you about another recent death. A friend of yours." She sat down.

His brow furrowed. "Ed, you mean?"

"Ed Barnes, yes. It's just routine, nothing to worry about. But I think you were one of the last people to see him alive?"

He was still standing. "You think... what exactly *do* you think?"

"Please sit down, Rob. We don't exactly think anything. We just look at anything unusual in the recent life of the victim or their family." It was, at best a half-truth, on top of an evasion. Sometimes, Katie felt like she was lying her head off.

He sat down in a recliner that complemented the sofa, hunching forwards, hands clasped together. "If you say so. What about Ed?"

"You were with him the night he died?"

"You obviously know I was."

"Could you talk me through it?"

He did so. Nothing she didn't already know. A drinking session. Ed having too much.

"He was always a bit too fond of his beer," Rob said. "I don't mean he had a problem. He just enjoyed a pint or several. But he was always sensible, for all that. Knew when he was over the limit. That's why we tended to meet at that pub. He'd often drive there, but was always happy to walk home on a half-decent night, although I always offered him a lift. He'd only accept if it was chucking it down."

"And it was a half-decent night then?"

"Decent enough that he insisted on walking. He reckoned the night air sobered him up."

"So him walking home that night was nothing unusual?"

"Nope. Happened all the time, and he was always fine. I assumed he was fine that time too, until the police got in touch, to say what had happened. They were trying to piece together his last movements. Seems some scumbag ran him down and didn't even have the decency to stop. No one seems to know for sure if Ed could have been saved if they had. Probably not. Massive head injuries, they said." His lower lip trembled. "He was my best mate, even though Dad never liked him. We went back to our first days at senior school."

"Why didn't your dad like him?"

"Ed's dad had been in some trouble."

"Jacko?"

"You know, then?" He shrugged. "Ed played the wide boy, too, but I always reckoned he was all talk. But my dad reckoned he was a chip off the old block and not a good influence. He never really knew him. Ed was a great laugh, and he'd do anything for a friend."

"But his dad blamed you for what happened to him. That's right, isn't it?"

"Yeah, he was all over the local press for a couple of weeks. Lashing out. Like I wasn't already blaming myself." He leaned back in his seat. "But what are you saying? You can't think this has anything to do with Dad. Can you?"

Katie watched Libby come back in with two mugs, setting one down in front of Rob and one in Katie's reach. The FLO disappeared back into the kitchen and Katie sidestepped the question.

"There was something about the car that hit Ed, wasn't there? Someone the police spoke to and let go?"

"Some rich lawyer's son. Jacko seemed to think the dad had pulled strings for him."

"What do you think?"

"Honestly?" Rob shrugged again. "I really don't know. It sounds unlikely. I'm guessing they didn't have enough on him.

Maybe he *was* the driver, maybe not. I wonder if he took as much shit on social media as I did, thanks to Jacko."

There was a first note of indignation in his voice. "I had to shut down my accounts. All this crap, saying I was a bad friend, as much to blame for Ed's death as the driver. I got death threats. Threats to rape my girlfriend, even though I haven't even got one at the moment. Threats to kill my family..." He paused, shock registering in his eyes. "You don't think..."

It wasn't an angle that had crossed Katie's mind. But vigilante justice fuelled by online outrage?

Both victims' sons had been in the public eye for a while. The team had been wondering if Jacko Barnes might have been punishing those he blamed for his son's death through their fathers, applying some twisted eye-for-an-eye logic. The thought that there could be any number of keyboard warriors out there, taking justice into their own hands, was a chilling one.

Libby returned with a mug for herself and sat down beside Katie.

"Like I say," Katie said, "we're just covering all the bases."

"But that guy who was found this morning," he said, horror on his face. "They said on the news *he* was a lawyer. A QC. Don't tell me he was the driver's dad?"

This was getting out of control. Later, Katie could run over the conversation and see if she might have handled it differently. But right now she needed to stop Rob spiralling into speculation that would be unhelpful, especially if he started articulating it outside this room.

"Look, Rob," she said, "you have to trust us to do our jobs. Right now, our job is to ask a lot of questions and build up a picture of your dad and those closest to him. There's no need for you to go reading things into it. As for the other death we're investigating, we're not saying there's a connection at the moment." That was at least technically true.

"I'll be keeping in close touch," Libby added. "As soon as we have something to say, you'll be the first to hear."

"Try not to worry," Katie said.

"But my sister. Is *she* safe?"

She couldn't promise that, not yet. But it was premature to start saying she should take precautions or needed protection. Most likely she'd be fine. Although, if the current theory held up and the murders were retribution for Ed Barnes's death, it was always possible that the killer wouldn't stop at the fathers of the men held responsible.

"Just remind her to take care with her personal security," she said. "Like she should do anyway. I'm sure she'll be fine."

"Bloody Jacko. Jacko the Lad, with his friends in the police, his mates in the music business…"

"Music?" Her ears pricked up.

"Rock stars. Old ones. I think he hung around the circuit back in the day. Probably dealing drugs," he sneered.

"Jimmy Steele?"

"Never heard of him."

"Did your dad ever mention a woman he was working with on some church projects? Anthea?"

His eyes were blank. "He was always doing churchy stuff. Like I think I said before, I'm not that into religion. My best mate run down, my mum gone from cancer. Now this. He talked about the church and it washed over me. Yeah, this Anthea might ring a bell. Not sure, really."

"She used to be a famous model. She's married to Jimmy Steele, the rock star. Your dad used to do his accounts." She chose not to mention that Steele was the client Alastair had fallen out with.

"I don't think Dad mentioned any of that. Celebrities meant nothing to him. And he'd never say who his clients were. A famous model?" He shook his head. "I'd remember that."

13

"Luke, why didn't you tell us you'd been questioned by the police in connection with a hit and run?" Katie wanted to know.

St Albans police had sent their own family liaison officer, Carol Nugent, along to sit in on Katie's return visit to the Woodleys' Harpenden home. But DS Appleby had decided to pass. Michael Woodley had been his missing person, but he was Katie's murder victim. Nugent would remain the family's FLO, offering them continuity, and would be a point of contact between the two divisions.

They were back in that *Home and Garden* kitchen. Both Luke and Clare were red-eyed, almost certainly from a great deal of crying. For Katie, this intrusion into raw grief was one of the most horrible aspects of the job.

Luke Woodley's expression was hard to read. Defensive? Belligerent? Confused? Or maybe a bit of all three.

"Why would I?" he said. "I mean, you knew that, surely?"

Katie had already quizzed Appleby on this. It seemed the hit and run hadn't been his case and, apart from Jacko's brief spell in the media spotlight, Luke's possible involvement in Ed Barnes's death had been a brief, circumstantial lead that had gone nowhere.

Plus, Appleby had admitted, the leaking of Luke's name to Jacko had left a bad smell around the station that everyone was trying to forget.

It still felt sloppy, but pointing fingers wasn't going to help. And it wouldn't undo Michael Woodley's murder.

"*I* didn't know," Katie said. "Not when I came to see you earlier. I'm not based in this area, remember."

"I still don't see the relevance," he said.

"I do," Luke's mother said. "You think it has something to do with Michael's death? That horrible man, Jacko Barnes.

Luke was hung out to dry in the press. Trolled on social media. Death threats. Threats to his family. To me. To Michael..."

"Jesus." Luke was wide-eyed. "You think someone killed Dad because—"

"No." Katie held up her palm, as if she could block the thoughts going through his mind. It was impossible to ask these questions without provoking those thoughts. "We've no reason to suspect anything like that, not at the moment. We're just building up a picture. But we can't rule out anyone with a grudge against you, or who might have threatened you or your family."

"I see," Luke snarled. "So that's all right, is it? I swear on my life that I didn't knock that guy down. I was just in the wrong place at the wrong time. I'd been out, I went home, and I passed by the outskirts of Marshalswick where the accident happened. You lot admitted that you couldn't even say for sure it was a Corsa that hit him. Some clown had dinged my car in a car park earlier in the day—"

"Did you report it to anyone?"

"What's the point? It happens all the time. People hit your car and drive off. I was going to get a quote for the repair and see if it was worth making an insurance claim."

"But did you mention it to anyone? Earlier in the day, I mean?"

"I didn't even notice until the following morning. It must have happened in the supermarket car park. I stopped off on the way home from work to get some chocolates for a work colleague's birthday the next day. I was going to ask them to check their CCTV, to see if they could see it happening."

"And did you?"

"I didn't get a chance. The police came to my work the next day, questioning me. I told them everything. They looked at the tapes, said they were 'inconclusive', whatever that meant. But that appeared to be that. Until someone gave my name to the victim's dad, and it was a nightmare for months afterwards. I shut down my Facebook. Maybe the trolls have moved on. Maybe not. I don't look."

"If your loose tongues got my husband murdered—" Clare started.

"We don't know any of that yet," Katie said.

"This trolling," Libby said. "Was it reported to the police?"

"Of course," Luke said. "Oh, we were assured they took it seriously. Nothing seems to have come of it though."

Katie made a note to see where that investigation had got to.

There wasn't much to add, and they left soon afterwards. Driving past rows of trees and open fields on the road out of Harpenden, she ran through the various strands of the investigation so far.

"We've got Jimmy Steele, who made veiled threats to Alastair Murdoch over his accounts," she said to Libby. "And Alastair was working closely with Steele's wife. They also knew a tattooist. And Jacko Barnes appears to have had connections in the music business. Maybe Barnes and Steele got talking. Found they both had a grudge against the Murdoch family and decided to do something about it, and about Luke Woodley too, through his father."

"I don't know. It feels a bit far-fetched. What about these trolls?"

"Trolls make death threats all the time. It doesn't mean they all carry them out. If it even happens, it's very rare."

"It just takes one twisted individual to be influenced by them. Or maybe it *was* Jacko Barnes, but Jimmy Steele had nothing to do with it."

"Too many maybes," Katie acknowledged. They were passing the outskirts of Redbourn, with its Iron Age and Roman connections and home to the Hertfordshire County Show. "We need to speak to Mr Barnes. I wonder how the guv got on with the post mortem."

*

Izzy Cole couldn't deny she's had butterflies in her stomach as she'd taken her seat in the incident room for the first briefing on the Murdoch and Woodley murders. A quick catch up, apparently.

When her boss, Sergeant Sally Todd, had taken her aside earlier today and told her she'd been asked for by name, she'd been stunned. She'd wished she could be in on the investigation, and now it was happening.

"You evidently made quite an impression on this DI Quarrel," Sally had said. "Either he likes the way you work, or he's got the hots for you," she'd added slyly.

Izzy doubted very much it was the latter. Quarrel had been all business the two times they'd met. Not unfriendly, but serious. She was flattered to think he wanted her on this team. Maybe by next week she'd be back to altercations in pub car parks or petty shoplifting. But in the meantime, she was determined to make the most of this opportunity.

"It's pretty clear that this is the same killer," Quarrel was saying. "Not that there was ever much doubt. Identical restraint marks, same marks where the heads were immobilised, and the tape across the mouths seems identical too. And the victim had inhaled cotton fibres, just as Alastair did, when he was smothered. It can't be a copycat. There's just too much information – including, of course, the tattoos and their nature – that isn't in the public domain."

"I don't suppose there's anything back from the tox screens yet?" DCI Sharp asked, her tone more hope than expectation.

"No chance, ma'am. Even fast-tracked, we're talking at least a week, maybe two. Obviously, if – as we think likely – some substance was used to incapacitate these men, it might help point us towards the killer. Although you can order so much stuff on the Internet now, and that's without the dark web. And we don't even know if he used anything that will show up on a tox screen."

"Fair enough," Sharp acknowledged. "I still want someone to keep pushing. Twice a day, please."

"Izzy, can you do that?"

She started. So far, she'd spent her time settling in – reading herself in, finding her way around the station and learning who really made this place tick. Now she was being given her first small piece of work. Not a great challenge to her deductive skills, but it was a beginning.

"I'll get straight on it," she said.

She privately thought that being a nuisance to the lab might be counterproductive, but she could imagine the pressure the DCI was under. It had been a very long time since Tring had seen so much media activity, and there was open speculation on the TV news that the two deaths were connected, even though the press office had declined to comment on that.

Sally Todd had said more than once that Izzy should have been a diplomat. Polite, non-aggressive persistence was the approach she'd take to getting those lab results as soon as possible.

"Okay," DI Quarrel said. "So we've heard back from DS Gray, and this hit and run remains the only connection between Alastair and Michael that we've unearthed so far. So she and I will be visiting Jacko Barnes next, to see what he has to say for himself. But we've also got these trolls. Can someone – Ricky? – make a start on seeing what malicious messages were sent to Rob and Luke and what progress St Albans have made with tracking down the originators?"

"Sure," Ricky drawled. "Although, as we know, a really clever troll is hard to pin down. Multiple fake online profiles, moving around Internet cafés so the IP address won't lead to their door..."

"As you say," Quarrel said, "we know all that. But let's see where we're at anyway. I'm sure St Albans are as stretched as we are. There's a difference between making online threats and actually carrying them out. No disrespect to our colleagues, but..."

He left it at that. Everyone knew there often wasn't enough time to go round. Things got put on a back burner, or just required too much effort when higher priorities arose. There was no reason to suppose a thorough job hadn't been done, but Izzy understood why he wanted to be sure.

Aliya Nazir raised an index finger.

"Yes, Aliya?"

"Guv, if we're revisiting the trolls, we should look for references to tattoos or Tarot cards, even if they're a bit oblique.

Say, for instance, someone tweeted 'Your death is on the cards'."

"Good point. Ricky, see if that sort of thing can be isolated. It might narrow the communications down, give us a focus."

"Will do."

One of the other uniforms, Sophie Monahan, had given Izzy a quick run-down on the team. Apparently Ricky had a bit of an action man self-image, but the DC also understood techie stuff better than anyone on the team and loved his social media – making him the natural choice for this job.

"Right," Quarrel said. "Anything else?"

"CCTV footage from Harpenden and other stations," Sophie said. "St Albans are still reviewing. No sign of Michael Woodley having got off at Harpenden. Interestingly, two cameras at the next stop, Luton Airport Parkway, are out. Smashed by vandals the night before last."

"Quite the coincidence," Quarrel mused. "If I was planning to play the Good Samaritan to a man who'd missed his stop, I might want to make sure the cameras didn't spot me doing it. I suppose local CSIs are checking to see if the so-called vandals left any clues?"

"Nothing definitive so far."

"Why am I not surprised?" He made another note on the Wall. "We know he was in the Harpenden area just before 8pm, so let's pinpoint when his train would most likely have got into the Parkway and see what cars departed the station around that time. We could be looking for a dark saloon or a white van."

"I'll get back to them," Sophie said.

"Good. Well done, everyone. Let's keep at it."

*

Quarrel watched them file out. Sharp hovered until the last of them had departed.

"Anything you need from me?" she asked.

"Nothing specific," he said. "If you can placate the Super when he and the other brass start expecting miracles, that'd be good."

She smiled. "We both know Superintendent Taylor isn't the most patient of men, but I'll do my best. He's probably going to want to do a press conference soon."

"I'm sure. The longer we can hold off, though, the better I'd like it. If the media sense that there's a serial killer at work on our patch, then the coverage we're already getting will be a teddy bear's picnic, compared to the feeding frenzy we'll likely see. It won't be helpful, Rachel."

"I'll tell him all that. But it might make him all the more keen. You know how he likes the spotlight."

14

Jacko Barnes's 1970s terraced house was tucked away in a cul-de-sac in the village of Markyate, once a rural and agricultural area, but now more of a dormitory village for Luton and the surrounding region.

Whatever Quarrel had expected Jacko Barnes to look like, it wasn't the man who opened the door. Short, wide, bald on top, and sporting what used to be called a 'National Health' spectacles frame with the thickest pair of lenses Quarrel had ever seen. Barnes wore a grubby grey tank top, a faded green polo shirt, and a pair of rumpled brown trousers, with more folds than a concertina. Tattoos crawled over his arms and neck.

He flashed yellow teeth. "You must be DI Quarrel." There was a smoker's rasp to his voice. "And this lovely lady must be DS Gray. Still, I'd best see some ID before I let you in. Can't be too careful."

They duly showed him their warrant cards and he made a meal of inspecting them.

"Seems in order," he finally said. "Come in."

He showed them into a reasonable sized lounge/dining room. Quarrel's first impression was that the place was well enough kept. 'Lived in,' his grandmother would have called it. A place for everything, but not necessarily everything in its place.

Barnes looked down at himself, then grinned at them. "Sorry about the glad rags. I did a bit in the garden today and never got round to changing. Cuppa?"

"We're fine," Quarrel said, eager to get on.

"Fair enough." Barnes sprawled on the only sofa. "Grab a seat."

Quarrel and Katie took the two easy chairs that flanked the sofa.

"We're investigating two murders in the Tring area, Mr Barnes," Quarrel said. "You might have heard about them on the news."

"Murdoch and Woodley." Barnes nodded, a small smile teasing his lips. "I did wonder. Are they the fathers of those two little sods who killed my Ed?"

"They were the fathers of Rob Murdoch and Luke Woodley," Quarrel responded. "I wouldn't characterise either of the sons in that way, though."

"No?" Jacko Barnes was grinning openly now. "Oh, but this is rich. Now they'll find out what it feels like to lose someone."

"And you approve of that, Mr Barnes?" Katie asked.

"I believe in karma. Did you know it'll be Ed's birthday on Friday?"

"Interesting choice of words," she said. "Interesting timing, too. Do you also believe some things are written in the stars – or maybe in the *cards*?"

His eyes narrowed. "Have you come here for a philosophy debate, or do you have a point? Only I've things to do."

"Where were you last night?" Quarrel brought the interview back on track.

"What, all night?"

"Let's start with between seven and nine."

"Having my dinner. Sainsbury's lasagne, if you're interested. Watching the soaps. *Emmerdale, Corrie, EastEnders…*"

"Can anyone confirm that?"

"Not unless my neighbours are spying on me, no. I'm divorced, Inspector, and I've never found true love since, despite me being such a great catch. Ed was all that mattered to me. So if you're wondering if I'd kill those boys' fathers, to get back at them… well, it's not a bad idea. But I'm not a violent man. You'll have seen my record?"

Quarrel nodded.

"Well, you know I've done wrong in the past, but those days are long gone. And I've never hurt anyone. I tell you what, though."

"We're listening."

"If I wanted to do anything to those lads, I'd go after them, not their dads."

"And yet," Katie said, "you're on record as hoping Rob and Luke suffer loss like you suffered."

"Am I?" He shrugged. "You remember better than I do, sweetheart. But am I sorry this has happened to them? No. It's just that I had nothing to do with it."

"You must admit it's quite a coincidence, though," Quarrel said.

"Not really," Barnes said dismissively. "For all I know, the dads were as big a pair of shits as the sons. I don't know who they've pissed off, do I?"

"We didn't see a car on your drive," Katie said.

"I keep it in the garage." He grinned again. "I know that's not the norm, these days – using a garage for the car, instead of storing junk in it. But I've always done it. I like driving off on a frosty morning when everyone else is scraping the windows."

"What car do you drive?"

"A Mondeo. Dark blue."

Katie and Quarrel exchanged a quick glance.

"Do you happen to have access to a white van?" Katie asked.

"I'm a delivery driver these days, so yes."

"And where's that?"

"At the depot. I drive there, pick up the van, drop it off at the end of the day. So what?"

"What time did you pick it up yesterday?"

"About half eight. You really think I did this, don't you." He looked amused. "Good luck proving that."

"But," she persisted, "could you have picked it up earlier? What time does the depot open?"

"Seven." Harry Baker, who'd found Woodley's body, reckoned he'd seen a speeding white van near Startops before 5.30am. "And you have to book the keys in and out. Why the interest in a van, though? Do you think your killer used one?"

"Let's stick to us asking the questions and you answering," Quarrel said. "What did you do on Sunday?"

"I'd have to think, if you want a blow by blow," said Barnes. "But I'm what you'd call a creature of habit. Wash the car and cut the grass on a Sunday morning, then lunch at the pub and a couple of pints – they know me in there." He named the pub and Katie made a note. "Then home, bit of telly and bed. Boring, aren't I?"

"And you've no keys to the depot? No spare keys to the van?"

"You can check."

"We will. Now," Quarrel altered tack, "I gather you spent a bit of time on the fringes of the music scene a few years ago."

"A lot of years ago. That was when I got fitted up over some drugs that weren't mine. What of it?"

"Did you know Jimmy Steele?"

"Jimmy? Yeah, I met him a few times. Knew him before and after he was famous. Not that well, mind. And he wouldn't give me the time of day after the drugs thing. Very protective of his gorgeous missus. She used to have a habit, you know."

"So when did you last see him?"

"To speak to?" He screwed up his face. "Could be twenty-five years. More, maybe."

"Not recently?"

"Like I said, we were never bosom buddies. I doubt he even remembers me."

"I see you like your tattoos," Katie said. "Who did them?"

"Why?" he asked. "Fancy one yourself?"

"I fancy an answer."

"Christ, you're a barrel of laughs, love. I bet you're single. Married to the job."

"She's not your love, or your sweetheart," Quarrel said, wearying of this man and his attitude. "Perhaps we should do this at the station."

"All right." Barnes held up his hands in surrender. "I got my tats years ago. The Ink Place in Luton. What's that got to do with anything?"

"How many years?" Katie asked.

"Twenty? Thirty?"

"Do you still have contact with them?"

"No. But why—"

"What about Tarot cards?" Quarrel asked. "Have you had anything to do with them?"

"Do I look it? Do me a favour."

He looked genuinely bemused, inasmuch as Quarrel believed there was anything genuine about Jacko Barnes. But, if they had hoped to find a man still up to his neck in criminal activity, with underworld connections who could help him abduct, mutilate and kill the fathers of men he wanted to punish, that wasn't what Quarrel was seeing. Just a sad man with a dull job and a dull life.

Or was that what he wanted them to see?

"That'll be all for now," Quarrel said, rising. "We'll want the details of your employer, so we can check out what you say about the van."

Barnes grimaced. "All right. But you'll watch what you say, right?" The cockiness had evaporated, replaced be a more wheedling tone. "I'm straight these days and I need this job. I can do without the police making trouble for me."

"We'll be the soul of discretion," said Quarrel.

*

There had been a late catch up with the team at the end of Izzy's first day. So far she hadn't done much hands-on investigating, but then she knew the uniforms on the team were all about gathering information in support of the detectives. And she was the new girl. It was to be expected that some fairly humdrum tasks were thrown her way, at least to start with.

All the same, she found she was really enjoying the buzz of an incident room and a major investigation. The energy levels were high, with everyone mucking in and doing what was asked of them without question. Nobody – not even DI Quarrel – seemed to think any job was beneath them.

When the meeting wrapped up, Quarrel sent everyone home. Izzy knew she was going back to an empty flat. Matt was working away again, for a couple of nights. It was a shame. She'd have loved to have told him about her secondment face to face, but she'd have to content herself with a phone call.

His business trips seemed to be on the increase lately. With her own work commitments, it wasn't ideal when you were building what was still a relatively new relationship. They'd been seeing each other for just over six months. When they were both free, Matt often stayed over at her place. Sometimes she stayed at his small house just off Hemel's Old Town.

Her best mate, Bethany, was in no doubt that Matt was 'a keeper'.

"I'll have him, if you finish with him," she'd said after Izzy had introduced them: a night at the pub, just the three of them. It had been important to Izzy to get her friend's seal of approval.

She supposed finding someone you could get on with was something to cherish these days. Bethany's last relationship had ended in tears, Gavin dumping her and accusing her of clinginess. Izzy had been too tactful to say anything, but she knew what he meant.

Meeting Matt had been a twist of fate. Two strangers sitting together on a crowded train, a stop-go journey, a conversation struck up. The exchange of contact details had been the most natural thing in the world.

She just wished they could get more time together, to find out what it was they really had.

One thing was certain. He'd be delighted with her news. He knew her ambitions and encouraged them. She couldn't wait to tell him about her day.

*

Quarrel had wanted to speak to Jimmy Steele again before calling it a day, but the musician wasn't at home and wasn't answering his mobile. So, after sending everyone else home, he'd headed off himself. Laura was off shift for four days and would be home; he was eager to see her.

On the way, he mulled over the latest information that had come to light. There was precious little, but Ricky James had some preliminary details about the online trolls that had targeted Rob Murdoch and Luke Woodley. It was no real surprise that there were a handful who had savaged both men. A couple had been easy enough to track down and had been scared off from further maliciousness. A few remained undetected. Most of those had moved on to other targets, but one still wouldn't let it go.

The troll using the handle Ace of Spades – of which there were many in the online universe – clearly had multiple other identities, but the very similar language they all used, plus the fact that they all alternated between the same six online cafés, was the giveaway.

"Cards again," Ricky had said. "Interesting, don't you think?"

"Ace of Spades." Katie looked sceptical. "The death card. But why not a Tarot card?"

"Maybe he or she's trying to be clever," Ricky had speculated.

"I don't get it. If these accounts are known to be abusing people, can't they be closed down?"

"I asked the same question. It seems that, rather than try to get those accounts closed, the St Albans force has taken the view that they would only open new ones and carry on. They live in hope of making an arrest under the Malicious Communications Act. The trouble is, to stand any real chance of doing so, all six cafés would need to be staked out, to catch this creep in the act – and there simply isn't the manpower."

"We might have to find it," Quarrel had said. "Or another way."

Home at last, he let himself in and slung his jacket over the bannisters at the bottom of the stairs.

"Hi!" he shouted.

Laura appeared at the top of the stairs. "Hello, you."

She was about nine inches shorter than Quarrel, but then most people were shorter than him. She kept herself at peak fitness for her job and was lean and well-muscled. Her dark hair was cut short. But there was nothing masculine about her. She'd always been a woman in a predominantly male job, doing it on her own terms.

He used his long stride to take the stairs two at a time and took her in his arms, stooping in for a kiss.

"There's a bottle of white chilling, if you're interested," she said after a long hug.

"Very interested."

"Oh," she said, "and there's a letter on the side for you."

He wandered over to the corner of the worktop where post tended to get dumped. He recognised the envelope and the handwriting immediately, his stomach tying itself in a knot.

"It's from her," he said flatly. He sighed. "I'll take it up and shred it."

"One of these days, Nate, you're going to have to open one of them."

"Yes?" He tried not to go all belligerent on her, not now they were together at last. "You know I opened the first three. They all said the same thing. This'll be just the same."

He picked it up between thumb and forefinger and headed for the stairs up to his office.

"Maybe *I* ought to read it," Laura suggested.

He stopped. "Let's not do this again. I made my mind up years ago, before I even met you, and nothing's going to change it. Let me put this through the shredder, and then we can forget it."

He saw the concern etched on her face as he turned back towards the stairs. He knew she didn't agree with him, but it wasn't her decision to make. Even so, he hesitated for a few seconds before consigning the envelope and its contents to the shredder.

"So how was your shift?" he asked, snuggled up with her on the sofa, wine in hand. "Quiet?"

"We had a small barn fire, so a bit of excitement. No one hurt, and we managed to save most of it. How about you? I've..." She took a sip of wine. "I've been hearing about the murders on the news. I bet you've got them?"

"That's me," he said. "Mr Murder."

"Do you think there'll be more, or is that it?"

"Honestly? I don't know." He told her about the Tarot tattoos. "We're not releasing that for now." He completely trusted her discretion, and he valued the insights she sometimes had. But she had none of those tonight.

"Will you catch him?"

"Or her. Eventually. Got to. But you know me. I'm already worried I missed something that could have prevented the second death."

She kissed him on the cheek. "I told you when we first met. You can't save everyone."

*

Three years ago.
An evening walk by one of the Tring reservoirs that feeds the canal.

Quarrel hears a commotion. A woman in the water, struggling with what looks like a man's body, face down. He doesn't hesitate. He kicks off his shoes and plunges into the ice-cold water to help.

The cold stirs all-too-familiar feelings that threaten to overwhelm him for a few seconds, but he somehow fights them down.

"I don't think he's breathing," she says as he comes up the other side of the man in the water, taking a one-handed grip on his collar. "Can we get him on his back?"

Together, they manage to turn him over, so his face is out of the water before, with no need for further consultation, starting to swim for the bank, progress slowed by their burden and needing to paddle with only one hand. Between them, they get the man onto the towpath.

"Definitely not breathing," the woman says. "Call an ambulance. I'll try CPR"

She keeps trying, Quarrel a helpless, shivering bystander, until the paramedics arrive and take over.

They wait by the ambulance, blankets around their shoulders. Quarrel isn't sure whether he's shivering purely with the cold, or because he already knows in his heart that the man isn't going to make it.

There's something about the woman he likes though, some connection beyond what they have just gone through. She's told him her name is Laura.

When a paramedic finally tells them the man they tried to save is dead, Quarrel takes it as a personal failure. Laura seems to see it in his eyes. She gives his arm a squeeze.

"You can't save everyone," she says. "I'm a firefighter. If I let it eat me up every time I couldn't get to someone in time, I'd have lost my sanity by now."

"You're a fireman?"

"Fire person." But she's grinning. It's the first time he's seen her smile. He likes it.

"I'm a policeman."

She gasps. "No way! What are the chances?" Another grin, cheeky this time. "It must be fate."

Before they part, she gives him her phone number.

*

"Earth to Nathan?" Laura dragged him back to the present.

"Sorry. Yes, you're right, of course. I know I can't save everyone. It doesn't stop me wanting to try."

"I know. It's one of the things I love about you." She put her glass down and hugged him. "I just worry about you sometimes."

"Says the woman who runs into burning buildings for a living."

"Used to," she said. "Until someone not a million miles from here persuaded me to go into management."

As crew manager, she supervised her crew members' activities at the station, made sure her fire appliance and equipment were in working order and took charge of smaller incidents. She also supported her watch manager at more major incidents. Her role was supposed to be more supervisory these days, but he knew that, on at least two occasions, she'd been berated and praised in equal measure for taking calculated personal risks when members of her crew had been in danger.

"Best thing I ever did," he said. "Bad enough when you come home smelling all smoky."

She was silent for a moment. "These murders," she said. "I know what you're like. You'll look back and decide, with hindsight, that there was more you should have done. Remember, hindsight's a wonderful thing."

"So you always tell me," he said. But they both knew he wasn't convinced.

15

For Megan Jacobs, it had been a good day. Work had gone well, and she'd been busy from start to finish. The time had flown by. Then, outside the office, she'd bumped into an old acquaintance who'd suggested a quick drink. It had been a nice surprise, a good chance to catch up and to chat about shared memories. The only down side had been how woozy she felt after just one drink. Her companion had expressed concern about her driving in that condition and had offered to drive her home.

The last thing she remembered before waking up here was some sort of cloth being pressed over her face.

Where exactly *here* was, she had no idea. She couldn't see very much, with her head immobilised by something hard and cold that pressed tightly enough to be uncomfortable, but without actually hurting. There were bright lights and the ceiling was high and yellowing. There was a musty smell in the air.

She could hear someone moving about above her.

Again Megan tested whatever the bindings were that lashed her to a hard surface that might be wood, or possibly metal. There was no give in them at all. The attempt at movement, and the fresh wave of terror that washed over her, made her head spin. For a moment she fancied she felt nauseous, and that was especially terrifying. She dare not vomit behind the tape that sealed her lips together. With nowhere to go, the vomit would choke her.

She was twenty-four years old. She desperately didn't want to die.

She fought down the urge to be sick and willed herself to keep as calm as she could. She had to think. Think about why this was happening to her, and how she might be able to get out of it.

She worked in PR, after all. A lot of what she did was to do with shaping ideas and opinions. If she could only get inside this person's head, understand their motivation, then maybe she could somehow talk her way out of this situation.

Of course, she realised, she couldn't do much talking with this tape over her mouth. Perhaps her captor would remove it. Perhaps they'd want to talk. If not, how might she persuade them to remove it? She didn't think making *'Mmmph!'* noises was the answer.

She wondered how long she'd been here. Long enough for her parents to wonder where she'd got to, and worry?

Footsteps upstairs again, above the ceiling she was forced to stare up at. Then the sound of a door opening. The footsteps were coming downstairs, walking towards her. A face coming into view.

"Good," her abductor said. "You're awake. About time too. You've been asleep a bit longer than the others."

Oh, Christ, there'd been others. What had become of them? Nothing good, she suspected. Nothing good at all.

For the first time, total despair ran through her. No one knew she was here. In all likelihood, no one even knew she was missing yet. And she was in the hands of... what exactly? A serial killer? Someone who tortured their victims first – or, perhaps, to death?

Why else would she be strapped down and totally immobilised?

The only saving grace was that she seemed to still be fully clothed. Somehow she thought that, if some kind of sexual perversion was intended, she would have been stripped naked.

Or, perhaps, the monster who held her intended cutting off her clothes. Perhaps that would be part of some sort of obscene gratification.

Monster. In all her nightmares, if she'd ever imagined finding herself in this sort of mess, she didn't think she would have envisaged her kidnapper taking this form. It was almost laughable.

Almost.

Megan attempted to speak behind the tape. The muffled noises she made provoked nothing more than a smile.

"What's that? You're not making any sense. Not that I'd expect you to."

The taunt infuriated her. She bellowed behind the gag, only muted animal noises coming out.

The response was a giggle.

"Oh, my, what a temper. Who'd have thought it?" A sad shake of the head. "Oh, well. Can't stand around chatting all night. It's getting late." And then the words that chilled her to the bone. "We've got an awful lot of work ahead of us."

16

Quarrel had got to the office early, thoughts of the case having gone round in his head all night, denying him sleep, yet bringing him no fresh insights. Katie had arrived soon after him, then Izzy Cole. Quarrel might have interpreted the latter's keenness as a newcomer trying too hard to impress, but he was fairly confident that the diligence was genuine in this officer.

By 7.30am, the whole team had assembled. Less than half an hour later, the call had come in.

The dark-haired young woman would have been pretty, Quarrel thought. Before a maniac had desecrated her face with yet another Tarot abomination. Before death had stolen her vitality and its pallor had replaced the bloom in her cheeks.

Her bag sat by her side, like a faithful dog beside its mistress. Whatever these tableaux were about, the bag was part of the staging here. They were resisting the temptation to open it until Debbie Brown and the team arrived.

He felt the familiar gnaw of failure in his guts like some black dog of shame. If he'd missed something that could have seen the killer in custody yesterday, or even sooner, then this outrage would lie at his door.

They were standing in a space behind the DeadlineZ nightclub in the Marlowes, just a stone's throw from the police station. It was a service area where delivery vans could unload, and also where the big bins were stored. The dead woman was propped up, like her predecessors, this time against one of the bins. It was as if she was just one more item of trash.

The body had been discovered by a cleaner, putting out some rubbish from last night. Quarrel had got a uniform to drive the cleaner, Sheila Ellis, up to the hospital to be treated for shock. She'd looked on the verge of collapse.

"This one's the Ten of Swords," Katie was saying wearily, holding up her phone so he could see the same image on the screen as the one inked into the flesh of this once-attractive woman's face.

This card, Rider Waite like the others, depicted a male figure lying face down in the dirt by a calm sea under a dark, brooding sky. Ten swords protruded from his back, in a line from neck to buttocks. A red cape covered the lower half of his body. The tattoo was a pretty good monochrome copy.

"Even I can read the meaning of this," Quarrel said. "She stabbed someone in the back."

"You'd think," Katie agreed. "Let's see what it actually says." She fiddled with the phone. "You notice this one's upright – not reversed like the other two? I wonder if that's significant."

"The whole thing's a bit of a departure. We had two middle-aged men. Now suddenly we have a woman. She must only be mid-twenties, wouldn't you say?"

"I would. Although, if this is all about Ed Barnes, and people being held to blame are being punished through family members, maybe this victim's parents or siblings did something."

"Makes sense." How many more were being blamed for that hit and run?

"So this is what it says about Ten of Swords. When you receive this card in a Tarot reading, it denotes a painful but inevitable ending – perhaps of a relationship, a job, or some sort of trust. You might be the victim of betrayal or deceit, as if you've been stabbed in the back. It happens out of the blue, and you feel your world has fallen apart. Along with the pain, there's also grief over what's been lost."

"So what are we saying? That this woman isn't being punished, but was herself a victim of some sort?"

"It does say the card can suggest you're taking on the role of 'victim', and hoping others will pity you and save you. But it also puts responsibility for letting go and accepting the situation on the person who gets the card. There has to be change, and you have to accept it rather than fight it. If you can pick yourself up and learn from the experience, the pain will fade, and you'll see this needed to happen."

Quarrel wondered if he was overtired or just plain stupid. "But this doesn't make sense, does it? I mean, we could see in the previous two victims how the cards might be hinting at wrongdoing on their parts. In crude terms, Alastair's son was a fool to let Ed drive home. Michael's son had escaped justice for his hit and run crime. But this seems to say someone else has betrayed this victim in some way. Why kill her, and not the betrayer?"

"Maybe we have to look at the sort of wrongdoings the cards are about and ignore the rest. Some sort of loss or betrayal, in this case. So perhaps this woman was the betrayer. Or, if her death has paid for what one of her loved ones did, then they were the ones guilty of betrayal."

"Oh, Christ," he said. "This is like Groundhog Day, isn't it?" Another day, another murder. And the real possibility that the pattern would repeat, day after day, until the killer was stopped.

If they could be stopped.

"All right." He reached for calm. "It's going to be more of the same. Who was this victim? What were her last movements? Who might wish her harm? Is there a link with the other victims? Has she been trolled online?"

"And what exactly might this Tarot design mean for her personally?"

Quarrel looked around the dirty space they were in. Rubbish overflowed from one of the bins. Some cans and bottles were scattered around. A gust of wind disturbed discarded crisp packets and Styrofoam takeaway packaging.

"And why this place?" He puzzled. "It's pretty obvious the killer wants these bodies found. Makes sense, if you go to the trouble of making these tattoos, that you want to display them. But why here? Why Tring Church?"

"Why a canal bridge?"

"There's significance, and we're missing it. All three body dumps in the borough of Dacorum, yet we know this wasn't Ed Barnes's stamping ground."

"Like you say, maybe it's not Ed Barnes," Katie said. "I know we don't believe in coincidences, but maybe we've got the wrong coincidence here. You said yourself that maybe we've been too quick to fasten on him. Whatever the connection is, we're just not seeing it yet."

He found that his head was starting to hurt. Rummaged in a pocket and found a blister pack of paracetamol. "Got any water?" he asked.

She fished a bottle from her bag and offered it to him. He washed down two of the tablets with a couple of sips.

"Thanks." He wiped his mouth with the back of his hand. "I suppose if you believe in six points of contact, there might be something in it. Alastair Murdoch and Michael Woodley aren't directly blamed for Ed Barnes's death, and we've been thinking their deaths were proxies to punish the sons. But maybe they, and our new victim, all have a more direct connection to whatever motivates the killer. Bloody hell." He shook his head. "Too many damned theories. And Jimmy Steele, Anthea Swallow, even their tattooist, Conor Burke... they could be involved in some way, or not at all."

"There's a key to all this," Katie said. "And we *will* find it. When we do, everything else will start to fall into place."

"I'm sure you're right." He tried to match her positive tone, but his gloom only lifted for an instant, before settling back on his shoulders. "But how many days will it take? How many more deaths?"

17

The dead woman's name was Megan Jacobs. Amongst the items in her bag had been a driving licence and a DeadlineZ membership card. Quarrel couldn't help thinking the killer had left the bag because he'd wanted the body identified, like all the others. At the same time, that card was a third departure from victim type, compared with Murdoch and Woodley. Different gender, different age bracket and now, for the first time, an association with the location where the body had been found.

Megan Jacobs had lived with her parents in Adeyfield, the first planned neighbourhood built in Hemel's new town expansion. The Jacobs' home was a semi-detached house which sat behind a high hedge, with a driveway running up the side to the front porch.

Megan's mother, Valerie, was at home on her own and perplexed to find three police officers on her doorstep. Quarrel had asked Libby Statham to accompany him and Katie, although he suspected they'd need to introduce another FLO to the case if the body-a-day pattern kept on repeating.

Valerie led them into an almost square kitchen that Quarrel supposed looked a bit tired and out of date. She was slim to the point of thinness, with elfin-cut blonde hair and a hint of dark roots. She wore no make-up and looked a little washed-out.

She offered them chrome-legged stalls around a narrow breakfast bar and put the kettle on.

"So what's this about?" she said finally.

"You ought to sit down," Quarrel said, gently but firmly.

Whatever Valerie Jacobs had imagined was the purpose of their call, her whole demeanour changed now, her expression turning from curiosity to naked fear. She pulled up a stool. Quarrel wondered if he'd made an error not insisting they do this in the living room. He imagined a whole range of reactions, each one toppling the stool over, her head smashing on the hard tiled floor.

He prepared to jump up and grab her if there was any risk of that happening.

"I'm afraid we have some terrible news about your daughter, Megan," he said. "A body has been discovered in the town, and we believe it to be her. We're so sorry, Mrs Jacobs."

As he spoke, the blood leeched from her face, her mouth making a tight line. Her hands gripped the edge of the breakfast bar, the knuckles whitening. But she didn't faint, nor did she show any sign of losing her equilibrium.

"Are you sure?" she whispered. "That it's her, I mean?"

"She had her driving licence with her. She looks very much like the photograph. Obviously, she'll need to be formally identified."

"Obviously. Can you tell me what happened to her?"

Quarrel would have almost preferred her to fall apart. He thought the real shock would set in later, and it could be bad when it came.

"Can we call someone for you?"

"My husband. He's not long left for work in London." She checked her watch. "He'll be on his train by now."

Libby Statham took his mobile number and went outside, saying she would arrange for him to be met at one of the stops and the news broken discreetly. Then someone would drive him home and pick up his car for him.

Valerie agreed to all this like an automaton.

"I'm so sorry," Quarrel said again, "but we do need to ask you some questions."

"You haven't answered mine yet. Was it an accident?"

"We don't believe so."

The woman's mouth fell open, but she didn't say anything. She just sat gaping.

"Mrs Jacobs, we believe that Megan lived here with you. Weren't you expecting her home last night?"

She gave her head the faintest of shakes. "We've long since stopped expecting anything of Megan. She comes and goes as she pleases. In fairness, she'll usually call us if she's going to be especially late, and certainly if she's not coming home. But there's been a couple of times she's forgotten. Do you have kids, Inspector?"

"Me? Sadly, no." Not that he'd ever wanted any.

"One thing you never stop doing, as long as they're under your roof, is lying awake, listening for their key in the door. We probably should have picked her up on it, asked her to be a bit more considerate. But she's had a difficult couple of years. Now this." She locked eyes with him. "Did she suffer? Was she... you know?"

The tattooing alone would have been torture. Then those final moments, when her body craved the oxygen it was being denied by a cold-blooded killer with a pillow or cushion. Quarrel thought Megan Jacobs, Alastair Murdoch and Michael Woodley had probably suffered more than many murder victims he'd encountered.

"There'll have to be a post mortem," he dodged. "We'll know more then. I hope she didn't suffer too much."

He knew it was a lame evasion, and he could somehow tell she'd seen right through him.

"Can you think of anyone who'd wish her harm?" he asked.

"Yes," she said fiercely. "The Snows for a start. And some horrible people on social media, although they're probably only brave sitting behind a computer."

Was one of those people Ace of Spades? If so, they really did need to unmask him. But he was more interested in the name she'd just supplied.

"Tell me about the Snows."

"Emily Snow was Megan's best friend. They worked together in PR, in Watford. Started in the same week and hit it off straight away." She smiled. "Emily was very vivacious. In many ways she was good for Megan. Brought her out of her shell."

"But not all good?"

"I think she also led her astray a bit. Don't get me wrong," she said hastily, "nothing awful. Megan came home the worse for drink a few times – she'd never been much of a drinker before. And I think Emily was a bit cavalier about her own family, although she had her own flat. Not far from her parents."

"In Hemel?"

"Tring."

He glanced across at Katie, to see if she'd registered the significance. She raised an eyebrow.

"Emily's parents live in Grove Park, if you know it?" Valerie said.

"Off Station Road, right?"

"Yes. Emily rented a little flat in the town centre. Frogmore Street."

Quarrel knew it, a longish road that ran up to the High Street.

"You keep talking about Emily in the past tense," Katie observed.

"She died. It was awful. She killed herself."

"And would that have anything to do with why her family might wish Megan harm?"

Valerie Jacobs bit her lip. "Well. Maybe that's a bit strong. But they do blame her, at least in part." She stared at the surface of the breakfast bar. Brushed off a tiny crumb. "A bit unfair in one way, but I might have felt the same."

"What happened?"

"Emily was raped by a colleague. She claimed he spiked her drink and she found herself in his flat, in his bed. She complained, and it went to trial. The defence had a field day with her. Made her seem like some loose-morals good-time girl. A slapper who'd sleep with anyone."

Quarrel had been thinking the name Emily Snow rang a bell. Now he vaguely remembered the case.

"And Megan?" Katie asked gently.

"They used every trick to discredit Emily, make it seem like she almost certainly consented to sex, maybe even initiated it. Then got embarrassed about sleeping with a colleague and cried rape. They latched onto Megan pretty quickly. They were almost inseparable, so Megan knew what Emily was like when they went out clubbing, for instance."

"I can imagine. Every flirt, every drunken snog…"

"And she did have a couple of one-night stands. It didn't mean she wasn't choosy. But they dragged every lurid detail out of Megan, made it look as bad as they could. She was under oath. What could she do? She came home in bits after giving evidence. Oh, that wasn't all they relied on, I don't think, but it didn't help. And the rapist was acquitted. Two weeks later, Emily hanged herself in her bedroom."

Quarrel was processing this, seeing new connections. "It was about two years ago, wasn't it?"

"That's right. Emily had anonymity during the trial, but the media got hold of Megan's name after Emily died and Megan was abused savagely online. There were death threats. Rape threats. She would never let us see them, so I set up my own Twitter account to see for myself. It was horrendous. In the end she came off all social media and never went back on."

"Can you remember if one of them called themselves Ace of Spades?"

"I really can't remember. I've just tried to wipe the whole thing from my mind." The first tears spilled from her eyes, sliding down her cheeks. She swiped them away. "No one could make her feel worse than she did already. It's taken ages to get her life back on track. She had to leave her job – the rapist was still there, and she couldn't stand to see him every day. But now she's got a job in Hemel that she likes, and she's found herself a nice boyfriend, Scott."

She looked Quarrel square in the eye. "My Megan wasn't perfect, Inspector, but she was basically a nice person. I don't know what we're going to do without her." Her face hardened. "Promise me you'll find the person who did this."

"We'll do all that we can."

She shook her head vehemently. "Not good enough. You find them. Find them and put them away."

18

PC Michelle McGrath nodded slowly. "Yes," she said. "Emily Snow was one of my cases. She was the rape victim I told you about – the one who killed herself after Michael bloody Woodley, QC used every scummy trick in his book to discredit her in court. I believed every word of her complaint but, by the time he'd done with her, the jury would have looked out the window to check, if she'd told them it was raining."

She grimaced. "You must have seen it before. Sometimes you can tell how a case is going to go, well before the verdict is delivered. You can see the jury's reaction to evidence or, in this case, so-called evidence. They thought Ben Newell was an innocent man accused, and Emily was a trollop who'd chosen the wrong man to sleep with and regretted it."

"That's a bit illogical, isn't it?" Katie said. "If she was really one to put it about, she'd most likely have slept with all sorts of unsuitable men. Why accuse that one of rape?"

"I know. The fiction Woodley wove was that Newell was different because she worked with him – well, the same firm, anyway. She'd shat on a doorstep too close to home, thought Newell would brag about it in the office, so she decided to get her retaliation in first."

"By putting herself through the hell of a rape trial?"

"Well, exactly. It takes courage to even report a sex crime. I made it clear what Emily was letting herself in for, and she did have some wobbles before she decided to go through with it. She saw that if he got away with drugging and raping *her*, he might well do it again. Might even have done it before."

"And had he?" Quarrel wondered. "Or has he?"

"If there have been other victims, they haven't come forward." She sighed heavily. "After the trial, Ben Newell made a statement about how unfair it was that men accused of sex crimes didn't enjoy the same anonymity as their alleged victims. How his good name had been dragged through the mud."

"But Emily *did* have anonymity," Quarrel pointed out.

Michelle sighed. "That's true, up to a point. But her family knew she'd made the complaint, Megan knew, obviously. And she was pretty sure people at work either knew or had surmised. That could have been paranoia, but Ben's name was in the media and Emily was missing from the office throughout the trial and at other times. It doesn't take a genius."

"I don't suppose any of that helped Emily's state of mind."

"It's exactly why so many sex crimes go unreported. Newell had a point, but the fact is, other victims are sometimes emboldened to come forward once they see their attacker has been charged. It didn't happen here, although that doesn't necessarily mean Emily Snow was his first victim."

They were in Quarrel's small, beige, functional office. He'd never felt the urge to personalise it in any way. He leaned back in his chair, thinking.

"So we have a whole new connection," he said. "The man who defended Emily's alleged attacker and one of the witnesses whose evidence helped acquit him." He'd seen it immediately. Valerie Jacobs either didn't know or couldn't remember if the defence barrister's name had been Woodley, but Quarrel would have been more surprised if it hadn't. It seemed a long way from their earlier tentative suspicions about ageing rock stars and their petty grudges.

"What about Alastair Murdoch?" he asked Michelle. "I'm guessing the name didn't mean anything to you when his body was found, but now you have a context? Could he have been anything to do with the case?"

Michelle stared at the ceiling as if seeking inspiration there. After a few moments, she shook her head. "Sorry, no."

"We'll speak to Emily's family. Maybe the name will mean something to them."

Katie was frowning. "Hang on a bit," she said. "Let's think about the cards again. Megan Jacobs, Ten of Swords – the backstabbing betrayer of her best friend. Michael Woodley, Justice Reversed – injustice. Alastair is The Fool Reversed.

Among other things, stupid and negligent. Who might that description apply to if you didn't like the outcome of a trial?"

"Pretty well anyone," Michelle said.

"But what about the jury?" Quarrel suggested.

"My thoughts exactly." Katie nodded. "Gullible fools."

"Oh, God, seriously?" Michelle looked horrified. "You think there's at least eleven more?"

"Let's not get carried away," said Quarrel. "If they were going after the entire jury, why not go through them all first? Why move on to Woodley and then Megan?"

"More to the point," Katie said, "how would the killer even get the names of all the jurors?"

"He wouldn't need to," Quarrel replied. "Just the foreman."

"You think Alastair was the jury foreman?"

"His business partner mentioned him doing jury service a couple of years ago. I'm not saying that proves anything."

"But you're thinking the foreman would stand for the whole jury in the killer's campaign?" said Michelle.

"It would make sense, wouldn't it? The man who actually delivered the verdict? The whole pack of them are reckless idiots taken in by a deceitful lawyer and treacherous witnesses, and he symbolises them all."

"I'd buy that," said Katie. She frowned again. "But how on earth could the killer identify the foreman? Jury IDs are not in the public arena."

"Your guess is as good as mine. Even *we'd* have to get a judicial order to find out who served on a particular jury, and we'd need a pretty good reason. Which, by the way, I think we have here," he added. "But Michelle," he turned to her, "cast your mind back to that case, that verdict. Can you remember it being delivered, the foreman saying 'Not guilty'?"

"I know what you're asking," she said, "but I'm sorry. I just can't see his face in my mind's eye. Woodley, yes. Megan Jacobs actually. Poor kid."

Quarrel could tell that just the memory made her blood boil. How much angrier might someone close to Emily Snow, someone who had loved her, be when that verdict was delivered?

How much angrier still, after Emily had taken her own life?

"Anything else you can remember about the case, Michelle?" he asked.

"You say Megan was found outside the DeadlineZ club? That's significant. It's where they met Ben Newell the night of the rape, apparently by chance. He was chatting to them at the bar. Megan went to the loo. When she came back, they'd both gone. Megan assumed Emily had gone off with him willingly. He must have already spiked Emily's drink." She looked him in the eye. "You're thinking, at its core, this is vigilante justice?"

"I really do," he confirmed. "Someone who wants to right what they see as a wrong done to Emily. The Tarot images symbolise each victim's role in that wrong, and the bodies are being placed in chosen locations. We've been thinking the dump sites are significant. We need to talk to Emily's family and friends and see if they know what their significance might be."

"That'll be an interesting conversation," Katie said, "considering one of them could be the killer."

19

Superintendent Taylor was making a statement later today in which he would be confirming that three people had now been murdered in the Borough of Dacorum in as many days, and the police were treating the cases as connected. In doing so, he would effectively be admitting that there was a serial killer at large, but media speculation had already reached the point where Taylor believed something had to be said.

Only that morning, one of the local newspapers had carried a story on its website connecting the first two victims through their sons and the death of Ed Barnes. Quarrel wasn't surprised. All it would take them was an Internet search. It was, after all, exactly how the police had found the link. Quotes from Jacko Barnes had been lifted from earlier articles.

"We can't be wasting our time with this sideshow," Taylor had said. "Unless there's some other connection between Megan Jacobs and Ed Barnes that we're missing, then Jacko's in the clear and that case isn't the motive for these murders."

Quarrel had asked Valerie Jacobs if she was aware of Megan knowing Rob Murdoch, Luke Woodley or Ed Barnes. The names had meant nothing to her. So Quarrel was mostly inclined to agree with Taylor, but experience had taught him never to rule anything out completely.

Meanwhile, DCI Sharp was seeking a judicial order to determine whether Alastair Murdoch had served on the jury in Emily Snow's rape trial. And Ricky James and Aliya Nazir were on their way to London, where the alleged rapist, Ben Newell, now worked, to warn him to be vigilant. It was premature – to say nothing of expensive – to start putting serious police protection in place for him, even though Quarrel would have liked nothing better than to put him in protective custody.

Quarrel wasn't looking forward to the media reaction to Taylor's announcement. To broadcasters' vans all over the place and people with microphones lurking around crime scenes and victims' houses. At the same time, he knew it was sometimes a necessary evil. You never knew what might jog a member of the public's memory. And at least he could be straight with Emily's family about why she had become a focus for their enquiries.

Tring's Grove Park estate was a fair sized development, about midway between the local station and the town centre. It was considered one of the town's more desirable areas: less than a mile from the centre and the shops, but close enough to fields to inject some rural soul into an urban setting. Quarrel and Laura had viewed a couple of properties there in their house hunting days.

There were quite a number of bungalows, but the Snows' home was a modest detached house, probably built in the 70s or 80s. Quarrel and Katie were in luck. Both Emily's parents were at home. Helen Snow worked part-time at a local charity shop and her husband, Mark, worked from home.

"We've just finished lunch," Helen said apologetically as she removed mugs and crumb-scattered plates from the glass-topped coffee table. Once the offending items had gone, the living room was immaculate. There were family photographs dotted around. Quarrel had looked up the reports of Emily's suicide online and recognised her in several pictures from the couple he'd seen there: a pretty, vivacious young woman with a cascade of blonde hair and a wide smile.

Helen wouldn't take no for an answer when it came to offering refreshments, so they made small talk with Mark while she brewed up. The couple had had two daughters, including Emily. The eldest, Naomi, was married and living in France.

"We see them four or five times a year," Mark said. "They come to us and we go to them. Provence. It's beautiful."

"How long have they been married?" Katie asked.

"Coming up for four years. Emily moved out a year later. It upset Helen a bit, but I could understand her wanting her own space." His face clouded. "Of course, after she died... well, we both wondered if it would have happened if she'd still been living here."

He seemed to be waiting for the detectives to pass comment on that. Quarrel knew better and so, apparently, did Katie. No one would ever know for sure, one way or the other, although Quarrel entirely understood why anyone would look for what ifs, seek to blame themselves, when a loved one committed suicide. Should they have seen the signs? Was there something they might have said or done that day that might have made a difference?

Quarrel's opinion wasn't going to alter the extent to which Emily Snow's parents beat themselves up over what might have been.

When tea and biscuits had arrived and Helen had sat down, Quarrel told them why they were here. The couple looked at Quarrel incredulously.

"You're thinking these murders are to do with Emily's case?" Mark was first to break the silence. "That someone's out to avenge her death?"

"As I said," Quarrel answered, "we have to look for connections when we have similar crimes within a short distance of each other, and at least two of the victims were involved with the trial."

"Well," Mark said, "I can't pretend I give a damn about either of them. That defence lawyer didn't care about justice – just getting his client off so more rapists would pay him fat fees to defend them. And Megan must have known she was weakening the case against that Newell creature."

"What was Megan supposed to do?" Katie asked. "Lie under oath?" She spoke gently. A question, not a challenge.

"If need be. She was supposed to be Emily's best friend. She didn't even make it clear that Emily wasn't the kind of girl the defence were making her out to be."

"You were in court?" Quarrel asked.

"Every day," said Helen.

Quarrel never ceased to be amazed by people's capacity for selective memory. He knew the tricks lawyers pulled in court. He'd have wagered that Woodley cut off any qualifying remarks

Megan tried to make, once he'd got the answer he wanted. The prosecution could try to recover the situation during re-examination, but by then the impression had been made on the jury.

The Snows must have seen how the case had played out. Michelle McGrath had said Michael Woodley had twisted Megan's words. But anger would have blinded them to that. In Mark Snow's eyes, at least, Megan had stabbed her best friend in the back.

The Ten of Swords. A body face down, with ten blades in the back.

"So do you agree with your husband, Mrs Snow?" he asked. "Do you think Megan shared some of the blame for the verdict?"

"I blame her for letting Emily out of her sight, the night she was raped," Helen said with a vehemence that startled Quarrel. "She went off to the ladies' and left Emily all on her own with that bastard. Now she's come to a sticky end herself. I call that karma."

Karma. Jacko Barnes had used the same word to describe Rob Murdoch and Luke Woodley losing their fathers. Whatever the conclusion to this case, retribution seemed to hang over it all like a dark and twisted shadow. These angry, bitter, broken parents definitely had a motive for the murders of Michael Woodley and Megan Jacobs. Alastair Murdoch's too, if his role in the jury was confirmed. Whether they had means and opportunity remained to be seen.

He asked them to account for their movements over the past three nights.

"We don't go out much," Helen said. "I know it's been two years but, since Emily died, we just haven't had the heart for anything. We get a bit of shopping. I think we've maybe been to the cinema twice, although I really didn't take the film in. We put on a brave face for Naomi when we see her. The last three days?" She looked thoughtful. "Nothing on Sunday. I popped to the supermarket Monday morning. A shift in the charity shop yesterday afternoon. Nothing much else." She gave a wry, mirthless smile. "You're looking for an alibi, aren't you? We can't really give you one. We're each other's alibi for most of the time, which I suppose is a bit rubbish."

She held her wrists out to them. "Better snap the cuffs on."

"We'll leave that for now," Quarrel said. "But we've got a few more questions for you. First of all, we know Emily went to the DeadlineZ club a lot. Did St Peter and St Paul Church have any significance for her?"

Helen nodded. "And for me."

"You're churchgoers?" Helen hadn't mentioned going to church on Sunday.

"No. Well maybe the odd Christmastime. But no, we've never been big church people. It was a choir. It does its concerts in the church. I was a member for years and Emily joined when she finished uni. She loved it. Even did a couple of little solos."

Katie frowned. "I was a member too, just for one concert. I don't think I remember you, though." She froze, looking mortified. "Oh, God, I'm sorry. It was probably just after..."

Helen sighed and nodded. "Quite likely. I haven't been since she died. There doesn't seem to be much to sing about any more."

"That bloody trial," Mark said. "She wished afterwards she'd never bothered reporting the rape. So do I."

Quarrel had seen this before, grief ripping the heart out of a family so they ceased to be really living, just plodding through time as the days and weeks shuffled by. He wondered if this couple could even be bothered with the effort of revenge. But the hate he'd seen in Helen's eyes a few moments ago told him not to write the possibility off.

"What about Little Tring Bridge? Along the canal?"

Mark smiled. "Her favourite walk, along the towpath. She liked to see the narrow boats, in the summer especially, even if they were just moored up. She was always going to hire one with Megan for a holiday. It never happened." His voice caught. "Never will, now, of course."

"Could you do something for us?" Quarrel hesitated, wondering if these people would be in the least bit interested in helping them catch this killer. He could only try. "Could you make a list of any other places that meant anything to Emily?"

Somewhat to his surprise, Emily's father smiled. "Sure. I can do that now. Just a sec."

He got up, walked out of the room, and returned less than a minute later with a pad and pen.

"Carry on," he said. "I'll be jotting things down. It'll be nice to remember."

It occurred to Quarrel then that, whoever was killing people associated with that rape trial, it wasn't some faceless troll behind a keyboard who'd never known Emily. This killer clearly knew her well enough to know the places that had meant something to her. This wasn't just about revenge. It was about building a macabre memorial, body by body.

If Ace of Spades, or another of the online peddlers of hate, was responsible for these deaths, it was someone who'd known and cared about Emily. The handful of trolls who had targeted the first two victims' sons were being reviewed to see if any had also directed their abuse at Megan. Quarrel made a note to himself to find out if any of those hate accounts had been opened only after the verdict in Emily's rape case, or perhaps in the aftermath of her suicide.

"Something else we're interested in," Katie was saying, "is, was Emily interested in Tarot cards?"

Mark Snow looked at her quizzically. "How on earth did you know that?"

"So she was?" Katie prompted.

"Yes. I don't know where it came from, but she was always interested in magic and fortune telling. Not serious occult stuff with Ouija boards and the like – at least, I don't think so."

"She read a lot of fantasy books as a child," Helen added. "I think she still did as an adult. Maybe that was where it began. But she really got into it. Did readings for friends and colleagues. Loved collecting Tarot decks." Her tone softened as she remembered.

"Did she own a Rider Waite deck?" Quarrel asked.

Helen shrugged. "I don't know. Lots of different decks, that's all I know. Mark?" She shot a glance at her husband, who was still scribbling on the pad.

"No, I wouldn't know either," he said.

Katie took out her phone, fiddled for a moment, then showed the screen to the couple. "It would have looked like this. That one's The Fool."

"I think so," Helen said. "Yes."

"I didn't know that was what it was called," Mark added. "Or if I did, I've forgotten. But yes, I remember that. A nice set. She said it was a bit old fashioned, and she would probably never use it for readings. She just loved the pictures. They were her favourite."

Things were finally coming together in Quarrel's mind. The choice of body dumps. The Tarot tattoos. The choice of Rider Waite.

This was all about Emily Snow.

"And tattoos?" he asked. "Did she go in for tattoos?"

"She had one," Helen said, but the bitterness had crept back into her tone. "Just a small one, on her right thigh."

"What was it?"

"Red lips. Like a kiss. I wished she hadn't got it, but at least it was cute, or so I thought. But the defence even made something of that. Called it flirtatious."

"It was nothing of the sort," Mark said, looking up from his pad. "It certainly wasn't an invitation to rape."

"She only got it because she went out with a tattooist for a while," Helen added. "I think it got her interested, but she didn't want anything big and showy."

Quarrel found himself leaning forwards, as if he needed to bridge the gap between them somehow. "So was this tattooist a serious thing?"

"For him more than her, I think," Helen said. "She broke it off when he started getting *too* serious. He wanted them to get a place together. She wasn't ready for anything like that."

With an awful certainty, he knew the answer to his next question, but he asked it anyway.

"Oh, yes," Helen said, "she got the tattoo done at his studio. It's still there, off the top of the High Street. Conor's Body Images."

20

"Conor's just popped out for coffees," the female tattoo artist, whose name Quarrel remembered was Jane Dorcas, said. She seemed to be the only one in the shop. There was no sign of surly Tabitha. And no clients at the moment.

"Slow day?" he asked.

"It's like that sometimes. Like any business, I suppose. Ebbs and flows. Have a seat, though, and I'll make some drinks. Not the good stuff Conor's getting." She grinned. "I could give him a buzz, ask him to get two more."

"I'm okay," Quarrel said.

"Me too, thanks," said Katie. But they sat down to wait. Jane seemed unsure whether to make small talk or get back to what she'd been doing, so she just hovered.

"Have you worked here long?" Quarrel asked.

"Couple of years."

"Do you remember a girlfriend of his? Emily Snow. He did a tattoo for her – a red lipstick kiss, I think."

"Emily? Yes, I remember her. Conor was really down when they broke up. You know she died, and how? It took him ages to come to terms with it. But he didn't do the tattoo."

"No?"

"No, that was Tabby. The kiss is one of her specialities, and that was what Emily chose."

Quarrel mentally adjusted his thinking. When Emily's parents had revealed where she got her tattoo, he and Katie had remembered their previous conversation with the tattooist. They'd asked Conor Burke about Tarot and he'd mentioned a former girlfriend, whose favourite deck had been Rider Waite. Quarrel remembered the sadness in his voice, the wistfulness of his expression, when he'd spoken of her.

They'd assumed that Burke himself had done Emily's tattoo, and her parents hadn't said otherwise. But that was beside the point. Everything Quarrel had heard so far about Burke and Emily suggested that he'd had strong feelings for her and had taken her death hard. It wasn't so much of a reach to imagine him taking revenge on those he blamed, using his professional skills to make a statement in ink on their faces before snuffing them out.

It was true that he had an alibi for Sunday afternoon, almost certainly when Alastair Murdoch had been abducted. But maybe he had an accomplice. A friend or relative of Emily's? Under questioning at the station – something Quarrel had now decided to do – if Burke cracked, the whole story would probably come out.

Jane was still hovering, shifting her weight from foot to foot. "So what's the interest in Emily? Last time you came here, Conor said you were asking about two guys. One, he knew had been murdered the day before, and it was on the news that the other one was murdered too. What's it got to do with Emily? Or Conor?"

"Did you meet Emily's best friend?" Katie asked. "Megan Jacobs?"

"Megan? Couple of times, yeah. She was nice, or I thought she was."

"*Thought* she was?"

"You're cops. You must know about the trial?"

"Say we don't," Quarrel said, wanting her take on it.

"Emily accused a colleague of drugging and raping her. We all believed her, but he got off, and Megan's evidence helped him too. She made out Emily was a total slapper. Bitch." Jane wrinkled her nose as if a bad smell had stolen into the shop.

"Megan was murdered last night."

Jane's eyes widened. But if Quarrel had expected shock, horror – maybe dismay at having spoken ill of the dead – instead the faintest of smiles quirked across her lips.

"Well, good," she said. "Emily killed herself. You must know that. She couldn't live with being branded The Girl Who

Cried Rape, nor with Megan betraying her like that. So now Megan's dead?" She shrugged. "Karma."

There was that word again. Karma and Tarot seemed to be the words of the week.

Quarrel thought it was interesting. It seemed that Conor Burke wasn't the only tattooist who wasn't going to be grieving for Megan Jacobs. Was the use of the same word by Jane and Helen a coincidence? Or was it possible that not one, not two, but several people were involved in a conspiracy of revenge?

Jane had been at the same Sunday lunch as Burke, giving them both alibis for Alistair Murdoch's abduction. But Mark Snow, for example, could have taken care of that bit of business.

"Were you close to Emily yourself?" Katie was asking.

"I wouldn't say that, no. She was nice. Conor loved her. And Conor's a good friend of mine."

Before they could question her further, they heard the door to the shop opening. Conor Burke was entering backwards, using his backside to push the door while he juggled a papier mâché tray bearing two Costa coffee cups. As he turned, he took in his visitors. Something flashed across his face, too quickly for Quarrel to read it.

"Detectives," he said. "Hello again." He raised the tray slightly. "Sorry. I'd have got four, if I'd known. One of you can have my flat white, if you like."

"It's fine," Quarrel assured him, even though the thought of a good cup of coffee appealed to him.

Jane was already investigating the cups and helping herself to one.

"Only two?" Katie commented. "No Tabitha today?" She'd clearly assumed, as had Quarrel, that the other woman was somewhere about.

"She called in sick." Burke set his own cup down on a surface and binned the tray. "More tattooing questions?"

"I think we'd like you to come to the station for a chat, if that's okay," Quarrel said.

Burke stared at him. "What?" He glanced at Jane, as if she had the answers, then back at Quarrel. "Why?"

"We'll explain at the station."

"But am I being arrested?"

"Not at the moment, no."

"What does that mean?"

"Oh my actual God," Jane said, gaping. "They think you murdered Megan."

"Megan? What—?"

"We really don't suspect you of anything at the moment, sir," Katie said.

"But you keep saying 'at the moment'. Megan who?"

"Emily's so-called friend." Jane wasn't going to keep her mouth shut. "Apparently the back-stabbing cow is dead."

"*Back-stabbing?*" Quarrel echoed. "Interesting turn of phrase. Maybe you should come too, Miss Dorcas…"

"Seriously?" She shook her head. "Now you think we *both* killed her?"

"Megan *Jacobs?*" Burke locked eyes with Quarrel. "She's *dead?* Murdered?"

"We can discuss all this at the station," Quarrel said, more firmly.

"But we've got clients booked in. Can't it wait until this evening?"

"I'm afraid not." He turned to his colleague. "DS Gray, would you turn the sign on the door to 'Closed'?"

"Of course." She got up and walked towards the door.

"Hey!" Burke protested. "You can't do that."

Jane Dorcas stepped into Katie's path. The DS stepped around her and reached for the sign, but Jane grabbed her arm.

Quarrel wasn't about to intervene.

Katie looked at the restraining hand, then at Jane. "You really don't want to do this."

For an instant, Jane squared her shoulders. Then she shrugged and backed off.

"Thank you," said Katie, turning the sign.

"You can drink your coffees before we go," Quarrel said.

"Hang on, though," protested Jane. "If we're not under arrest, we don't have to come, right?"

Quarrel sighed, getting fed up. "Ms Dorcas, we're conducting a murder enquiry. We'd like you and Mr Burke to come to Hemel Hempstead with us, of your own free will, and help us with our enquiries. If you don't come voluntarily…" He shrugged. "Well, then we'll have to decide what to make of that."

"Let's just go, Jane," Burke said wearily. "Get it over with."

"We should talk to Ms Hunt, Tabitha, too," Katie said.

"Is that really necessary?" Burke protested. "She said she thought she had flu."

"Does she take a lot of time off sick?" Quarrel asked.

"Tabby? No. She's not always people person of the year, but she's pretty dedicated. If she says she's ill, she must be feeling really crap."

During their previous visit, she'd given an address in Bennetts End, Hemel Hempstead. Quarrel got Burke to remind them of it, and also noted the woman's phone number.

"Okay," he said. "DS Gray, can you call the office? Get someone to check on Ms Hunt? If she's really not up to coming to the station, we can have a chat to her in her home."

Katie took out her phone and moved into the office, without seeking permission.

Quarrel said nothing, watching the two tattooists. Conor Burke had one hand in his jeans pocket. In the other, he held his coffee, taking sips, trying to appear cool. Jane Dorcas had her arms folded across her chest, and was tapping her foot.

But now Quarrel was more interested in the staff member who wasn't here, the one who had done Emily Snow's tattoo. Because he thought it interesting that Megan Jacobs, who everyone here seemed to blame – at least in part – for Emily's suicide, had been murdered last night; and this morning Tabitha Hunt was a no show at work.

*

Quarrel had brought Conor Burke to the station himself and had left Katie and Jane Dorcas awaiting a local squad car to bring them in, so the two tattooists had no chance to converse and get their stories straight en route. Meanwhile, PC Izzy Cole had been round to Tabitha Hunt's small house in Acorn Road, Bennetts End and got no reply to the doorbell.

She'd phoned and, when the call had gone to voicemail, looked through the windows and the letter box; but she had seen nothing untoward. Quarrel supposed that, in all likelihood, the woman really was sick and was simply ignoring all attempts to communicate.

Or was she still in bed, sleeping off her latest murder? Or maybe stalking another victim? Perhaps even Ben Newell, the alleged rapist?

When Quarrel had arrived back at the station, he'd checked with Ricky James that he and Aliya had warned Newell to be on his guard and not to accept lifts or drinks from anyone.

"Not only warned him, but scared him," Ricky had told him. "He was talking about taking some leave, going home and staying there for a while."

"Good," Quarrel had said. If Newell did that, at least he would be safe – although there was an irony that the one potential victim they'd managed to keep alive was possibly the one most to blame for Emily's suicide. Certainly Michelle McGrath thought his acquittal had been a travesty.

When this round of interviews was over, Quarrel would take a view on whether to formally arrest anyone and whether to send a forensics team into Burke's studio looking for traces of any of the victims. Now, with Ricky James beside him, he sat opposite Burke in one of the interview rooms.

It seemed there had been talk of smartening up the interview suite ever since Quarrel could remember, but year on year the budget never quite stretched to it. As a result, the rooms were even more austere and, yes, intimidating, than they had ever been meant to be. The magnolia walls were scuffed and faded in more places than not, and the furniture – bolted to the floor in case an irate suspect decided to try chucking it about – had undoubtedly seen better days. It was just that no one here owned up to having been around whenever those better days had been.

But if Conor Burke felt intimidated, it didn't show. He almost looked too cool, sitting upright in his chair waiting for the questioning to begin. He'd said he didn't need a lawyer present as he had nothing to hide.

"I just want to get on with this and get back to work."

Quarrel took a sip of water, scribbled on his pad to make sure his pen was working, and nodded to Ricky to start the video recording.

"Thanks for coming in voluntarily, Mr Burke," he began.

"Yeah, sure. I didn't exactly have a choice, did I?"

"Let's talk about Emily Snow. How long were you two dating?"

"About five or six months. I really liked her. To tell the truth, I was in love with her."

"How did you meet?"

He shrugged. "Tinder. The 21st century cliché."

Quarrel resisted the temptation to shrug back. He understood that Tinder was an online dating app. The whole concept was alien to him, even though Laura had laughed at him when he'd said as much.

"You're right," she'd giggled. "Your method is so much more the thing. A casual meeting in a reservoir over a dead body."

"So you got a match," Ricky James, who Quarrel knew swore by Tinder, was saying, "and when you hooked up, you clicked?"

"For a while, yes. She even decided to get a small tattoo, something she never thought she would."

"Tabitha did that?" Quarrel checked.

"The kiss was one of her specialities."

"But why didn't *you* do it? She was your girlfriend. I'd have thought it was a nice thing to do for her."

Burke smiled. "I see where you're coming from and, yes, it *is* an intimate procedure. But it involves a degree of pain, blood and mess too, so it's not exactly romantic. She preferred someone else to do it, and so did I. Tabby did a nice job. She's very good."

"But the relationship, it didn't last?"

The smile left the tattooist's face. "My fault. I fell too hard, too soon. Story of my life. I think I tried to take things too quickly. I scared her off. She said we should cool it for a while. We said we'd keep in touch as friends, and I did text her a couple of times, suggesting coffee or a drink, but she obviously wasn't really keen and made excuses. I could take a hint. A year later, she was dead, and the stuff about the rape trial came out."

"How did that make you feel?"

"Sad. Guilty, I suppose, that I hadn't been there for her, even though she'd long since moved on from me. Angry."

"At the rapist?" Ricky asked.

"And at the system. I looked it up. I guess you know how many reported rapes make it to trial?"

"Less than two per cent," Ricky said. He might try to act cool and laid back, but he did his homework.

"And only about a third of those prosecutions lead to a conviction. Of course, I didn't even know the trial was about her when it was in the news. At least she had public anonymity, but that didn't help her with people she knew. When she died, I went over the trial reports. It was horrible."

"So you were angry with the defence?"

"And the jury, who were too stupid to see they were being played. And Megan, who made it worse. They even dragged Tabby's tat into it. Made an innocent little motif into something dirty."

"You hated them all?" Quarrel pressed.

Burke hesitated, then nodded. "Pretty much so, yeah."

"Enough to kill them?"

"No. I couldn't take a life, no matter what."

"Sure you couldn't," Ricky said, allowing a little sarcasm to show.

"I couldn't."

"You and your workforce are pretty close, aren't you?" Quarrel said. "Sunday lunches and all that?"

"I suppose."

"So if you wanted to get justice for Emily, they'd help?"

"Help me take the law into my own hands? I doubt it. And it's academic."

"What about Emily's family?" Ricky said. "Have you had contact with them since Emily's death?"

"I did get in touch at the time, yes. To express my sympathy."

"So no contact for the last two years?" Quarrel asked.

"No."

"We'd like to borrow your phone and verify that."

"My phone? No way. I need it. It's got all my contacts and everything for my business, and there's private stuff on there."

"We can get an order," Quarrel said, "or you can be cooperative and show you've nothing to hide."

Burke looked ready to protest further. Then he sighed, fished the phone out of a pocket and slid it across the table. "How long will you keep it?"

"If there's nothing untoward? We'll get it back to you as soon as we can."

"Is it PIN-protected?" asked Ricky.

Conor Burke trotted out a short string of numbers and the DC jotted them down, slipping his note in a bag with the phone.

"Where were you last night?" Quarrel wanted to know.

"Home. I caught up on some paperwork with one eye on Netflix. I was half-watching *Lucifer*. Have you seen it?"

Quarrel shook his head, but Ricky leaned forward a little. "Cool, isn't it? The Devil fighting crime."

"I prefer the graphic novels, to be honest."

"Yeah? I ought to read some. Have you ever done any of the illustrations as tattoos?"

Burke smiled. "I don't suppose there'd be much demand. Interesting idea, though, if someone brought one of the comics in."

"So you prefer Tarot cards?"

"What?" The suspect had been leaning in, mirroring Ricky's body language. Now he snapped back in his chair. "What is it with Tarot tattoos?" He looked at Quarrel. "I told you. I've never done that sort of thing. What have they got to do with Megan? Or your other murders?"

"I'd like to send a forensics team into your shop," Quarrel said. "I'd prefer it to be voluntary."

Burke made a face. "How long's that going to take?"

"If it's clean, I'm sure they'd be finished by the end of tomorrow at the absolute latest."

Burke looked furious. Quarrel was convinced he'd refuse. Then his shoulders sagged. "If it puts me in the clear, knock yourselves out. Can I at least contact my clients and reschedule my bookings? The details are in the shop."

"That should be fine. Someone will accompany you." Quarrel paused. "One more thing. Tabitha Hunt. Was she angry about Emily's death?"

"We all were. Everyone liked Emily. Tabby? She wears her heart on her sleeve and sees things in black and white terms. She was more than just angry. She couldn't stop talking about it."

"She wanted retribution?"

Burke frowned. "You think—" He shook his head emphatically. "No. Tabby's a lot of things…"

"Interview concluded," Quarrel said, and he quoted the time before Ricky terminated the recording.

Burke was returned to reception and given coffee while he waited for Jane Dorcas's interview to be completed. Unless any grounds for holding her emerged, Ricky would drive the pair back to the shop to cancel appointments under his supervision.

Meanwhile, Izzy Cole had arranged for a uniformed officer from Tring to control access to the shop until Debbie Brown and her CSIs turned up. If any of the victims had been held, tattooed and murdered there, Quarrel was prepared to wager that no clean up would be good enough to eradicate every trace – and that, if anyone could find something left behind, Debbie and her team would. At least, if Burke was involved in the murders, his salon couldn't be used for creating Tarot tattoos for a couple of days.

Quarrel retreated to the incident room and went to the Wall of Death, adding a few notes. They needed pictures of Conor Burke, Jane Dorcas and Tabitha Hunt to add focus to their strands of narrative.

Tabitha Hunt. Quarrel hadn't taken to her sullen, abrasive attitude and, thinking back to his brief encounter with her, he thought there was something altogether off about her. Maybe the pink hair just went with a slightly different approach to life. Burke had admitted she was 'more than just angry' about Emily Snow's suicide and its circumstances, and he hadn't denied that she might even hanker after some payback.

Quarrel had wondered if Emily's family and the tattoo shop staff were working together on the murders. Now he wondered if Tabitha could be working alone. What if she'd thought that by now the police might have worked out the connection with Emily, and thus with Conor Burke and his team? Was that why she was laying low?

He backed up his thinking. Two men and a young woman had, in all probability, been drugged, manhandled to wherever the tattooing went on – not the shop, if Burke wasn't involved. He lived in the flat above.

And then their bodies had been dumped at the church, on the towpath and behind the club. Was Tabitha really capable of such physical feats? Living with Laura had taught Quarrel not to underrate the strength of a woman, but this one seemed rather slight for humping the dead weight of an adult male around.

And she was supposed to have been lunching with friends and colleagues while Alastair Murdoch was being abducted. If that was true, she had to have an accomplice.

Or, even now, were they on yet another false trail?

He reminded himself that they didn't even know for sure yet whether Murdoch had been the jury foreman in Emily's rape case. DCI Sharp had obtained her judicial order and that fact would be checked, if not by close of business today, certainly by lunchtime tomorrow. Some wheels turned slowly, and now there was the added pressure of the media response to Superintendent Taylor's announcement.

West Hertfordshire wasn't exactly known as the murder capital of the world, and the tabloids in particular were pressing for ever more details for their front pages. The television companies were also out and about. Quarrel was just grateful that the tattoos, and the connection to Emily Snow, were being held back. That would be more than sensational enough for a full feeding frenzy to ensue.

In the meantime, at least Ben Newell was taking precautions, so Quarrel thought they could relax a little over the safety of Emily's alleged rapist. But who knew who else might be on the killer's list?

He took out his phone and called PC Michelle McGrath.

"Have you got time for a chat?"

"Sorry, Nate. One of my cases is being heard in court this afternoon, and I'm already running late. But what about a quick drink after work?"

21

The Market Arms Tavern was a single-storey white building on Waterhouse Street, two minutes' walk from the police station. It had fruit machines, a dartboard, pool tables, and a quirky, bespoke 'Ye Olde Library' area, with shelves stuffed with books. It prided itself on being family friendly with a 'fun' atmosphere.

Michelle McGrath had changed into her civilian clothes – denim jacket, jeans and a striped shirt. She and Quarrel should have blended in with the rest of the after-work set, but Quarrel suspected they were still giving off that police aura that some people could detect a hundred yards away.

They found a relatively secluded corner. The jukebox was belting out something loud and bassy that Quarrel couldn't recognise. He trusted the music, and the babble of the bar, would mask their conversation.

"I need you to think hard about the Emily Snow case," Quarrel said after a brief chat about their respective days. "So far we've got probably the jury foreman, although that's to be confirmed; the defence barrister; and the best friend whose evidence helped make the defence's case for them. Apart from Ben Newell himself, who else might be blamed for his acquittal? Or, I suppose, for Emily's suicide?"

She frowned, sucking on the straw sticking out of her non-alcoholic cocktail.

"Like I said when we talked about this before, there's eleven more members of the jury. But you're probably right. The foreman would likely be enough to make the killer's point, and not so hard to track one man down. In fact, I've been thinking about that."

"Go on," said Quarrel, who had his own theory.

"Well, suppose your killer decided there and then, as soon as the not guilty verdict was announced, that they were going to do something about it. He could have just hung around outside the court, waited until the foreman came out, and followed him home."

"You're thinking he or she would have been planning this ever since? For two years?"

She nodded.

"Then we're on the same page," he acknowledged. "A death a day can't be something you can just orchestrate on a whim. Someone's been observing these people over a period and deciding how best to get to them."

"I suppose it's just possible that the plan has come together a little more recently," she said. "Say the killer sees Alastair Murdoch by chance – in the street, in a shop – and recognises him. Emily's death's been festering for a while. Now they decide to follow Mr Murdoch and see where he lives. And a plan to kill him, and everyone else they blame, starts coming together."

"Also possible," he agreed. "Although we're still talking about a decent interval between starting to plan and starting to kill." A thought came to him. "Either way, it's surely got to be someone who was in court for at least part of the trial."

"What about Emily's family? Or her colleagues? Or friends other than Megan?" Michelle wondered.

"Who knew she was the complainant?"

"She didn't give me a list. It would have to be people she was comfortable telling. Of course," she added, "depending on who the actual killer is, they might also blame any of those groups for not seeing that Emily was suicidal."

This was a new thought for Quarrel. "You mean the killer might blame them for not preventing her death? But that's ridiculous. Quite often the signs are easy to miss. How many times have those closest to a suicide never seen it coming?"

"That's true, and you can't make generalisations about how someone like Emily might be affected by their experience. She isn't the only rape survivor I've known take their own life and, even if Newell had been convicted, we can't be sure she'd have been able to cope with what happened to her. But on the other hand, I've known victims of horrendous abuse come out of it with a positive attitude to their future."

Quarrel wondered if that was true; whether people ever really put great trauma completely behind them.

"I suppose that isn't the point though, is it?" he said. "It doesn't matter whether it's fair to blame those people. If we were talking about someone rational, they'd be unlikely to be conducting a killing spree in the first place." He thought for a moment. "Family, friends, colleagues. If we can identify them all, the chances are the killer's in there somewhere, as well as a whole lot of potential victims."

"I'd be surprised if the pool's very wide when it comes to the killer. I worked pretty closely with Emily after she reported her rape. Apart from her family and Megan, I didn't get the impression she was close to anyone. Whoever's killing people to avenge her is surely more than an acquaintance. Unless..." She looked thoughtful. "Maybe someone cared more about her than she knew?"

"A secret admirer?"

"Something like that. Maybe."

He looked at his watch. "Too late to talk to Emily's old employers now. I might swing by her parents' house." He sighed. "They gave me a list of places that were important to her, but we don't have the manpower to stake them all out."

He could feel his frustration rising. If there was another death tonight, could he have avoided it? Was he even thinking clearly enough?

But, if Connor Burke's shop wasn't the killing ground, where else would the Tarot tattoos be done? Suddenly it seemed all too obvious.

One way or another, it was time to get into Tabitha Hunt's home.

*

In numerous situations, the police might have to get into a house urgently. In extremis they would break the door down. But, in the case of Tabitha Hunt's property, there was a reasonable cause for concern about her safety, but no compelling need for such destruction. And, as luck would have it, the Hemel Hempstead force had Sergeant Colin Webster.

Webster had a set of lock picks, had been on a course to learn how to use them, and had put his skills to use a few times in helping out people who'd managed to lock themselves out of their homes. He'd just been sitting down to dinner when the callout had come, but he was no less cheerful for that. Quarrel suspected he rather enjoyed showing off his talents.

Bennett's End was on the south-east side of the town. The neighbourhood was fairly unremarkable, and almost all the housing had been council-owned until Margaret Thatcher's Right To Buy policy in the 80s.

Tabitha Hunt's house in Acorn Road was a modest terraced property with faux-Georgian-style windows and a porch over the matching front door. Quarrel regarded it dubiously, trying to imagine victims being brought in, restrained, tattooed and killed, then removed again – night after night – without neighbours noticing. It seemed unlikely, and yet people these days could be oblivious to all manner of things going on under their noses.

Katie Gray had been happy enough to abandon her plans for a microwave dinner for one and an evening in front of indifferent TV in favour of accompanying Quarrel and Webster to the Hunt residence. Now they were there, Quarrel had a moment's trepidation about what they might find inside. He hoped he wasn't about to regret putting this off for so long. He knocked and announced, getting was no response.

"All right," he said. "Let's get this done."

Webster crouched down, peered at the Yale lock, made a show of eyeballing it close up, then took a small leather pouch from his pocket. It was zipped around the outside and it opened up to reveal a selection of perhaps two dozen plastic-handled tools in a range of shapes, and a few slim lengths of metal. Humming to himself, he studied them and selected one of each.

Quarrel recognised the tune Webster was humming; something from Gilbert and Sullivan: 'A policeman's lot is not a happy one'?

Crouching again, the sergeant carefully inserted his plastic-handled, fork-like tool into the lock and then slid the slimmer pick in. He then withdrew it, wiggling it as he did so. Quarrel heard a series of clicks.

"Et voila!" Webster said, pushing the door open.

They stepped into a small, white-painted hallway with a couple of oriental prints on the walls. From there, they moved into a rectangular lounge/diner.

Quarrel reeled.

Blood-red splashes on white snow. For an instant, he was sure it was real, not a trick of his mind. Even the temperature seemed to plummet.

He was breathing hard, close to hyperventilation. The room took on a shade of grey.

"Guv?" Anxiety in Katie's voice. "Nate?"

He closed his eyes, rocked on his heels. Forced himself to breathe in and out, slowly, regularly. The feelings of panic, of not quite *being there*, subsided. He opened his eyes again.

The room was painted white, like the hallway, but someone – in all likelihood, Tabitha herself – had painted blood-red rosebuds on the walls. Not to his taste, but nothing like...

"Nate?" More urgency in Katie's tone this time. She'd seen this once before. Her hand was on his arm.

"I'm okay," he said, hearing the shake in his voice. He fought to master that, as he'd managed to master his breathing. "I'm okay. Just... maybe my blood sugar is low. I can't remember when I last ate."

It was glib, but Katie seemed satisfied. She rummaged in her bag, came up with a roll of mints and offered him one.

"This might help."

Sucking on the mint, he looked around the now unthreatening room. Neat and tidy, not necessarily what he'd expected. The kitchen was much the same. They checked drawers and cupboards for anything significant. Tattooing equipment would have been ideal, but they found nothing out of the ordinary. Upstairs, the same applied to the bathroom.

There were two bedrooms, and the larger was obviously the one Tabitha used. The smaller bedroom contained a bed and a chest of drawers, but seemed to double as storage space, items packed in transparent plastic packing boxes.

Quarrel and Katie stood in the main bedroom. Here was the most sense of personal space. A bottle-green tee shirt was carefully folded on the bed. Quarrel would have wagered it was precisely dead centre.

"A neat freak," Katie remarked. "Who would have thought it?"

They'd both donned latex gloves before entering. Quarrel turned to the double wardrobe just by the door and opened it. Katie stood beside him as he checked out the clothes. Mostly jeans, shirts and smock tops and dresses. One very dressy little black number. Most of the shoes at the bottom of the wardrobe were practical, but there were a couple of strappy pairs, one with quite formidable heels.

They checked out the drawers, careful not to disturb too much. A jumper drawer, one full of tee shirts, one containing tights, socks and underwear. Most of the latter were workaday, but there were three quite pretty sets, one of them black and whispery and presumably intended to be sexy. Quarrel wondered if they were for anyone in particular.

Katie pointed to a laundry basket under the window.

"I can't see anywhere in here that looks like a makeshift tattoo parlour," she said, "but if she *has* been bringing the victims here to work on, then maybe we'll find blood on some of her discarded clothes."

So they rummaged through the basket, finding nothing remarkable.

"If Tabitha's involved in the killings, I don't think she's doing them here," Quarrel said. "So far, everything's pointing to Conor, Tabitha, maybe Jane, doing the tattoos and probably the killing from the shop, maybe even working with some accomplices from outside the team."

Katie's mouth made a grim line. "If that's right, then we don't know who we can believe. You talked about speaking to Emily's family, maybe her work, to get a handle on who else they might blame for her death, and who cared about her. But we could be asking people who are part of the conspiracy."

"Does it sound crazy to you?"

"I wish it did."

"Look, not everyone who knew Emily is going to be part of this revenge agenda. It would be just too big. My money's on the family working with at least one of Conor's team, so let's leave them for now. But someone should visit her old workplace in the morning. At least we might see another side of her."

"By tomorrow, we might have another body."

"You think I don't know that?" he snapped.

Katie flinched and he held up his hands. "Sorry, Katie. It's just…"

"Frustrating. I get it."

"I shouldn't have snapped." He felt drained. He had no intention of going back to that white and red living room. "Let's call it a day and get some rest. It's been a long day, and tomorrow will be more of the same, body or no."

"Maybe no," Katie said. "If Conor Burke's shop is where they've been bringing their victims, they won't be getting in there tonight. And maybe this time tomorrow, Debbie Brown will have some evidence and we can start to make arrests. It only wants one of them to start talking…"

"You're right." He felt a little more positive. "We might be closer to solving this thing than I thought."

He led the way downstairs. He was almost at the bottom when a female voice croaked, "What the actual fuck?"

In the front doorway, a carrier bag hanging from her left hand, stood a diminutive figure with pink hair and a washed out complexion.

"Well?" Tabitha Hunt demanded. "What are you people doing in my house?"

22

Tabitha Hunt had, Quarrel was forced to admit, looked so ill that he was convinced she wasn't putting on an act. She claimed to have gone to bed early, feeling like a walking corpse, and then spent most of the day in bed with earplugs in, trying to sleep it off.

"No, I didn't hear no one knocking. I wouldn't have got to the door without falling down, even if I had."

She'd finally felt up to dragging herself up, and decided to walk the half-mile to the pharmacy to buy cough mixture, throat pastels and Lemsip.

"You walked?" There was no mistaking the scepticism in Katie Gray's voice.

"Yeah, silly cow that I am. Hoped the fresh air would help. It didn't." She'd tipped her purchases out on her kitchen table. "In case you don't believe me."

"I take it no one can confirm you were here all night?"

"I wish. They could have gone and picked up this lot."

Such as shock could register on the face of someone already looking so dreadful, she seemed shocked at Megan's death. Yes, she'd liked Emily and been both upset and angry about what had happened to her. Yes, she'd felt Megan had let her friend down. No, she wasn't pleased she was dead.

"Now can you fuck off and let me dose myself up and get back to bed? I've a good mind to make a complaint."

At home, he'd told Laura about the wobble he'd experienced in Tabitha's living room, knowing she was the only person he could confide in. The only person who could understand. It wasn't the first time something like that had happened, and he doubted it would be the last. She hadn't nagged him about what he should do about it. She'd listened and held him, and empathised.

It had helped, but not enough to keep his sleep from being troubled by red and white dreams.

At least, for the second night running, he wasn't disturbed by early morning calls with news of grim discoveries – although he knew that was no guarantee no new body would turn up at some point in the day.

Laura was still sleeping when he set off for work. Faint mist was still rising from the canal as he drove away. The team had assembled a little after 8am. One little piece of progress had been made, in that it had been confirmed first thing that Alastair Murdoch had indeed been the jury foreman in Ben Newell's trial.

"So, what if there *is* no body today?" he mused out loud. "What do we make of that?"

"It could be simply that Ben Newell's last on the list and the killer couldn't get to him," Katie said. "We know he studies their habits. Ben was apparently going home early, taking a different route to usual, and staying there."

"Or maybe sealing off Conor Burke's tat shop has floored them," Izzy Cole added.

He nodded. "Assuming it's him or one of his team. Maybe they need to find a new killing ground elsewhere, or maybe we're looking at another tattooist altogether." He sighed. "Nothing's simple, is it?"

"We were thinking Emily's family might be pulling the strings," Katie reminded him, "but someone else is doing the actual abduction, tattooing and killing for money."

"We're going to have to haul them in and ask them."

"That'll go down well. Grieving family questioned over mad serial killer plot. It's not going to attract the most popular of press coverage. Unless they break down and confess, of course."

"We can only hope," Quarrel said.

*

As well as bringing Emily Snow's parents in, questions also needed to be asked at the Watford PR firm where she and Ben

Newell had been working at the time of the alleged rape. To Izzy Cole's delight, Quarrel decided that she should sit in on his interviews with Mark and Helen Snow, while Katie headed to Watford with Ricky James. And Aliya Nazir and Libby Statham would drop by at Ben Newell's place in Bushey to check on him and reassure him that the police were keeping an eye on him.

Now, while Helen Snow kicked her heels, Izzy and Quarrel sat opposite her husband in an interview room. As a preliminary, Quarrel had taken him through his and his wife's movements again from Sunday and the time of Alastair Murdoch's abduction onwards. It was the same story as before – mundane stuff, and Mark admitted that, in the main, only he and Helen could alibi each other.

A quiet Sunday at home together, with a bit of work in the garden. Helen had done the supermarket run on Monday morning and done a shift in the charity shop on Tuesday afternoon. Mark had worked at home and seen no one, although he'd made a few phone calls. They were on his work mobile, but phone records should be able to verify time and location.

Izzy scribbled notes, underlining things she thought needed to be double-checked.

Quarrel went on to ask him what his feelings were now about his daughter's death and people involved in the trial verdict.

He sat back in his seat. "You know I'm angry about Emily's death, Inspector. But I'm not stupid. I wanted to kill the animal who raped her. Probably still do. And I can't shed any tears for that pig of a lawyer, who blackened my daughter's name and reputation all through the trial. As for Megan, she didn't look out for Emily the night she was attacked and she helped the defence at the trial. We haven't forgiven her."

"So why not hate the jury too?"

"They're different. Like I said, I'm not stupid. They were taken in by the lies they heard. I'm sure they did the best job they could. I don't care either way about what happened to the foreman."

"But you must see, sir, that every victim has a connection to that court case?"

Of course I do. Someone felt strongly about Emily and has a twisted sense of justice. But that isn't me." He looked her in the eye. "For the record, I was angry with Megan, but I didn't hate her."

"What about Helen? She called Megan's death karma. Sounds a lot like hatred to me."

"Maybe. But the only person we truly hate is the... the *thing* that raped Emily. Put me in a room with him, and I don't know what I'd do."

"Well, *someone* seems to be killing people associated with the trial," Quarrel observed. "Can you think of anyone else close to Emily who might do something like that?"

"Emily didn't have that many close friends, to be honest. After the case, she didn't want any more to do with Megan, and I think she must have felt pretty isolated. I think she was well liked at work, but she never went back there. I don't suppose it helped her mentally."

"I have to ask you this," Quarrel asked. "What about her sister?"

"Naomi? I can't imagine that. She's a gentle soul. Besides, as I told you before, she's in France?"

"Are you sure about that?"

"Absolutely. Helen calls her there every day."

It didn't rule out Naomi having hired someone to do the job, Izzy thought. Nor Emily's parents. Izzy supposed they could get a warrant to investigate their bank accounts, but such suspicions as they had were somewhat flimsy at present.

"So what did you make of him?" Quarrel asked her as they grabbed a quick coffee between interviews. She was buzzing with the experience. It made her all the more certain that she wanted a career as a detective.

"He sounded plausible," she said, "but that doesn't mean much. I've met plenty of plausible people who don't know the meaning of the word 'truth'. It'll be interesting to see how the wife's story compares. If it's too word perfect, I'll be wondering if they colluded."

"Me too. Although, in my experience, even when two people think they've got their story straight, there can be differences.

But you're right. I'm not liking these two for the killings at the moment. I hope Katie or Aliya are having better luck."

*

Time was when Katie Gray might have headed into Watford to do some serious shopping but, these days, even the local council recognised that parts of the town centre were looking tired, and ambitious plans for transformation were apparently in development. Emily Snow's former employers had offices just off Watford's main Hempstead Road, on the edge of the proposed development area. Watford police station had sent a young DC by the name of Greg Fuller to accompany them as a point of contact between the two patches.

Katie thought the firm's reception area, with its ultra-modern furniture, framed magazine covers and articles, and general pristine spotlessness, had a hip glossiness about it that was trying almost too hard. The receptionist's accent was posh, but with West London notes.

Katie and Ricky James were shown into a meeting room in similar vein to reception, with a glass table covered in smeary fingerprints. The managing director, Ray Marsden, was a fifty-something in a sharp suit, and the head of human resources was a besuited blonde perhaps ten years younger by the name of Chantelle Price.

"Of course I remember Emily," Marsden said. "None of us who were here at the time will forget those awful days. Ben's trial… what happened to Emily afterwards. The damage to our reputation," he added, as if that was the worst thing of all.

"Your reputation," Ricky repeated.

"Well, Emily and Ben Newell both worked with clients. Emily had anonymity, of course. Only a handful of people here who needed to know what was going on were aware she was the accuser. But a number of Ben's clients distanced themselves from us when the case was in the news. We work with a lot of local companies, and the trial was all over the local media."

"Ben doesn't work here any more, does he?" Katie checked.

"No, we had to let him go," Chantelle Price said. "It was quite awkward, as you can imagine. We sent him home on full pay when the trial and all the publicity was happening but, once he was acquitted, that's when it got really difficult. He'd been found not guilty, so we couldn't actually fire him. Emily resigned, of course. She couldn't bear to be in the same place as him."

"But you let him go eventually?"

"A number of clients thought there was no smoke without fire and didn't want to work with him, nor with a firm that employed him. We had to make him a healthy offer to go away. Not that I thought he ever felt comfortable here after what happened."

"Mr Marsden mentioned that a few people here knew she was Ben's alleged victim."

"I knew, of course, as head of HR but, to be honest, there was some pretty accurate speculation here. It's a small firm. No one let on to Emily what was being said, but that just made for an awkward atmosphere. She must have sensed it."

"And what was the view? Did Ben do it? Or was Emily making it up?"

"Who really knows?" Marsden said. "We've all done things we're not proud of, or regret. Maybe Emily felt mortified about a one-night stand with a colleague and had to justify it to herself by denying any responsibility."

"On the other hand, Ben often sailed close to the wind, when it came to appropriate behaviour," Price said. "He fancied himself as quite the ladies' man and was flirty with every female that crossed his path."

"It was just banter," Marsden protested. "I've seen Emily engage in a bit of banter too."

"Sure," Price acknowledged, "and we'll never know for certain whether Ben misread the signals. But there can be a thin line between banter and harassment. You know, Ray, that I had to warn him once, after a client complained."

"About what, exactly?" asked Katie.

"That woman's a bit of a drama queen," Marsden declared, wrinkling his nose. "She didn't like him complimenting her on her appearance, for some reason."

"It was a bit more than that, Ray." Price seemed irked. "People need to be so careful these days. Telling her how well her jewellery matched her eyes was a bit personal for her taste. She thought he was hitting on her, and I don't know that he wasn't."

"You sound like you thought he was guilty," Ricky remarked.

"I wouldn't go that far," Price said. "I could never decide. He and Emily were nice people, basically, who liked a laugh and weren't entirely politically correct. I think Ben had some boundary issues. It doesn't make him a sex fiend."

"So what did you think about the case, Mr Marsden?" Katie pressed. "You must have had an opinion."

The CEO fixed his gaze on a sizeable smear on the glass table top. "What I think is academic. You can't be in our line of work and keep a man with that sort of taint on the payroll."

"What about the staff? You didn't really give me a straight answer on that. Did Emily find support amongst any of her colleagues? Or did they believe Ben's story?"

"Put it this way," Chantelle Price said. "The whole thing divided the crowd, and not just on gender lines, either. There was a group – mostly women, but some men too, who weren't sorry to see the back of Ben. But a smaller hard core of men, plus a couple of women, sympathised with him and thought Emily was a liar. Even after she died."

No wonder Emily had resigned. If Price's assessment was correct, and she'd sensed she was being talked about, everyone having an opinion about her… She would imagine even the sympathetic colleagues picturing her ordeal. Not everyone was tough enough to come into work, day after day, in such circumstances.

"To tell the honest truth," Marsden said, "I don't think our *esprit de corps* has ever really recovered. The whole thing drove a wedge between people who previously rubbed along well enough. Now a fair chunk of our workforce is polarised, with some fairly naked dislike. Sniping at meetings, pettiness, that sort of thing."

"But was there anyone in particular?" Katie asked. "Someone who especially took Emily's side and might have been angry enough about what happened to want to dish out some justice on her behalf?"

"What sort of justice?" asked Marsden. He looked at her sharply. "You said you were investigating Megan's murder. I know about the evidence she gave at the trial, and I know the defence twisted it against Emily. Megan was mortified. You think someone here killed her in revenge for Emily? That's crazy."

"I can't see it," Price agreed. "Quite a few of the staff hated Ben after what happened. Enough to harm him? Maybe. But Megan? Surely not."

"So who hated Ben that much?" Katie thought it would be a start.

"Enough to kill him?" Price shook her head. "How well do you really know your colleagues? I wouldn't have expected people to turn against Emily. She was extremely popular until Ben's arrest. In fact..." She stood up. "I won't be a moment. I've got something to show you."

She left the room. Katie looked a question at Marsden. He shrugged.

"Apart from Megan, did Emily have other close friends here?" Ricky asked.

"I don't know about close. As Chantelle said, everyone liked her. But Ben was well-liked too." He sighed. "The workplace is such a minefield these days, isn't it? Everyone has to be so careful not to give offence. No wonder so many people date online. If I was young and single now, I'd think long and hard about asking a colleague out for an innocent coffee, let alone anything romantic."

Katie chose not to comment. She still had the occasional nightmare about a frightening incident with a colleague, the best part of a decade ago. A well-liked colleague, whose so-called banter and occasional unwelcome touching were laughed off as friendliness, concerns dismissed as politically correct prudery.

Until a dull night on surveillance together when things had taken a darker turn.

She was beginning to think this visit was just another dead end. She remained convinced that Emily's rape case, the verdict, and its tragic aftermath, lay behind the current spate of murders. But she was getting no sense that anyone here, however high passions over the case might have run, was likely to have gone on a killing spree two years later. Her money was still on Emily's family, probably hiring in people to do their dirty work for them.

Maybe that was the key. Except that the Snows seemed ordinary enough folk. How would they get into contact with the kind of people who would abduct and murder to order? With a skilled tattooist who'd be happy to be a part of it? She knew money talked, but you still needed the contacts.

Chantelle Price returned with a large photograph, something like A4 size. Its focus was a beaming Emily Snow, wearing a strappy dress and holding a champagne glass. She was surrounded by men and women of various ages, mostly smartly dressed. All smiling at Emily, most also holding glasses. Katie spotted Megan Jacobs nearby.

"Happier times," Price said. "Emily's birthday, a couple of months before everything went wrong. She brought in some bottles of fizz and a few nibbles, and we had a little party after work. We put the picture on the noticeboard and in the social section of the staff intranet."

"Is that a tradition here?" asked Ricky James. "Birthday parties?"

"No. But she said she'd already had her twenty-first when she started here. She was twenty-two that birthday and reckoned it was the next best date for a celebration. You can see everyone likes her."

It was true. Katie scanned some of the faces in the picture, detecting only genuine warmth. One face seemed to jog a faint memory, but she couldn't place it. Maybe a resemblance to someone on TV.

"Can I keep this?" she asked.

"I'll make you a copy," Price said. The HR manager looked

wistful. "Looking at that, who'd have thought...?" She shook her head. "Don't you sometimes wish you could turn the clock back?"

23

Back in the incident room, Katie Gray completed her report on the visit to Emily Snow's old workplace and returned to her seat. The photograph of a happy Emily Snow at her office birthday drinks had been added to the Wall. The impression of an attractive young woman sparkling, enjoying a moment in her life, saddened Quarrel. Was this when Ben Newell had set his sights on her? Decided he had to have her, one way or another?

Now Emily and three other people were dead. Four families torn apart. A killer still out there, working their way through a list. All Quarrel knew for certain was that Ben Newell must surely be on that list and was likely earmarked as the final victim.

Quarrel hoped Newell was keeping himself safe. He invited Aliya Nazir to report on her visit to Bushey to check on him.

"He's pretty rattled," Aliya said. "I don't think he can quite believe that rape case has come back to threaten him. He thought he was putting it behind him. But it seems he's called in sick and plans on staying at home for the next few days. When we called round, he had the door chain on and had a damn good look at our ID. Anything he needs, he'll be having delivered."

"What did you make of him?" Quarrel wondered. "This is all about a rape he was acquitted of, that someone thinks he actually did. You say he was putting it behind him, but did you get the sense of an innocent man forced to relive a nightmare?"

"As opposed to a sex offender who got away with it?" She glanced at Libby Statham. "You didn't like him, did you, Lib?"

The FLO shook her head. "Not a lot, no. He might be rattled, but that didn't stop him flirting with us, nor staring at our chests. I wouldn't like to be stuck in a lift with him. But I guess that doesn't mean he was guilty."

"Well, at least it sounds like he's safe for now," Quarrel said. "If he's the last name on the killer's list, we've at least brought ourselves some time." He checked the list on his notepad as Aliya sat down. "Now, that white van seen near the scene of the second body dump – Little Tring Bridge. I know none of the local CCTV picked it up but, Ricky, weren't you going to broaden the trawl and take in the other body dumps too? Where are we on that?"

Ricky James fidgeted. "Yes, guv, sorry. Nothing so far. A few vans close enough to the action at the right times, but none common to all the first three crime scenes. I tried focusing down on the second site. On our patch, two white vans on the move around the time our witness says he saw it. I got uniforms to speak to both drivers."

"And?"

"And neither has anything obvious to do with the victims, or with Emily Snow. They gave convincing enough reasons why they were where they were at those times, reasons that check out."

"What if someone's paying them for involvement in the killings?"

Ricky shrugged. "Always possible, I suppose, but no criminal records there, apart from traffic offences. I'm not liking them for being involved, guv. By the way, I also spoke to DC Will Tyler, at Aylesbury Vale in Thames Valley. As you know, Startops, where that jogger says he saw the van, is actually on their patch. I chased Will yesterday, and apparently something's been kicking off in the Vale and he hasn't got round to it, but he promised to get back to me today. Let me check my email when we're done here."

"Okay," Quarrel said, irked by the loose end. "Let me know if you think you're getting the bum's rush, and I'll escalate it."

"Sure, guv," Ricky said, "but I really think it's just work pressure. I've had dealings with Will before and he's pretty efficient."

"Then he'd better deliver," Quarrel all but snapped. "That van didn't just appear in a puff of smoke. It could be a real lead."

He scanned the faces in the room. "Izzy," he said, "can you work with Ricky on that? Top priority?"

"On it," she said.

"And, Izzy, weren't you checking out those online accounts that trolled Ben Newell?"

"Yes, guv. None of them is Ace of Spades, and they were all active well before the rape trial – before the alleged rape, for that matter. I'd say they're nasty, malicious keyboard warriors. I can't see them branching out into murder. And none of their profiles is local."

"Profiles can be entirely fictitious," Quarrel pointed out, "but okay. Let's put that on a back-burner for now." He checked his list again, scanned the Wall. "I think we're done, unless anyone can think of anything else."

No one could. Sharp stood up.

"I reckon you're doing all that's necessary, Nathan," she said. "Getting Ben Newell to stay home and be careful about opening the door, and keeping in touch with him. If he's really the last on the list – and we can't think of any others, can we? – then at least there won't be any more murders."

"And if there are?" The thought appalled him. Made him feel sick.

"Then we investigate it," Sharp said. "We can't protect people if we don't even know they're a target."

*

After the others had dispersed, Izzy Cole remained in the incident room, staring at the Wall. There had been something bugging her, something she hadn't quite been able to put her finger on until just before the briefing, when she'd taken her mug to rinse in the kitchen area and had a brief conversation with Ricky James, who'd slipped in for a quick drink of water.

They'd hurried along to the incident room, and Izzy's thoughts had turned to the matters under discussion. But the feeling that something was off had obviously been ticking away at the back of her mind. Now she saw what it was. It had been in plain sight on this board all along.

The door opened behind her.

"Great minds think alike," Katie Gray said, coming to stand alongside her. "Do you think we're missing something too?"

Izzy was grateful that she wasn't the only one. She was still finding her feet. She wanted to contribute, and she wanted to make an impression – but the right impression.

"I do," she said, "and I think I know what it might be. But I don't want to make an idiot of myself."

"I get it," the DCI said. "Want to try it out on me first?"

"Okay, then."

She'd liked Katie from that first day in the churchyard. She didn't know her well, but she thought the DS might be a receptive ear.

She jabbed her finger at the relevant note on the board.

"It's that white van," she said. "Our jogger, the one who found Michael Woodley's body and called it in? He told us he'd seen a van that might have been speeding away from the body dump, right?"

"Right."

"Yet we can find no conclusive trace of it on CCTV, even though we're supposed to be one of the most watched societies in the world."

"There's still Ricky's man in Aylesbury Vale to get back to us," Katie pointed out. "And Ricky picked up on a couple of vans in the vicinity."

"Not really. I was talking to Ricky just before the briefing, and I know he wants to tick the boxes. Thing is though, they were both on the edges of quite a radius from the dump site. And Ricky's a bit bemused, actually. He reckons it'd be quite hard for a van coming from the direction our man – Harry Baker?"

"That's the one."

"Well, the direction Harry said the van was coming from, there's various cameras. Even if you knew where they all were, it'd be hard to avoid them all."

"Hard, but not impossible?"

Izzy waggled her hand from side to side. "I'd have to see them plotted on a map, but Ricky thinks it would be *bloody* hard."

Katie chewed her lip. "So what are we saying? That Baker's lying? Why would he do that?"

Izzy swallowed. Had she gone too far?

"I'm not saying that's a conclusion we can jump to. He just could be mistaken."

"Or maybe he simply embroidered his story. Still," Katie squared her shoulders. "Right. Can you pull Harry Bloody Baker's statement, with his contact details? I'll have a word with the guv. I think someone needs to have a little chat with him."

*

Harry Baker had given his address as Katherine Close, a cul-de-sac just outside Hemel Hempstead's Apsley village. Much of Apsley retained a slightly old-world identity that dated back to its days as a mill town, dominated by the now defunct John Dickinson's paper mill, but this house was more recent – a small yellow-brick terraced property with a tiny front garden and a block paved drive.

Since this was Izzy Cole's hunch, Quarrel and Katie had brought her along. Izzy rang the doorbell. She was about to press the button again when the door opened to reveal a flustered-looking young woman. The officers flashed their ID and Quarrel did the introductions.

"We're looking for Harry Baker," he said. "Is he at home?"

The woman's brow furrowed. "No one of that name here."

"Are you sure?"

She rolled her eyes. "Let me see. I've got a small lounge, a tiny kitchen, one bedroom and a bathroom." She ticked the rooms off on her fingers. "There was no one else in any of those rooms last time I looked. Unless he's hiding under the bed. You're welcome to check."

"Sorry." Quarrel held up his hands. "Maybe we've got the wrong house number." But his stomach was churning.

"I think you have."

"Do you know Harry Baker?"

Another Olympic standard eye roll. "Oh, yes, of course. Best friends, me and Harry."

"Really?"

"No." Her tone oozed withering sarcasm. "Don't you think I'd have said? Now, if that's all…"

"Look, Mrs…" Katie said, her voice friendly.

"De Souza. And it's Ms."

"Ms De Souza, we're sorry to have disturbed you."

"Yeah, well, I just got in from work. I don't know no Harry Baker, and I don't know why you've got my address." She softened a little. "Look, maybe it's the wrong house number, like you said. I don't really know my neighbours. What's he look like?"

Katie described him. "Goes running."

"I don't think I've seen him. You could try next door."

They tried a few more houses. None was Harry Baker's address, and no one knew him, nor recognised his description.

The three of them sat in the Volvo. "I'm getting a bad feeling," Quarrel said.

"I've got his mobile number," said Katie. "I'll call it."

She pulled out her phone and notebook, dialled a number. Seconds later, she cancelled the call and tried again. Looking worried, she hung up.

"Temporarily unavailable."

"We need to check if that number's registered," Quarrel said. "I'm betting it isn't."

"Pay as you go?"

"Yes, and it's served its purpose. I'm guessing the SIM card is out, or the phone's on a skip or at the bottom of the canal. Either way, we can't trace it."

A hideous truth was dawning on him, but it was Izzy who voiced what they were all thinking.

"Oh, Christ," she said. "He didn't *find* Woodley's body under the bridge, did he?"

"No," said Quarrel, a pulse beginning to beat in his ears. "I think he put it there."

24

Ben Newell was scared and bored at the same time. Scared because the police believed someone might want to kill him. Bored because he was going stir crazy here in his flat in Bushey.

He'd spent two years trying to put the trial behind him. Had avoided dating or relationships because of what had happened, even though a few seriously fit women had come on to him. He had a fear of history repeating itself, and a dread of getting involved with someone only for them to find out about his past.

His name had been splashed all over the news after his acquittal, and again after Emily's death, but it was perfectly true that, even in this age of online information overload, today's news was tomorrow's virtual fish and chip paper.

Except that, unlike physical chip wrapping, his story was still there if anyone cared to put his name into an Internet search.

Whatever mistakes he'd made with Emily, he wasn't going to repeat them. He knew what he'd done then, and he wasn't proud of himself, but he was sure he was a different man to the one she'd met in DeadlineZ that fateful night. Oh, some people had stood by him and believed his version of events. But most had melted away. The law had found him not guilty, but the doubts had remained.

Still, things could have been worse. They say that, when things are bad, that's when you find out who your friends are, and he'd found support in one or two unlikely places. The person he now considered his best friend had stuck by him in the weeks after Emily's suicide, when his life had been at rock bottom. A friend who'd helped him get his confidence back, accept that he had no future at the firm where he'd worked with Emily, and move on. Now he had an even better job than the one he'd had to leave.

Still, he hadn't felt able to tell even his best friend why he was confining himself to home. He'd concocted a mystery fatigue illness that he hoped would blow over in a few days – even though he knew it would only blow over if the police did their bloody job and caught the killer who was rampaging around killing people associated with his trial. People the killer apparently blamed for Emily's death.

That cute Asian detective, Aliya, had told him they still didn't know how many more potential victims were on the list. The only thing she seemed sure about was that he was at the top of it, and that the killer may well be saving him for last.

Great. And not much help if you didn't know how many dead people it would take before he was the last man standing.

Self-pity washed over him. Sometimes it was as though he hadn't walked free from the court at all, the day the verdict had been delivered. There had been a whole new debate about effectively putting the so-called victim's morals on trial, much of which had only served to undermine his innocence. It was almost as if he was in a prison without bars.

And now he was a prisoner in his own home.

The doorbell rang, and he jumped, like a child jumping at his own shadow. God, this was making him such a wuss. Even so, he felt terror beginning to spread from the pit of his guts. Was this the police checking up on him again? He supposed seeing the gorgeous DC Nazir would bring a few moments' sunshine into his life. She might even have that PC Libby Statham with her again. There was something about a woman in uniform…

What if it wasn't the police, though? What if it was the killer, posing as pizza delivery, or something? Best take no chances.

The bell rang again, and Ben realised he hadn't moved. On legs that seemed reluctant to carry him, he stepped into his small hallway, walked up to the front door, and peered through the spy hole.

He felt his shoulders sagging with relief at the sight of a familiar face.

"Come on, mate," his friend said. "I know you're in there. Look what I got!"

A four pack of beer was held up for inspection, and a grin split his face.

"Just a sec," he said, and he took the chain off the door and turned the key in the lock.

*

"Well, we've been had," Katie admitted, slumped in a chair in front of Quarrel's desk. "We took Harry Baker at face value. Why wouldn't we? Now it's beginning to look like he doesn't exist. He's not in DVLA records as far as we can tell, at least by that name. I mean, there's a lot of Harry Bakers in the system, but we've whittled it down by age and area and looked at the records. None of the photos looks remotely like our jogger."

Quarrel wasn't surprised. From the moment the Katherine Close address had proved false, he'd suspected that the man who'd called in the discovery of Michael Woodley's body had used a false identity. Whoever Harry Baker really was, he was no random jogger. Either he was the killer, or he was involved in a murderous conspiracy.

"It'll take a lot more checking to be sure," Katie was saying. "Not everyone drives, and I suppose his licence could be registered elsewhere. We need to check other databases…"

"Yes," groaned Quarrel, "and that all takes time that we haven't got. Jesus. We had him here in the station, making a statement and talking about how shaken he was, and how he was having flashbacks." He shook his head, furious with himself. "Remember how he banged on in detail about the route he takes on his run? All part of his persona, I'll bet. And that white van of his? No wonder we couldn't find any trace of it."

"He chucked that detail in just to send us down a rabbit hole," Izzy said.

"I think so."

"But why call it in?" Katie frowned. "And why *that* body in particular?"

Quarrel thought about that. "It was the second one," he decided. "We might have thought Alastair Murdoch was an isolated case. Then Michael Woodley made it a trend. He wanted to see if he could get some sense of what we were making of it."

"Damn it." The frustration in her tone matched what he was feeling. "It wouldn't be the first time the person who claimed to have found a body turned out to be the killer. But this guy seemed so random, didn't he?"

"He did. And there's something else. Remember how fit and muscly he looked? He could easily be strong enough to manhandle the victims in and out of cars and even carry the bodies from his vehicle to the dump sites." His head was pounding. "Megan Jacobs would still be alive if we'd checked him out there and then."

"We had no reason to," she insisted. "And we can't think that way. It won't help."

"You're right, of course," he conceded, even though the self-loathing persisted. "We need to focus on finding him. We don't even have a picture. Well, we have CCTV," he amended. We need to find any footage he's on. It's a start."

Katie was looking thoughtful.

"What?" he asked.

"A picture," she said. "Just a thought, but we know he's not one of Emily Snow's immediate family, and her parents said she didn't have a wide circle of friends."

"So…?"

"So, if our Harry Baker, or whoever the hell he really is, is someone who cared enough about Emily to be doing this, he must be someone who knew and liked her. Come with me."

He and Izzy followed her to the incident room and up to the Wall. She studied the picture of Emily's birthday party, then smiled.

"She was well liked at work," she said. "What if someone liked her rather more than her other colleagues?"

"You think Harry Baker could be in this picture?" He pored over it. "But he isn't."

"Look again." She stabbed the photograph with her index finger and Quarrel found himself focusing on a weedy, insignificant-looking figure with thick-rimmed glasses. The young man was looking directly at Emily. There was something about his smile that was somehow different to the others. Not just a man at a colleague's birthday drinks, enjoying the moment, maybe toasting the birthday girl.

Even fixed in a photograph, this man seemed to have eyes only for Emily, his expression bordering on pure adoration.

"All right," Quarrel said. "You've got my attention, sort of. You think this lad had a crush on Emily?"

She looked carefully at the picture. "Now you mention it, that could be. Maybe more than a crush. But that isn't what I mean."

"No." It was Izzy who spoke. "I see what you're getting at. You think he looks a lot like Harry Baker, don't you?"

Katie was nodding. "Build him up, take away the glasses…"

Quarrel stared at the face. He thought maybe they were all reaching, out of desperation, but right now he wasn't going to reject any new ideas. "You might be right. I'm not a hundred per cent convinced, but we certainly ought to check him out."

*

"Harry Baker?" Chantelle Price shook her head. "No one of that name has worked for us in the time I've been with the firm."

Price had gone home by the time Katie tried to contact her, but she had answered her phone quickly enough and had willingly agreed to talk further to her and Quarrel. Now the three of them sat on a sofa in her comfortable home office, the party picture between them.

"That," Price said, referring to the bespectacled man Katie had indicated, "is Howie – Howard Parker." She pursed her lips. "Not so different a name, I suppose. You're sure you haven't misheard or something?"

There was an earnestness about her that diminished any resentment Quarrel might have felt about such a question. He got no sense of patronisation, only a willingness to help.

"There's no mistake," he said. "We know this man as Harry Baker. What can you tell us about him?"

She looked thoughtful. "I suppose the word I'd use to sum him up is 'nerdy'. Not someone you'd have working directly with clients, but quite creative. Good with numbers and their interpretation. A bit under the radar, really. No serious friends here until…"

"What about Emily?" Katie asked, interrupting her. Quarrel wished she hadn't. "What sort of relationship did he have with her?"

Chantelle Price smiled. "Oh, I rather think he fancied her. I think everyone could see the way he looked at her. At social get-togethers, he was always on the fringes of any circle she was in, although never contributing much. I could never work out if he was shy, or if he wasn't that interested in their conversations."

"Was he aloof in any way?"

"No, I wouldn't call it that. He just had different interests. He was big on online gaming, a great reader of comic books, and he was quite an artist, if you like that sort of thing."

"What sort of thing?"

"Superheroes mainly, but also some quite romantic stuff, a bit like the Pre-Raphaelite paintings, but his own ideas."

Quarrel's ears pricked up. "Did he do any Tarot card designs?"

She looked at him. "Why do you ask that?"

"Did he?"

"Well, funny you should say that. Howie gave Emily an absolutely beautiful hand-made card for that birthday, with two Tarot cards on it. He said he'd been online and calculated her birth cards. I can't remember what they looked like now. I've got a vague recollection of a lion."

"Why would he do that?"

"Emily was interested in Tarot. She was a bit of a reader – did readings for quite a few of the staff, as a matter of fact. I guess he thought it would be a nice thing to do for her birthday. Maybe he hoped it would lead to something, who knows? I mean, they got on pretty well. You often saw them chatting by the water cooler. But I think that was all."

She made a face. "I do remember that he was off sick when the trial was happening. He had a doctor's certificate for depression. I remember hoping – a bit selfishly – that he wasn't going to be another HR headache at what was already a difficult time. But he came back soon after the verdict and Emily's resignation. It was strange though."

"Strange how?"

"I'd have banked on him being one of those who cold-shouldered Ben, or worse. But it was quite the opposite. The two seemed to get quite close, soon after Emily's death."

That was a jolt. "They became friends?"

"They were friendly enough before all that – Ben was an online gamer too, so they did have a shared passion. But after Emily died, they seemed to become as thick as thieves. Ben was a Watford fan and Howie – who'd never shown any interest in sport before – even started going with him. I know they did some after hours drinking too."

She pursed her lips. "To be honest, I found it a bit shocking – almost as if her death had pushed him *towards* Ben, when it seemed to push quite a few colleagues away. Some would only communicate with Ben by email, until we parted company with him."

"And Howie left too?"

"Yes," Price said. "A bit sad, really. His parents were quite well off, but both died quite young. His mum from cancer, then his dad had a heart attack about six months or so before the court case. Apparently Howie was going to be well provided for, once probate came through. There were some stocks and shares, and a fair bit of cash – they'd not long downsized to a house not far from Hemel station. He said he was going to live in it and devote more time to his art. Apparently it's got a basement, and he planned on setting up a studio down there."

25

The world swam into focus for Ben Newell. He found himself staring at a bare lightbulb suspended from a high ceiling. His mouth felt dry and fuzzy. He attempted to lick his lips, but they were somehow stuck together. He tried to move and realised he was tied or strapped to some sort of hard surface. Something gripped the sides of his head firmly.

Panic set in. He wanted to thrash about, but his mobility was so limited that he couldn't manage more than some vague jerking motions.

"About time, too," said a voice he knew, and Howie's face appeared before him.

Howie! Howie Parker, his mate? Confusion rippled through him. Confusion and a dawning, nightmarish understanding.

"We've got a lot of work ahead of us, Ben," Howie said. "But I need you awake, to fully appreciate the experience."

He smiled, and it was a smile that froze Ben's blood. That half-shy, familiar Howie smile, but with a madness behind the eyes that had always been concealed before.

Oh, God. It was coming back now. Despite all the police warnings, Ben had had no reason to fear his buddy. Howie had brought beer and a list of old films, available to stream, that he thought they could choose from. He'd gone into the kitchen to open a couple of brews while Ben chose a film. They'd had a few such evenings, so nothing strange there.

But, not long into the film, Ben had started feeling groggy and confused.

"You don't look at all good, mate," Howie had said. "I reckon I should get you to A and E."

Ben tried to protest, to say he probably just needed to sleep. But his tongue felt too thick and useless to work properly. Howie had got him to his feet and taken his beer from him.

He'd gone into the kitchen and Ben had heard Howie emptying both opened bottles down the sink. He'd come back, stashed the bottles in his messenger bag, and turned off the TV.

Then he'd pulled Ben to his feet and walked him to his front door, where he paused and put sunglasses and baseball caps on both of them, even though it was dark out. What was that all about? A disguise, in case they encountered anyone, Ben realised now.

Had they passed anyone on the way to Howie's car? Ben really couldn't remember. Howie had put him in the passenger seat, then walked around and got behind the wheel. Ben had an impression of him reaching for something behind him. He had turned around and pulled a cloth out of a plastic bag. Then he'd put one hand firmly behind Ben's head.

Ben seemed to recall the cloth coming towards his face. Then nothing, until he woke up in this place.

Howie was grinning again. "How much have they told you about the others?" he asked. "The others I killed, I mean. I'm guessing, with no real details in the papers, not too much. Nothing about tattoos, I bet. Well," he continued, "what do you think of this one?"

He held a sheet of tracing paper in front of Ben's face. There was some sort of carbon paper behind it. The paper bore a picture, a bit old-fashioned in style: a light-haired girl, robed in white, with laurels in her hair and a belt of garlanded flowers. She was opening the jaws of a lion. The beast seemed passive to her actions. Why was he being shown this? Lunacy!

"Strength," Howie said. "Ironically, one of Emily's two birth cards. That and The Star. You'd have seen them on the birthday card I gave her, if you could be bothered to look. I bet you didn't, though. Too full of yourself."

There wasn't a hint of rage in Howie's tone. Ben would have preferred it if there had been. It might have been a little less terrifying if his captor had been ranting. This calm control, this sense of earnest purpose, sent icy daggers into his heart. Whatever was coming, it wouldn't be good.

"I won't bore you too much," Howie said. "I know you won't care, but I want you to know. Emily was born on the seventh of April, 1995. There's a formula for working out a person's birth cards, in Tarot. Hers are The Star and Strength. The Star is a card of dreams and positive energy – of moving away from negative influences. Strength is about accepting life and trusting ourselves to make the right choices. The combination means positive forward movement, with the necessary resolve to make a success of things." He smiled fondly. "That was Emily, don't you think?"

He made a sour face. "But Strength is also known as the lust card. Perfect for you, you filthy animal." He brandished the picture. "This is going on your face, before I kill you. The last thing you'll see before you die is your face in a mirror, with this card tattooed all over it, proclaiming you for the rapist you are."

He laughed without humour. "You didn't question for a moment why I stuck by you after what happened to Emily. I loved her. I don't doubt some of our workmates could see that. But not a self-absorbed piece of dirt like you. But you know what? The weekend after you drugged her and raped her, Emily and I were going on our first date."

Perhaps Ben's surprise showed in his eyes.

"What, you don't believe me?" Howie sounded bitter. "No, you wouldn't would you? Well, *mate, she* asked *me* out. Just a drink and a movie. Maybe that was all it was. Just friendship. But I had hopes. I had dreams. We'll never know now, will we?" His face darkened. "It never happened, of course. But she told me what you did. Begged me not to tell anyone else. She trusted me. We had a connection. Who'd have thought it?"

Howie shrugged. "I wanted to kill you then but, like a fool, I decided I should let justice take its course. I didn't let on I knew, not even to you. Maybe I was even planning this, at the back of my mind, as a contingency – in case the verdict went wrong. You didn't see me sitting at the back of the court every day of the trial, did you? Even if you had, you'd have probably imagined I was there for you. But I wasn't. It was all about Emily. And so is this."

He put the paper aside and made quite a show of rolling up his sleeves. "Anyhow. I have work to do. You just lie there and relax." He started to turn away, then stopped and looked back at Ben. "Oh, by the way. It's going to hurt."

*

Katie had phoned the station as Quarrel drove them back, frantically dishing out tasks and setting up a meeting in the incident room for 6pm sharp. By the time the team had assembled, a slightly grainy image of Howard Parker, captured from station CCTV footage, had been added to the Wall.

The atmosphere in the room had transformed from previous meetings. The team had struggled a little to maintain energy as lead after lead had evaporated and frustration had mounted. Now there was a new buzz about the place, coupled with a sense of desperate urgency.

There were two reasons for the change. First, they'd been told they finally had a credible prime suspect who must be located without delay. And secondly, Aliya Nazir had tried to phone Ben Newell, to redouble the warning about not opening his door to anyone, specifically including Howard Parker.

But Ben wasn't answering his land line or his mobile. Local uniforms had gone to his flat, got no answer, and broken the door down. The flat was empty, with no sign of a struggle.

CSIs were on their way to check the flat for evidence, and the statement 'Harry Baker' had signed would also be dusted for prints for comparison. But, important though such evidence might be in slower time, the priority now was to find Parker and to find Ben.

If it wasn't already too late.

"Time's of the essence," Quarrel said, "so I'm going to make this quick." He tapped the new picture on the board. "We think Harry Baker here is in fact Howard Parker, a former colleague of both Ben Newell and Emily Snow. We have reason to believe that Parker had a serious crush on Emily. Might have fancied himself in love with her. Yet, after she took her own life, he became Ben's new best buddy. It's pretty obvious now he wanted to get close to him and gain his trust."

"He was probably planning all this from the moment Emily died," Katie put in. "Maybe even from Ben's acquittal. Thinking that, even if we worked out the connection between victims and warned Ben to be on his guard, he wouldn't fear a close friend. Now we must assume that Parker has him."

"There's something else," Quarrel added. "Parker's quite the artist, it seems – even gave Emily a Tarot-inspired birthday card. He'd certainly have the flair to do the tattoos, and it sounds like his late parents left him enough to live on while he quietly learned tattooing somewhere. They also left him a house with a basement, that would be ideal for what he's doing to his victims. We need to locate that house quickly."

That message had been relayed by Katie on the drive back, work set in hand.

"So," Quarrel said, "what have we got? Anyone?"

"His last known address," Izzy Cole said, "the one you got from his old employers. It's a rental flat in Watford. He moved out over a year ago."

"Forwarding address?"

"Nope. If he's moved into his parents' old house, then presumably he changed the address for his bank accounts and stuff before he left the flat. Obviously, we have no way of knowing where his mail is going. The present occupants have no forwarding address. They do get some stuff for him, but most of it's junk mail. Anything that looks important, they return to sender."

"Who was talking to DVLA?" Quarrel demanded.

"That'd be me," Ricky James said. "His driver's licence is still registered at the old address, and he doesn't seem to own a car. My guess is he rents them. He's doing all he can to fly under the radar, I reckon, to slow us down even if we do get onto him."

Quarrel pushed his fingers through his hair, panic threatening to overwhelm him. Since the beginning of this case, he'd done nothing but fail. Now he was sure they'd finally identified the killer, but they had no idea where he was. If they failed Ben Newell too...

He closed his eyes and saw blood-red spots on white snow.

He opened them again, batted those thoughts away. He couldn't go there, not now, not if he wanted to think straight. Not if he wanted to be of any use to Ben.

"The parents' house?" he demanded. "Come on, how hard can it be? A house in Boxmoor with a basement?"

Ironically, Parker's erstwhile employers had held that address as his next of kin at one time, when his father had been alive. But it been deleted under the firm's data retention policy soon after Howard had left. Neither Chantelle Price, nor anyone else in HR, could now remember the address, nor the parents' names.

Libby Statham raised a hand tentatively. "I had a sort of a wild idea and did an Internet search of the local papers' death notices. I filtered from three years ago and found three Parkers in Hemel Hempstead who would have died around the time we think we're looking at. Two are men, and only one's the right age to possibly be Howard's father."

"Assuming there was even a notice in the papers for our man's dad," DCI Sharp remarked gloomily.

"I know, ma'am," Libby said, "I was just trying to think outside the box. Anyhow, I've got our techie guys, who are much quicker than me, trying to find this man's death certificate. It'll have his address on it. Name of Martin Parker."

"Good thinking, Libby," Quarrel said. "But we don't know for sure he's Howard's dad?"

"No, guv."

"We must be able to get hold of Howie's birth certificate, with the parents' names on. His date of birth will be on his driver's licence. Ricky, did you note that down?"

Ricky was riffling through a sheaf of paperwork. "Better than that, guv. I printed off a copy. Here we go." He waved one of the sheets triumphantly, then peered at it. "Yep, 18 May 1988."

"Right, then. I want all that paperwork, I want that address, and I want it yesterday."

*

194

Ben could feel the almost paralysing panic building inside him as Howie worked on his immobilised face. The man he'd counted as a close friend seemed to delight in telling him in detail, almost like a teacher to a student, everything he was doing. He was painstakingly transferring the design for the tattoo onto Ben's face as a guide for the needles that would dispatch the ink into his skin.

There was no more than mild discomfort at the moment, but Howie had assured him, almost conversationally, that the actual tattooing would hurt like hell. Building up the fear, the anticipation, was evidently all part of the torture.

He'd smiled. "I could take the edge off with a topical anaesthetic. But I'm not going to."

Ben had felt his terror mounting. Had tried to beg for mercy, to reason with Howie, but the tape covering his mouth had rendered him unintelligible. Howie had ignored him anyway. All it had done was hurt his throat until he'd given up.

Howie had given a 'what can you do?' shrug. "Oh, well. Can't stand around chatting. Lots to do. First I need to get this pattern onto your face. That's the easy bit, Ben, so make the most of it."

He'd leaned over and patted Ben on the shoulder. "Meanwhile, here's something to think about. It might take your mind off the pain. When I've finished your tattoo, I'm going to take that tape off your mouth and you're going to confess to what you did to Emily. No more lies. It'll be a chance to purge your soul before you meet your maker. If he exists, of course."

While Howie worked on the transfer, Ben had played those words over in his mind. He was in for a great deal of pain, and who knew what might then be done to him to force a 'confession'? And then he was going to die.

He had no real idea what the time was, but surely Aliya Nazir had been trying to get in touch since their last conversation? The detective seemed very good at checking in regularly to make sure he was okay. Surely by now she'd realised something was wrong? People must be looking for him.

But what if they were? Why would they have any more of a clue as to where he was than he had? Three people had died before him, and he had no reason to suppose the police had a suspect in their sights, let alone a location.

He had to face the fact that he had only a few hours left to live. He felt a prickling behind his eyes. He blinked, determined not to let this monster who'd posed as his friend see him cry.

But would he be able to hold back the tears when the needles started?

26

Quarrel sat in his office, feeling impotent. Having dished out work to the others, he'd left himself little to do except wait and worry.

There had been one glimmer of light to lift his mood. It seemed that an elderly man had walked into St Albans police station this afternoon and confessed to the hit and run killing of Ed Barnes. DS Lewis Appleby had phoned as a courtesy to let Quarrel know. It seemed the incident had resurfaced in the local news in a story about Rob Murdoch's 'double tragedy' – first losing his best friend, then his father. Appleby had been short on details, but the story had pricked the driver's conscience.

At least Jacko Barnes would finally have a genuine focus for his anger.

Meanwhile, it was going to be a very long day, possibly going into the small hours. He decided to ring Laura. To warn her he might not make it home tonight, and just to hear her voice.

"That's a shame," she said when he'd broken the news. "We've got a visitor."

"Visitor?" They didn't exactly have a wide social circle. He couldn't imagine who'd casually drop round on a week night. "Who's that, then?"

There was a pause. Not a long one, but long enough.

"Your mother."

"What?" A cold, knifing shock cut through him. "Please tell me you haven't let her in."

"She's here now, having a cup of tea. I've offered her dinner."

He had the weirdest feeling that Laura had been replaced by a stranger. "Why would you do that? You know how I feel."

"Yes, I do," she said quietly. "That's exactly why I think you should finally listen to what she has to say?"

"Listen to her lies, you mean?" He was gripping the phone so hard, it hurt. But it was nothing compared to the pain in his heart.

"I don't believe this," he said. "All my life, there were only two people I trusted. My grandparents. Then you came along and made it three."

"Nate—"

"Since Grandma and Granddad have been gone, there's only been you. Now I find there's really no one at all I can trust."

"Now you're just being ridiculous."

"Am I?" He sighed. "We'll talk about this later. You know full well how I feel about this, yet you take it on yourself to let that – that *thing* in. I hope you can keep her away from the knife drawer!"

"You're overdramatising."

"Am I?"

"She's your mother."

"No. She's the woman who gave birth to me. The grandparent who raised me – she was my mother, in any real sense. She was always there for me. That creature you've got in our house, drinking our tea? You know what she is."

*

As Howie worked on the transfer, he continued to talk.

"When you stop and think, the symbolism is astonishing, isn't it? An innocent young girl and a lion. A beast. And, you know, it's funny. When I first found out you could calculate a person's Tarot birth cards, I wasn't so interested in the meaning of the cards. It was all about the art. I just wanted to create a beautiful birthday card for Emily. I chose the Rider Waite deck, because I knew it was her favourite, and that's why I'm using it for this project. Don't you love the romantic styling of the images?"

He heaved a heavy sigh. "I know it's a bit of a one-sided conversation, but that's okay. This is a bit like a confessional, in a way, Ben. I can say what I like, knowing you'll take my words to the grave.

"For instance, I'm actually hoping I can move on once this is over. Start again. Maybe even find someone new to love." He barked a laugh. "It's funny how one thing leads to another. When we first met, I was shy and weedy, and most women barely knew I existed. No way would I have dared ask one for a date. I couldn't believe Emily wanted to go out with me. But, after the verdict, when I realised you weren't the only one who had to pay for that travesty of a trial, I knew I needed to build myself up, both physically and mentally.

"And now things are different. Some stunning-looking women at the gym have gone out of their way to chat to me. A few have even invited me for drinks or coffee. Oh, I've always made polite excuses and declined, but I *have* been tempted. The thing is, though, I have to be strong. If I came to care for someone, I'm not sure I'd be able to see this through. I'd have more to lose if I got caught."

He worked in silence for a few minutes, then started talking again.

"If it's any consolation, I count my chances of getting away with this as no more than fifty-fifty in the long run. I accept I might well be caught and made to pay for what I've done. But I don't mind about that."

He worked on. The pen moved over Ben's face like a slug crawling across it. Finally it stopped and Howie stepped away. When he returned, he held up a mirror so Ben could see his reflection.

"What do you think?" he said. "Not bad at all, if I do say so myself."

He stepped away again. Moments later, a wasp-buzz drone began. The sound seemed to fill the room,

"Here we go, then," Howie said. "Time for some serious work."

*

Clearing his mind after Laura's bombshell was proving difficult for Quarrel. He knew all families had their frictions, and he understood why people might take it upon themselves to act as peacemakers between their partners and their kin. But this was a whole different level to most family rows.

He felt he'd spent all his life running from events he couldn't even remember. He barely remembered his parents either – just fragments of memories and impressions. He knew he'd seen things as a child that were so terrible he'd blocked them out, even when his grandparents had finally told him the truth. It explained the instants of visual flashback, and even his disquiet when it snowed or grew cold. But the memories remained mercifully out of reach. He was fine with that.

He supposed he'd always known that, if he ignored the letters for long enough, the woman who called herself his mother would finally turn up in person. She'd done it before, the first time she'd tracked him down. He'd closed the door in her face, changed his name and moved a long way away. Rationally, he knew it had been an extreme response, but her physical appearance on his doorstep had been the culmination of a lifetime of dread and horror associated with the very thought of her. He hadn't had the strength to fight those feelings, so he'd fled.

It had been in vain. In the end, she'd found him again and the letters had started over. After the first couple, he'd learned to recognise her handwriting and simply shredded them unopened. He had no reason to read her lies.

Laura was the only person who knew who he really was. And now, knowing his feelings, knowing he wanted nothing to do with this person, she had nevertheless invited the viper into their nest. Right now, he wasn't sure they could get past this. The sense of betrayal was absolute. He had never felt so utterly alone and isolated.

In the end, he'd done his best to shift the whole issue to the back of his mind. He simply couldn't allow it head space while there was a chance Ben Newell could be saved and a serial killer apprehended.

Since then, he'd been going over the case, trying to think of anything that could be done that wasn't already in hand. So far, nothing was coming to him.

A tap on his open office door broke his concentration. Katie Gray stood there. Behind her, James, Nazir, Statham and Cole. Quite a deputation.

"Anything?" he asked, guessing they hadn't decided to take a collective break.

Katie was grinning, visibly excited. "I think we've got it. We had to be pretty pushy to get people to do stuff out of hours, and the techie guys have been amazing in what they've ferreted out."

His pulse was racing. "So what have we got?"

"A detached in Boxmoor, formerly owned by Martin and Lynda Parker. Now owned by one Howard Parker. As luck would have it, they only bought it nine years ago, and we've managed to find some plans online. There's definitely a basement. Cowper Road."

Quarrel knew it well. Adrenaline surged through his veins. "I already asked the boss to have an armed squad on standby. I'll get her to scramble them. If he's there, and he's got Ben – and Ben is still alive – we could find ourselves with a hostage situation. Is there a direct way into that basement?"

"Not that we can see, Nate. Only through the front door and down some stairs."

"Damn. We're going to have to give him plenty of warning if we try to bust in. He could decide to just kill Ben. Is there a land line?"

"If there is, it's either not listed, or listed in a fake name."

"No matter. If we were going to phone him and try to talk him down, we'd really need a trained hostage negotiator, and we might not have time to organise that. Does the basement have windows?"

"Doesn't look like it."

He bit his lip. They might have the killer in their sights, but what was the best way of stopping him claiming his final victim?

"All right," he decided. "First things first. We get that armed team mobilised and we all get over there. Quietly, though. No blue lights or sirens. We'll have to make up a strategy once we know the lie of the land."

But he didn't like it. On top of everything else, he didn't think he could bear to lose Ben Newell, not when they were this close to saving him.

27

The little convoy drew up outside the house. It was one of the older properties in Cowper Road, although the front garden had at some point been converted to a block paved drive with an integral garage. In Quarrel's Volvo were Quarrel himself, Aliya, Ricky and DCI Sharp. Behind them was an armed response vehicle. Armoured and armed cops spilled out as soon as it halted. Quarrel and his passengers, all in stab vests, joined them on the pavement. Katie Gray's car stopped behind the ARV and she, Izzy Cole and one other passenger emerged.

He studied the house.

"This couldn't be better, could it?" he remarked. "If you wanted to get an unconscious person inside unseen by neighbours or passers-by."

"Just drive into the garage, close the door, and do what you like," Ricky James agreed.

The armed unit's leader, Sergeant Mike Ryan, jogged over to join the detectives. He looked to Sharp, the senior officer present.

"How are we playing this, ma'am?"

Sharp jabbed a thumb in Quarrel's direction. "This is DI Quarrel's show, but we've been talking on the way over. We think the suspect may be in the basement with his captive, which makes it all a bit tricky."

"According to the plans, there's no direct access to the basement," Quarrel told the firearms officer. "Our obvious first step should be to just knock on the door and hope he answers, but if he's in the middle of his tattooing, there's every chance he'll ignore us. All that leaves us is getting in and getting down to that basement fast."

Ryan squinted at him. "How fast?"

"Put it this way. We might not be dealing with the most rational of people, and we think this would be his final victim. He's killed three times already, so he might think adding one more won't make a great deal of difference to his sentence."

"You think he might kill his captive before we get down there?"

"I think the tattooing is the icing on the cake of what he wants to achieve. His main objective is to right what he sees as a great wrong by killing those he holds responsible. I think he'd cut his losses and despatch Ben Newell in a heartbeat."

"All right. So we need two things, then. We're going to have to be checking the other rooms while a couple of us go down to the basement. We'll look pretty stupid if he's in the kitchen, making a sandwich."

"Agreed."

"And somehow, we need an element of surprise," Ryan said. "You can't break a door down quietly."

For the first time in a while, Quarrel smiled. "Just as well we won't be breaking it down then." He placed a hand on the shoulder of Katie's second passenger. "Meet Sergeant Colin Webster, our resident lock picker."

Ryan looked from Webster to Quarrel. "Seriously?"

"He can get us in quietly. Then it's a matter of getting through that door to the basement – I hope to Christ it isn't locked – and down the stairs."

He outlined his plan to the group one more time. Faces were grim, some pale with anticipation. But nobody gave him any arguments.

He and Sharp walked up to the front door, Webster at their heels. Quarrel stooped, bending his tall frame, and gently opened the flap of the letter box.

"Mr Parker," he called, very softly. "Police. Open up please."

He lowered the flap and turned to Sharp. "There. We've announced ourselves."

He counted down from ten to zero, just in case his almost whispered call had been heard. Then he turned to Colin Webster.

"Right, Colin, do your stuff. Quieter the better."

*

Howie had completed the outlining, giving a running commentary as he worked. It seemed he'd used a single-tipped needle and a thin ink to create a permanent line over the stencilled outline.

"It's important to start at the bottom right-hand corner and work upwards," he'd lectured. "It reduces the risk of smearing the stencil when you clean any excess ink from the permanent line."

He'd cleaned the area with soap and water and now he was well into the shading stage, using a thicker ink and a variety of needles.

"The aim here is to create an even, solid line, with no shadowing. The technique I'm using also avoids excessive pain and delayed healing." He'd emitted a dry chuckle. "Although obviously I don't really care about that in this instance."

From Ben's perspective, there had been more than enough pain.

Howie paused now, surveying his work.

"I'm about to get started on the final stage now. I'll clean the tattoo again, then start to add dots, fine lines and hatching, to give some light and shade to the image. I need to take care to avoid blowouts – that's where the needle goes too deep and too much ink is delivered, creating a smudgy effect. After all, Ben, I'm a professional, and I need this body of work to be my finest."

Ben had become quiet, exhausted and nursing his pain. Howie could dress it up however he liked, but this was slow, painful torture. This was all about punishment.

"How do you like the music?" Howie asked. "I often have grime for background, but not today. Not for this job. This selection is more personal and appropriate. It's my own playlist with 'Emily' in the title or lyrics. Did you notice? It's quite an eclectic mix, isn't it? Sinatra, Streisand, Pink Floyd, Elton John and the Manic Street Preachers."

His voice became thick with emotion. "The track currently playing is The Zombies: 'A Rose for Emily'. I'm not ashamed to say, the first time I heard that one, I cried like a baby, because my Emily won't grow old like the one in the song. But you know what? It added to my resolve to see this work through. And, when this is all over, I'll leave a red rose on her grave every year –" his voice cracked – "on her birthday."

Howie fell silent for a moment. Walked out of Ben's limited field of vision. Blew his nose. After a few moments, he returned and, without another word, applied the needle and resumed his work.

As ink was delivered to Ben Newell's face, he hummed along with the music.

*

Colin Webster smiled and carefully pushed the door open. Ryan adjusted his grip on his weapon, nodded to Quarrel, then led his team inside. They moved surprisingly quietly. Quarrel hung back until they were all inside, then stepped over the threshold himself. Sharp, Katie and Aliya were close behind him. Ricky and Izzy were waiting outside just in case Parker somehow managed to make a getaway.

Not that Quarrel could see how that was going to happen.

While Colin Webster had worked on the lock, Ryan and his team had studied the floor plan Katie had brought along. Now Ryan took up position by the door leading to the basement. From behind that door wafted faint music, although Quarrel couldn't quite distinguish the tune. It reinforced the likelihood that Parker was down there with Ben Newell, but Ryan was taking no chances. Two of his team checked the other ground floor rooms, quietly, methodically, before mouthing 'clear', as each room was swept.

It was just possible, of course, that Howard Parker was working upstairs, but the least likely scenario. Even so, the two officers went up, as silently as they could. A floorboard creaked and Quarrel prayed that the music Parker was playing would drown the sound out.

The upper floor was swept as efficiently as the ground floor, and all attention turned to that basement door. Quarrel found that his mouth was dry as Ryan laid a hand on the handle. He turned it slowly, then gently pushed. It opened inwards by the slightest of cracks. Light filtered through. The music grew a little louder.

Ryan turned, locked eyes with each of his teammates in turn. Held up a closed hand then lifted first his index finger, then the middle, then the ring. On the third digit, he thrust the door open, his colleagues clattering in as he bellowed, "Armed police! Down on the floor!"

*

Ben somehow sensed that Howie had tensed. The drone of the machine ceased. The music played on.

"What was that?" Howie murmured, evidently listening hard. Ben had heard nothing but the buzz of the tattoo machine. He looked a question at Howie.

"Thought I heard…" He shook his head. "Spooking myself."

His words were barely out when Ben thought he heard something too.

Unmistakeable, the groan of a floorboard. Hope soared. Someone else was in the house. Surely it could only mean one thing.

He saw anguish in Howie's eyes as they lingered for a moment on the unfinished tattoo.

"Fuck," he said. "They've found us." He reached out and patted Ben's shoulder. "I have to go. Don't think this is over."

He walked briskly away, moving behind Ben's head. There was a click and a creak. The sound of a door opening. Cool air entered the space they were in.

"It's all in the planning, Ben," Howie said. Then there were scrambling sounds.

Seconds later, a voice bawled, "Armed police!"

*

Ryan burst through the door, his colleagues at his heels, yelling, "Armed police!" again. Then their movement ceased.

"Shit," muttered Ryan, starting to move again.

"What?" Quarrel demanded.

He stood at the top of the stairs, looking down, taking in the figure strapped to a bench. *Christ, his head really was in a vice!* He made out the black outlining on the face, the tattoo unfinished. He couldn't be sure it was Ben Newell, not from this distance, but he could see the reassuring rise and fall of the chest.

Of Howard Parker, there was no sign.

"We've missed him." Mike Ryan stated the obvious from the bottom of the stairs as Quarrel started down. Then the firearms officer added, "I can see where he got out."

He moved towards the rear of the room. Quarrel started to hurry after him, but paused by the bench. Yes, definitely Ben Newell.

"Aliya and I will look after him," Sharp said. "Catch the bastard."

With Katie tight at his back, he crossed the room to where Ryan stood. The opening couldn't be much more than three feet high and about as wide. It looked newish, new enough to not show on the plans, the workmanship rustic but adequate. The door hung open, a breeze blowing through.

Quarrel squeezed through, almost on his knees, cursing himself for not stationing anyone at the rear of the property. On his feet, he scanned the garden. The back fence looked the most likely route to take. He pelted towards it, sprang upwards, grabbed the top of the fence and hoisted himself up.

A path ran behind the fence. There was no sign of Parker. Katie was already dragging herself up beside him.

He looked at her. "He's got to have gone right."

Seconds later he had dropped down and was sprinting along the path. He heard Katie landing behind him, her footsteps pounding the tarmac. Before they reached the end of the path, he heard the unmistakeable sound of a motorcycle starting up and roaring away.

Katie, younger and fitter, overtook him. He caught her up at the junction where the path came out onto Crouchfield, which shared a name with the original hamlet that had grown into Boxmoor village.

Katie turned to him, grim-faced. "It was him on that bike. I'm sure of it." She pointed up the road to her left. "He went that way. I was just in time to see him disappear round the bend." Towards a network of residential roads and, beyond that, the town centre.

He groaned. "I don't suppose you got a reg number?"

"No chance, and don't ask me what make of bike it was. It was black. I think."

"Marvellous," he sighed. "Not your fault, obviously. He'd prepared his exit strategy, hadn't he?" He shrugged. "We may as well go back to the house. I'll call Debbie Brown and get a team taking the place apart. Can you get Parker's description out to all cars? I want every motorbike in the town stopped and the rider's ID verified."

"Just black ones?"

"You're sure it was black?"

"Not completely, no."

"Then I want every bloody bike pulled over. I don't care if it's sky blue pink."

They turned right off the path, doubling back into Cowper Road. Sharp stood outside, conversing with Ryan and Ricky James. The other firearms officers stood around.

"Izzy's inside with Aliya, looking after Ben," the DCI said. "Parker got away?"

"Took off on a motorbike." He outlined the steps he proposed to take.

She shook her head, her expression almost admiring. "He thinks of everything, doesn't he? An exit from the basement, a motorbike ready and waiting. I wouldn't be surprised if his escape plan included a bolt-hole somewhere, would you?"

Quarrel paused for thought. "I don't know. Maybe he'd planned to get out of the country once he'd finished the job."

"You think that's his plan now?"

"We ought to notify all ports to be on the lookout for him. But surely Ben Newell was his most important victim, and he didn't get to finish the job. Maybe it's not over."

"You think he'll stick around and try again?"

"I don't think Ben will ever be completely safe until we've got Howard Parker in custody."

28

Ben Newell was in a fragile state after his ordeal and obviously distraught about the disfiguring outlines tattooed on his face, even though they could be removed in time. He knew he was lucky to be alive, and he was also shaken by crushing betrayal by a man he'd counted as a close friend. The realisation that Parker had befriended him as part of a murderous plan, and had been simply biding his time until he was ready to strike, had turned his world upside down.

One thing his experience hadn't changed, however, was his insistence that he was innocent of Emily Snow's alleged rape. Quarrel didn't have to ask him about it. Ben had talked openly, bitterly.

"It's unbelievable. Emily lies, a jury doesn't believe her, and now three people are dead and I've barely escaped with my life. Poor Howie. I knew he'd been sweet on Emily. He claimed that the court case had changed all that, but now I can see it just unhinged him."

Quarrel still couldn't make up his mind as to whether the man was telling the truth or simply justifying himself. But he thought that, when it was decided that a police officer should stay with him for a couple of days, Libby Statham's response was telling.

"Could you find someone else?" she'd pleaded. "Preferably a male. Aliya and I found he made us both feel uncomfortable. Mentally undressing us, and not too subtly, either."

Quarrel had assigned a male PC to move into Ben's flat for protection. Were Libby's and Aliya's instincts reliable? Or were they reacting to what they knew the man had been accused of?

Either way, with Ben safe, Parker's campaign was surely effectively at an end, although he would need to be caught before they could truly relax.

Quarrel arrived home around 11pm. He hoped that their unwelcome visitor might have given up and gone home, but that hope was dashed as he walked through the front door and heard voices upstairs that didn't sound like the TV.

As he walked into the living room, the temperature seemed to plummet.

He'd had glimpses, not much more than impressions really, of Sandra Bowman, the woman who'd birthed him in mental flashbacks to his early childhood. He'd seen two photographs of her in archived news coverage: one, a vivacious, attractive young woman in a summer dress, laughing for the camera; the other, looking quite a bit older, her face like stone, eyes blank.

The woman setting down her mug and rising from an armchair looked much older than either image. Even allowing for the passage of perhaps fourteen years since he'd last seen her, just before closing the door in her face, she looked to have aged beyond her years. She must be, what? Early to mid-sixties? She looked at least ten years older than that.

"Hello, Nathan," she said. The years may have rounded out Quarrel's accent, but her Yorkshire twang was undiminished by prison and the years since.

He felt fresh anger and resentment towards Laura. Without another glance towards his mother, he marched over to her.

"Can we have a word? Upstairs?"

Laura shook her head. "Let's not."

Bitterness was like bile in his mouth. "I can't stay here. I'll find a hotel or something."

"You're being ridiculous."

And he knew he was. A wall he'd built and maintained all his adult life was suddenly in danger of collapse, and his hurt was making him childish.

"This was a mistake," Sandra said. "I'll go. I don't want to come between you."

"Oh," Laura said. "I think you've been doing that for years."

Annoyance flashed through Quarrel. "What's that supposed to mean?"

She looked at him. "Seriously?" She looked over at his mother. "No offence, Sandra, but you've been the spectre at the feast all the time Nate and I have been together."

Sandra wrung her hands. "I got that from what you said when we were talking."

Quarrel's anger notched up. "Oh, you've been *talking*? Very cosy."

Laura folded her arms. "Please, Nate. Isn't it time you stopped running from your past, turned around, and confronted it."

What gave her the right...?

Yet there was no arrogance in her tone. Just the same love and concern he always heard when she spoke to him. He still thought she was wrong, hated this situation. But he found he couldn't hate Laura for creating it. The blame lay with the other woman – he still couldn't think of her as his mother – for having the audacity to show up here.

Time seemed to stretch as the three of them stood frozen in a tableau. Then his shoulders sagged.

"All right," he said, turning at last to Sandra. "We'll talk. You've got five minutes."

"Oh, for God's sake," Laura said. He knew that tone. Beyond exasperated. "Don't be so bloody stupid, Nate. Thirty-six years of catching up to do? Something so profound that, in your own words, ruined your life? Do you really think five minutes will cut it?" She laid a hand on his shoulder, a tender gesture, her eyes brimming with a compassion that cut through his anger.

"I'll make you both a cup of tea," she said. "Then I'm going to make up the spare room for Sandra."

Fresh panic gripped him. "She can't stay here," he said.

"Oh, yes she can. It's late. It'll be later when you two run out of words, if you even do, and she doesn't know this part of the country. At least hear her out. She's here now, and she's been trying long enough to talk to you."

It had been a long, difficult day, and all he really wanted was to sleep. But these two women had him cornered, and he was too tired to argue any more.

"All right," he said finally. "Make that tea, and we'll see."

Seemingly satisfied, Laura headed for the kitchen. He looked, properly looked for the first time, at the woman he had hated – and feared, too – for so long. He realised his hands were trembling.

"You might as well sit, then," he told her, trying for curtness, but his voice shook too.

The events that had ignited his hatred... had they really happened thirty-six years ago?

*

Life for abusive wife who stabbed 'perfect dad' to death
Yorkshire News, Thursday 14 March, 1974

A violent, abusive mother who stabbed her husband to death in front of their young son has been jailed for life at Leeds Crown Court.

The court had heard that Sandra Bowman, 29, was known locally to have a drink problem, and heard evidence from the parents of the deceased, Philip Bowman, that she had a history of physically and mentally abusing him. Because male victims in abusive relationships are so rarely heard of, Mr Bowman had been too ashamed to report her violent behaviour. Only his parents knew what he had been going through.

In the end, he paid for that reluctance with his life on a winter's day, when his wife killed him in a rage after he returned from a rare Saturday lunchtime visit to his parents.

Mr Hallam Wallace, QC, prosecuting, said no one would ever know for sure what triggered the attack. Perhaps Mrs Bowman had been enraged by her husband walking snow into the house. But she appeared to have grabbed a kitchen knife and plunged it into his stomach.

The court heard how Mr Bowman, 33, had staggered outside and round to the side of their converted farmhouse before collapsing and dying from exsanguination. Police evidence told of a trail of blood in the snow. His six-year-old son, who cannot be named, was covered in blood, almost certainly through attempting to comfort his dying father.

Philip Bowman's parents, John and Margaret Bowman, both spoke of their daughter-in-law's 'bossy and controlling' behaviour towards their son, claiming that she hated him being out of the house for anything other than work, didn't like him seeing his family or friends, and resented her role of caring for their son. She was also obsessively house-proud and hated to see a speck of dirt or anything out of place.

The couple's nearest neighbour, Jean Clough, spoke of often hearing raised voices from the house, and also said she had on several occasions smelt alcohol on Sandra Bowman's breath during the day.

Mr Wallace said a clear picture had emerged of an obsessive woman who drank, both jealous and resentful, possibly already angry with her husband for 'daring to spend time with his parents', and pushed over the edge when he walked snow onto her clean floor.

Mr Clive Onslow, defending, rejected this characterisation, insisting that Philip Bowman had been the controlling one in the marriage, dividing his wife from her family and friends. Sandra Bowman only had the occasional glass of wine to give her 'Dutch courage' when she feared her husband would come home in a violent mood.

In her own evidence, Mrs Bowman said she had acted in self-defence and in defence of their son when the deceased had flown into a rage after tripping on a toy just inside the front door. She had grabbed the knife to try to get him to back down, but he had lunged at her and fallen on the blade in the struggle. But the jury rejected her evidence, taking less than two hours to reach a unanimous guilty verdict.

Sentencing, Judge Ainsley Ambrose said the defendant was a violent, manipulative woman who had tried to paint herself as a meek, downtrodden wife. But, he said, the jury had seen through her shameless attempts to gain their sympathy. Sentencing her to life, he recommended she serve a minimum of 15 years.

Outside the court, Philip Bowman's father, John, read a prepared statement. He said nothing could bring his son back, but at least his daughter-in-law would now have a long time to reflect on the enormity of what she had done.

"She has robbed us of a wonderful, loving son and our grandson of a perfect dad," he said.

Mr Bowman and his wife are now looking after their young grandson, who he said was still extremely traumatised by witnessing his father's violent death.

*

"Laura says you can't remember anything about the day your father died," Sandra said.

It felt like a fresh kick to the stomach. The boy she was talking about didn't really exist for him any more. Whatever snippets of very early memories he might once have had were more like the tattered remnants of faded dreams to him now. After the events of that day, a day that might as well never have happened, he'd never returned to the home where he'd lived with his parents. Even that boy's very name no longer existed, as if he had been entirely obliterated.

Nathan Bowman had become Nathan Quarrel and, since his grandparents had died, hardly anyone now knew him for who he'd once been, let alone that his mind had blanked out memories too traumatic for the child who had witnessed them.

And now Laura, whom he'd confided to more than anyone ever before, had been chatting about it, cosy in his own living room, with this woman.

He was perched on the edge of his seat, almost rigid with tension.

"Not just that day," he said. "The whole of the first six years of my life is pretty vague and confused. I barely remember you or Dad. I've got little in the way of concrete memories. As for the day of the..." – he swallowed hard – "the *murder*... well, that whole day is a blank. They call it dissociative amnesia."

She held out a hand to him, as if appealing for – or perhaps offering – something.

"But don't you see?" she implored. "If you don't remember, then you don't *know* what happened. What *really* happened. No one does. No one except me."

"I've read the press reports. And I know what my grandparents told me, once they thought I was old enough to hear it."

"Your *dad*'s parents." She nodded, her face devoid of expression. "Yes. I'm sure they gave you an unbiased account."

He felt a fresh stab of anger. "Don't you dare impugn them. They took me in. My dad was in the ground, and my mother was in prison. I had no one else. And they loved me like parents. Don't you dare say anything against them."

"Oh, Nathan," she said. "Your dad was the apple of their eyes. They were blind to what he was really like. But there were two versions of what happened that day. The prosecution's and mine. Your grandparents gave evidence that seemed to back the prosecution. I had no one. The jury didn't believe me."

"Because you were lying." He allowed himself a sip of tea. "I'm not stupid. I'm a police officer. I know there are two sides to every case. But the jury believed the case against you, and so did two people I've always trusted. I don't even know you."

"But your grandparents… they more or less *were* the prosecution case."

"And the neighbours."

"Neighbours your father had charmed, like he charmed everyone. I had no one who could speak for me. Didn't you think that was odd?"

"Not really. You were obsessively jealous. You drove everyone else out of your life and made Dad the centre of your universe. You were so controlling, you tried to drive his friends and family away, too."

Her eyes were glistening.

"For someone with no memories, you seem to have it all at your fingertips. But no one really knows what happens in a marriage, behind closed doors." She paused, as if composing herself. "I wrote you letters. Laura said you destroyed them all."

"I wanted nothing to do with you. I still want nothing to do with you."

"The truth is, by the time your father died, there was no one to speak up for me in that court because, one way and another, everyone I'd been close to had gone. Some had died. Most, he'd driven away." She looked at him. "Were you told how me and your dad met?"

He shook his head. She nodded as if he had confirmed a suspicion.

"It was the darkest, most vulnerable time of my life. It was about six months after both my parents had died in a car crash. I was an only child of only parents, so I'd effectively lost my whole family. Good friends at the time were doing their best to help me through it. And then I met your dad. Good-looking, charming, and he treated me like a princess. It really seemed like I'd found the man of my dreams, and he said he felt the same. It all happened in a whirlwind, and we were engaged and married inside nine months.

"You were born eleven months later, and that's when things really started to change. Although, looking back, the controlling behaviour had begun in small ways right from the start. What seemed like caring was actually chipping away at my insecurities. He was very good at sniffing those out. From the moment I fell pregnant it shifted up a gear. He said he didn't want me doing things in my condition, but he made me feel I *couldn't* do them. And he wanted his mother to be my guiding light in all things maternal. He said a girl needed her mother at such a time, and she was the next best thing. Well, the truth is, the apple hadn't landed far from the tree."

"What's that supposed to mean?"

She looked Quarrel in the eye. "She brought you up. Maybe you saw it for yourself. The way she seems so reasonable, always having your best interests at heart, while subtly interfering, giving you no say in your own life. Ironically, I think she was more your father's role model in that way than your granddad was. But, to give them their due, I don't know where he got his temper from."

"He didn't have a temper," he said flatly. "He was the calmest person you could meet. You were the one with the temper. He was a bag of nerves. He always dreaded coming home, in case you'd been drinking and were in one of your moods."

"Is that what you remember? Or what you were told?"

He didn't answer.

"I know the prosecution painted me as a drunk," she said quietly.

"Maybe that was because the neighbours and the postman testified that they often smelt alcohol on your breath during the day."

She nodded. "I did have the odd glass or two during the day sometimes. No more. I didn't get drunk. But it got so I knew what mood he'd be in when he got home. Not that the wine made me any braver, not really. Anyhow, that came much later. First he isolated me. By the time I got to the end of my maternity leave, he was already halfway to alienating, or cutting me off from, my friends. Then he insisted I didn't go back to work, because his son needed his mother around."

It was too horribly familiar a story. Quarrel had heard it often enough. Had dealt with a couple of cases that had ended in tragedy.

She continued. "First it was raising his voice, then shouting in my face. Then that first slap, that first punch, always my fault for making him angry. He was always contrite. He wouldn't get so angry if he didn't love me so much. Once he threw me against a wall like a rag doll. If I answered back, it would be worse. A couple of times it was his belt, lashing me like a dog.

"And I had no one to turn to. All my friends had given up on me, tired of my excuses when they suggested getting together. I was virtually a prisoner in the house. He sold my car and did the school run in the morning himself. His mum would pick you up at the end of the day. In that part of Yorkshire, public transport wasn't great. Plus, he didn't like me going out without him. Always wanted to know what I'd been doing. Who I'd been seeing."

Quarrel said nothing.

"I know what you're thinking," she said. "Why didn't I just leave?"

"Actually, no," he said. "I suppose you'd say he'd made you believe he was sorry. That he loved you. And you gave him another chance. And that he'd so undermined your self-esteem that you didn't have the courage or the confidence to leave him. That you were economically dependent on him. That there was nowhere for you to go. That you were afraid he'd find a way of keeping me and stopping you seeing me. That he'd find you and kill us both, perhaps himself too."

"Exactly. All that and more. I tried twice. And twice, fool that I was, I forgave him and went back." Hope glimmered in her eyes.

Quarrel knew that, on average, an abused woman would leave her partner seven times before finally leaving for good. Some were killed before they got anywhere near that number And, here, at this moment, it would be easy to feel sorry for her. To believe her story.

Except this particular woman had had the best part of sixteen years in prison, and two decades since her release, to become an expert on such cases, and all the sad, sickening details. Thirty-six years to twist the truth and make herself the victim. So she could try to wheedle her way back into his life through a door he'd kept firmly closed for so long.

"You're very good," he said. "But this is text book stuff. I bet you haunted the prison library. I bet the Internet has been your constant companion since you got out."

The faint light died in her eyes. Tears slid down her face. They didn't exactly douse the flame of hatred he'd fanned for so long but, for a moment, it burned less fiercely.

Following the murder, his grandparents, as his closest kin apart from his mother, had taken him in. After she was jailed, they successfully applied for guardianship. By then, they'd already moved to the Midlands, where they weren't known, where no one would guess his mother was serving a life sentence for killing his father. Instead, he was the kid whose parents were much older than anyone else's. Little wonder that he'd always been slightly strange, and a bit of a loner, with trust issues.

They'd intercepted letters from his mother until his twelfth birthday when they told him the truth. They handed him the bundle, held together with an elastic band, and he'd burned the letters himself, unopened, and continued to do so until he'd grown up and got his own place, and had started his police career. Then he'd instructed them to do the same with them.

He'd seen in the news that she'd been released and then, somehow, she'd tracked him down. A few letters, then she'd turned up on his doorstep, only to be turned away. It hadn't stopped the letters, nor the phone calls.

He'd supposed he could take out a restraining order, but he'd taken the more drastic step of changing his name and transferring to Hertfordshire. He'd left no forwarding address and hoped he'd finally seen the back of her. But she'd found him again and the letters – and birthday cards – had started afresh. And now, finally, she was here, this stranger who cast a long, dark shadow over his life.

Crying.

For thirty years, she had been a monster on his mind, some sort of bogeywoman to loathe and fear in equal measure. Now all he saw was a woman who looked older and more worn out than her years – and, yes, one in whom he could see a slight physical resemblance to himself – damaged and broken.

He wanted to harden his heart with the same iron that had guided his destruction of every communication from her. He knew she deserved not a jot of compassion from him, yet he felt something like that stirring inside him. He hated his weakness.

She controlled her crying.

"That day," she said. "Your dad had popped round to see his parents, and the snow had come down while he was out. Not that heavy, but enough to settle. Seeing his mum and dad was one of his Saturday rituals, whatever the weather. At least he didn't drag me along." She swallowed. "I always hated the weekends. Spending so much time together. It was like sitting on a time bomb.

"He came in, cursing the snow, and he'd barely got through the front door when he fell over one of your toys. A red fire engine. Do you remember it?"

He shook his head.

"You loved that thing." A smile ghosted across her lips. "Anyway, he got up in a rage and yelled at you. *'Come here!'* You were scared, walking towards him slowly. You were halfway to him when he stamped on your engine, not once but three or four times, smashing it to pieces. *'That'll teach you to put your junk away.'* You started crying. *'Stop that noise!'* It made you cry all the harder. And that's when his belt came off."

"My grandparents said he never laid a finger on me."

"That's not entirely true. He'd lash out, give you a slap. But he never beat you as such, that much is true. But there was something different about him this time. Normally his rages were directed at me. But you were the target this time, and I wasn't having him take his belt to you.

"I'd been preparing vegetables, and I grabbed the knife I'd been using – or maybe I'd never put it down, that bit's hazy. But I got between you. I only meant him to back off, maybe long enough to calm down."

He was so tired. "Do you know how clichéd that is? How often a stab victim runs onto the knife, or gets stabbed in a struggle?"

"Cliché or not, that's what happened, Nathan. So much blood! He called me a stupid bitch, and then he staggered outside. You ran after him, before I could stop you. I was stunned. Couldn't move for a few moments. By the time I caught up, he'd got around the side of the house, leaving a trail of blood."

Red on white.

"He'd passed out and you were cuddling him, begging him to wake up. I called the police and ambulance. You'd gone quiet and were shivering when they arrived. After that, it was all like some unstoppable machine swung into action. I think at first they thought it was a domestic thing gone wrong. But, once they started investigating, evidence seemed to be stacking up against me, with no one to back my side of the story.

"I know you won't want to hear this, but your grandparents, your gran in particular, lied and lied. Possibly they just parroted your dad's lies. But somehow it all got twisted around. I was the evil woman who abused her lovely husband and finally killed him. A new twist on an old story. And the media loved it."

He felt a stab of fresh anger that she was again blackening his grandparents' names, knowing they weren't around to defend themselves. They'd lost their only child. He'd lost his father and, to all intents, his mother too.

He knew his grandparents. He knew what they were like, and what they weren't.

Well, didn't he?

"A jury found the case they heard credible," he said.

"Juries get it wrong. You know they do."

He thought of Emily Snow, her rape complaint rejected by a jury after a clever QC had stacked up just enough evidence to plant a reasonable doubt. A woman disbelieved by a jury. Ben Newell still protested his innocence, but Michelle McGrath was convinced his acquittal had been a miscarriage of justice. And, at the other end of the spectrum, innocent people did go to prison.

The very notion that his mother might be innocent flew in the face of all he had ever known. He'd had his world turned upside down at the age of twelve. Could he question everything he thought he knew again?

"You said you barely remembered me or your dad," she said. "What do you remember?"

He searched his mind. "Little things. Dad carrying me on his back. All of us laughing at the seaside. Making sandcastles with him."

"Yes," she agreed. "It wasn't all bad times. What about me?"

He realised he was smiling. "Oh. Bedtime stories, though I can't remember what they were. The hugs that made me feel safe. The smell of cakes baking, for some reason."

"Fairy cakes," she said. "You loved them. I put coconut in them and lemon icing on top."

Just for a moment, thirty-six years melted away and he fancied he could taste those cakes. Sweet. That lemony sharpness.

But it was only a moment. "Maybe I've blanked all the bad stuff."

She sighed and stood up. "Well, I've said what I came to say. I'll leave now."

He stood himself. "Laura's made you a bed up." He felt confused. Surely he wanted to see the back of her?

"And please thank her. But I don't think I can stay here after all."

Part of him made him want to ask her to stay. But he didn't insist.

She shrugged her coat on. "Can I ask just one thing of you?"

"You can ask."

"Take a proper look at the evidence. I know you can read the papers, and maybe you even have access to police files. Look at it as a copper, not as the person who's been told a particular version of events all his life. See if it really adds up to a solid case."

She took a purse out of her handbag and rummaged out a till receipt. She found a pen in the bag, scribbled on the back of the receipt, and held it out to Quarrel.

"My mobile number. I beg you not to throw it away. Look at the evidence. If you think it's even slightly doubtful and think it's worth us talking again, call me. Please?"

He stared at the scrap of paper for a long moment, then took it, and stuffed it in his pocket. He followed her downstairs.

"I don't even know where you live," he said, wondering why he cared. "Have you come far? Where will you go?"

"I'll find a local hotel on my phone."

"There's a Premier Inn at Tring. It's not far. I can get you the details."

But she was already at the door.

"Thanks. I'm sure I'll find it." She paused. "Can I ask you one more thing? Why Quarrel?"

He found himself smiling again. "Just how my mind works, I suppose. I was Nathan Bowman. A bowman is an archer. A quarrel is an arrow for crossbows. Stupid, really."

"No. I rather like it."

"How did you find us, by the way?"

"Private detective. I came out of prison with next to nothing, but I managed to find work. I live in a bedsit and drive a clapped out old Ford. What little I could squirrel away went on the detective's fees."

"He must be good."

"I don't know how he did it. I never asked." She half-leaned towards him, perhaps to plant a kiss on his cheek, or attempt a hug, but then seemed to think better of it. She simply opened the door. "I'll hope to hear from you."

He watched her walk into the night, then closed the door. Shortly afterwards, he heard a car door slam and an engine starting. He thrust his hands in his pockets and encountered the receipt with her number on it. He took it up to the office. Thought about putting it straight through the shredder but, instead, he shoved it in a desk drawer.

He supposed Laura had gone to bed. Maybe she was sitting up, reading. He'd been angry with her for inviting his mother in, but maybe the conversation had been something he needed after all.

He suspected he hadn't seen the last of Sandra Bowman. And he was surprised to find he didn't know quite how he felt about that any more.

29

Quarrel had slept little, and not just due to the visit from his mother. He'd been convinced that either Howard Parker would have been picked up somewhere, or the CSIs would have found something in Parker's parents' house that required his immediate attention. He'd lain in bed with his mobile plugged in beside him, expecting it to ring.

Maybe even willing it to do so. Something to take his mind off his mother, and the events of his childhood that she'd forced him to dredge up again. Every time he did try to close his eyes, he saw those red splashes – his father's blood – on the white snow.

He'd sat in his office for ages last night, before finally heading for bed. He'd found Laura waiting up for him. He realised he could no longer be angry with her for inviting Sandra in. She'd been right after all. It had been time he finally faced his demons. Only time would tell whether it changed anything.

She asked him if he wanted to talk, which had mostly consisted of her listening to him. One of the things he loved about her was her stillness: her ability to be quiet while he spoke, and to sense when it was helpful to ask a question or help him clarify a thought.

Sandra had challenged a truth he'd received from the two people in the world he'd never had cause to doubt. And then she'd asked him to do some sort of cold case investigation into his own father's murder.

"I'm wondering if that was her real agenda all along," he'd said. "To sow seeds of doubt about the truth I grew up with." He'd chuckled without mirth. "You could say it's a truth I know better than the palms of my own hands."

"And it probably is the truth," she remarked. "Sandra saying it isn't doesn't make it a lie. But this review. Will you do it?"

It was a question that scared him. He felt panic sitting on his shoulder, chittering in his ears at the very thought of opening that door.

"I just don't know," he admitted. "There's an argument for letting sleeping dogs lie. Except the dogs are awake anyway now. I suppose the real question is whether any good can come of it. The Yorkshire police and the CPS obviously had faith in the case against her, and the jury believed it. So what am I going to find that'll make a difference? And how much will it hurt me to start prodding around in all that?"

"You were a little boy back then, Nate. Now you're a grown man. How much can the truth – one way or the other – really harm you?"

"You sound like you think I should do it."

"I'm not saying that. I honestly don't know. I think only you can decide, and I think you need time to process it. I'm always here to talk to, though."

He'd nodded, knowing she was right. "There's one thing," he said. "I don't think I can hate her any more, not like I did. It doesn't mean I ever want to see her again."

She'd hugged him then. "Give it all time, love. As much time as you need. Nothing's going to change while you think about it, is it?"

He hugged her back, inhaling her scent. "Why are you such a wise woman?"

He'd been at work since just before 7am. There was a brief email from Debbie Brown, saying they'd found a few things and she would attend the morning briefing.

He realised he ought to contact Michelle McGrath and catch her up on developments. The tattoo murders weren't her case, but the connection to her old rape case called for at least a courtesy call. He half-wondered how she'd feel about Ben Newell's rescue. She'd always worn her heart on her sleeve when it came to the cases she prosecuted, and Quarrel knew she had little regard or sympathy for Newell. Would she have secretly hoped that Parker would claim him as a victim before he was caught?

Probably not that. But Quarrel couldn't help wondering if she might feel a sneaking pleasure that the killer had at least managed to make a start on tattooing the man's face. Perhaps she'd see it as a small slice of rough justice for Emily Snow.

He'd try to make time for her after the briefing.

The mood in the meeting room was harder to read than usual. That they'd managed to avert a murder was a win, but the killer had got away, so as yet they lacked the satisfaction that an arrest would have brought.

"At least we can be reasonably confident that Ben Newell must have been the final victim on Parker's list," Quarrel told the team. "We've got him safe now, and it's to be hoped the cycle is over."

Debbie Brown, sitting in the second row, raised an index finger.

"Debbie?"

"Sorry to rain on your parade, Nate, but that might not be quite right."

His stomach did a little flip. "What do you mean?"

She rose from her seat and came forward, a sheaf of papers in her hand.

"Sorry. I would ideally have had a word before the briefing, but it's been a long night, and it's all a bit—"

"Don't worry about it," he said. "What have you got?"

"Lots of stuff to process," she said, "but we also found these. Tarot card designs and stencils."

"The ones used on the victims?"

"Yes. We don't have the benefit of Katie's Tarot reader, but we did do an Internet search. The card Parker had started to tattoo on Ben Newell's face is called Strength. I won't go on about all the things it stands for, but one of them is lust, which I suppose Parker would have considered fitting."

"Okay." Quarrel sensed there was something else coming, and that he wasn't going to like it.

"The trouble is," she said, "there's an extra template."

"Extra?" He felt a fresh chill in his bones.

She held up a sheet so everyone could see. The distinctive Rider Waite style once again, this time depicting two dogs – or perhaps a dog and a wolf – on a grassy path. Behind them, a crab was emerging from calm water. Ahead of them, the water seemed more turbulent under a blue sky, against which two towers flanked a round yellow sun with rays radiating from it.

Across the face of the sun, a white face in profile, shaped into a crescent, smiled enigmatically.

"I looked this one up, too," Debbie said. "The Moon."

"Did you look up what it means?"

The crime scene manager shrugged. "I read the words. Printed them out, too." She found another sheet and started reading. "The Moon card may suggest that you're embarking on an uncertain path on a dark night, with possible dangers lurking. The light of the moon can bring clarity and understanding, and your intuition will guide you through the darkness."

"In other words, more mumbo jumbo," Ricky James declared.

Katie was already busy with her phone. "It seems the card's all about duality, two different possibilities. The animals are a wolf and a dog, representing the two sides of our nature – the tame and civilised, and the wild and feral. The towers flanking the central path once again allude to the theme of two possibilities.

"What about the crab?" Quarrel urged.

"It's actually a crawfish. We are the crawfish—"

"Course we are," sniggered Ricky. "All crawfish together."

Katie gave him a hard look and he subsided. She continued. "We're faced with a path that is a fine line between conscious and unconscious, between civilisation and the wilder forces of nature. The towers represent the forces of good and evil, and their similar appearance highlights the difficulty in telling them apart."

Quarrel absorbed this. "And reversed?"

"Not so good. The Moon Reversed can indicate the presence of darker, more negative forces in your life. You might be deluding yourself, responding to an emotional, dramatised version of events rather than sticking to the facts."

"I'm not wholly sure what that means," said Debbie, deadpan, "but I was thinking he was probably planning a reversed image."

"Christ," DCI Sharp said. "There's another victim out there."

"But…" Quarrel raked his fingers through his hair. "That makes no sense. Parker had an agenda. Revenge for the woman he'd loved. Surely he'd see Ben Newell as the most to blame for her suicide. He had to be last. The icing on the cake."

Aliya raised a hand. "What if Alastair Murdoch wasn't the first victim? What if there's a fifth body that we just haven't found yet?"

"Killed perhaps on Saturday night, you mean? The night before Alastair?" He pursed his lips. "I can't see it. Parker's made a deliberate point of displaying his victims in places that meant something to Emily, wanting them to be discovered. Surely we'd have found this other victim by now, even if not on Sunday."

"We can't discount it though," said Sharp.

"I know. And it *is* a good point, Aliya. Can you get your hands on that list of her favourite places that her family concocted? I know we've been monitoring them, but take Sophie and go round all of them, having a proper look. We'll look pretty stupid if we've missed a body."

"Will do."

"You're right to do that, Nate," Debbie said, "but I don't think *this* design's been used. You can see the others have. I think we're going to have to face the possibility that there's still a potential victim out there."

"Jesus," Ricky intoned. "Just when you think it's over…"

"But surely it is," Libby Statham said. "I mean, he's lost his basement, where he was taking his victims, and he left all his equipment behind when he fled, right?"

"I don't know that we can assume that," Katie said. "He's already shown what a planner he is. The escape hatch from the basement, the motor bike… What if he's got another private tattoo parlour elsewhere?"

"We didn't come up with anywhere else before," Izzy Cole pointed out. "But suppose he's taken another property under a fake identity? Hired a car or van, too?"

"Do some more digging, would you, Izzy?" Quarrel said. "Ricky, work with her. Maybe there's a sequence we just can't see, but – much as I hate it – Debbie's right. Another template means another intended victim. Someone's possibly in danger even as we speak."

"The night before last," Katie said. "There was no victim. We assumed he just couldn't get to Ben but, of course, that's not right. Ben trusted him – that's how he got to him last night. Why not the night before?"

Quarrel shook himself. "You're right. It's been under our noses, and we missed it. There had to have been a target for that night – one who, for whatever reason, he wasn't able to get at. But what if he hasn't given up on them?"

"The Super was going to do a press conference just after nine," Sharp said, looking worried. "It was going to be about the positive stuff we've done and asking the public to keep a look out for Howard Parker. This puts a slightly different spin on it."

Aliya raised a hand. "Guv, even if he hasn't got the means to abduct another victim, or to tattoo them, there's nothing to stop him cutting his losses and just killing them. A knife, a blunt object… maybe push them under a bus or train."

"Little Miss Sunshine," Ricky muttered. Aliya put her tongue out at him.

"You've got a point, Aliya," Quarrel agreed. "But I don't quite buy it. This guy's on a mission. He'll want to finish as he started, to the letter – a Tarot tattoo and one of Emily's favourite haunts. He's either going to take time to regroup, or he's already got a Plan B in play."

He looked at Katie. "Katie, can you talk to your Tarot reader? Find out as much as you can about this new card and what it might say? I'll speak to Michelle McGrath and try again to identify any more people involved in Ben Newell's trial who might have played an influential part in his acquittal. And we need to move fast. If Howard Parker really is sticking to his agenda, he'll be wanting to kill again tonight."

"Unless we catch him first," Sharp pointed out. "His photograph is already with all the news services."

"Let's hope so," Quarrel agreed. "Although, if he's got another place to hole up, I'll bet he's keeping his head down as much as he can."

He tried to push back the waves of despair. Saving Ben Newell had been the one positive note in an otherwise bleak week. Now even that triumph tasted like ashes in his mouth.

30

Katie found Lucy Andrews, dressed in a stained tee shirt and threadbare jeans with grass stains on the knees, pulling weeds out of her front garden beds.

"Sorry I'm so scruffy, Katie," she said as the women shook hands. "I've been putting this off, and I was determined to make some progress this morning."

"Then I'm doubly sorry to interrupt," Katie said. "Thank you for making time for me."

Lucy waved a dismissive hand. "Glad to help. Although I'm sure I heard on the news that you had a suspect."

"There's still some loose ends," Katie said carefully. "You know how it is."

"How's that brother of yours?"

"Mick? I haven't spoken to him since he gave me your number. I'm sure he's fine." She was close to her brother. Sometimes they didn't speak for weeks, but she knew he'd be on the phone like a shot if he had problems.

"Good to hear. Cake? I have coffee and walnut."

Having sampled Lucy's baking before, she accepted enthusiastically, and she sat at the kitchen table while the kettle boiled and the cake was sliced. She took out her phone, opened the Tarot website she had found most useful, and pulled up The Moon.

"Ah," Lucy said when she showed it to her. "Another victim?"

"Not yet but, between ourselves, we think it was planned for one."

"I see." She'd placed a Rider Waite deck on the table in advance of their meeting. She took it up, found the relevant card and placed it face up on the table.

"You want to know more about what the card might mean?"

"Anything you can tell me. We don't know who this was intended for but, since our suspect is still at large, we're anxious to identify the potential victim."

Lucy nodded. "I take it you've already looked it up online?"

Katie told her what they'd read about the duality of the card – the path between two very different possibilities that might be hard to differentiate.

"Okay, that's a good start. Traditionally, The Moon card is all about sensitivity and imaginative impressionability. In a state of deep relaxation, we dream, go into trances, have visions, receive insights, and go with the flow of psychic tides. We might experience deep realities that might be mystical, or terrifying, or both, and we can't always control what happens."

Katie struggled to get her head around this.

"I'm sorry. That's all a bit too deep."

"Sorry." She held up the card. "The Moon card represents a test – the ultimate test of a soul's integrity, if you like. The veil between the self and the unknown is parted, and the outcome is between a soul and its maker."

Katie swallowed a mouthful of cake. "That's clear as mud."

Lucy grinned. "I know. In simple terms, The Moon suggests a misunderstanding or a truth you can't admit, even to yourself. So, confusion, deception. Fear, maybe."

"Okay. What about reversed?"

"Again, it could represent confusion – a need to make progress, but uncertainty as to which path to take. You need to believe in yourself and move forward by managing your fears and anxiety."

Katie felt frustration gnawing at her. "Upright or reversed, you seem to be saying that this card says our victim's at some sort of crossroads and has to make a choice? I'm not sure where that gets us."

Lucy smiled. "Are you able to tell me how much of a practitioner your suspect is yet?"

"We can't be a hundred per cent sure, but my guess is that he's probably just looking it up like I am, trying to find cards that make a point about the victim. He's got an agenda, and his targets are hand-picked."

Katie hesitated. The connection to the Emily Snow case wasn't in the public domain, but she was sure she could trust this woman. She gave her a quick summary of what the murders were about.

"Right," Lucy said when she'd finished. "That helps. And I'd say he's cherry-picked whatever he wants to say, so the connections to the cards could be crude or even tenuous. But yes, I suspect he'll be putting negative connotations on The Moon and would probably have been planning a reversed presentation. Quite possibly he'd simply be saying the victim had made bad choices, perhaps with misguided intentions."

"Wilfully doing what they didn't think was right?"

"It's possible."

"Well, that's something. Thanks, Lucy. Can I just step outside and call my boss? Then I'll be back to finish my cake. It's really yummy."

"I'll cut you another slice."

Katie patted her stomach. "I really shouldn't…"

"Oh, go on," Lucy goaded. "You know you want to." She grinned. "Give in to the Moon – go with the flow."

*

Quarrel had no cake to offer Michelle McGrath, but he'd made her a cup of coffee. She took a couple of sips while he brought her up to date on the case.

She'd asked for an hour to wrap something up before joining him, and he'd swallowed his impatience. As it turned out, the time was well spent. Aliya Nazir had done a whistle stop tour of Emily Snow's favourite haunts and phoned to confirm that there were no undiscovered bodies lurking anywhere.

He'd also checked with Izzy Cole and Ricky James, but neither of them had been unable to unearth any other properties or cars that Parker might have access to. Of course, if the killer had managed to furnish himself with a credible fake identity, they could search all week and find nothing.

Katie Gray called in with the details she'd gleaned from her Tarot expert. Quarrel couldn't decide if it was useful or not, but he'd made notes. Maybe something would strike a chord with Michelle.

"I'm really not sure," she said when he finished updating her. "It could mean something specific or something vague, couldn't it?"

"It's been a bit like this with this entire case," he agreed. "At its heart, you've got a man with a simple agenda – revenge. This whole thing with Tarot tattoos and choosing where to put the next one on show is, on one level, just theatrical window dressing. But, on another level, it's a bit more complex. He's building a memorial to Emily, is how I read it."

He looked at her. "You know her case as well as anyone. So far, he's gone for the jury foreman; for the defence barrister; Emily's best friend, whose evidence sunk her case; and the man she accused of raping her. There's going to be one more, someone perhaps who went against their instincts and maybe led Emily to a bad choice or decision. Does that sound like anyone involved in the case to you?"

"I really don't know, Nate."

"Think," he urged. "Imagine you're the killer. Who's left that you'd still be angry with?"

"Well, there's the rest of the jury. I suppose he might think they knew in their hearts that Ben Newell was guilty, but still decided to acquit him on the evidence. Say he's somehow been able to identify all or most of them – could he be planning to slap this Moon tattoo on every one of them?"

He thought about that. "I don't think that really fits, Michelle. If he wanted to do the jury as a job lot, why not repeat The Fool – the design he used on the foreman? I think we're looking at a single, separate victim."

"I think you're probably right." She stared off into space. "So, in addition to the people he's already attacked, who, or what, is left?" Her gaze returned to Quarrel. "Damned if I know."

"The judge?" he wondered. "Did they show anything that someone less than rational might see as misguided bias towards the defence, in their summing up, or their conduct of the case?"

"I'd say the opposite, if anything. She did rein Woodley in a few times. Asked him if a line of questioning was strictly necessary, reminded him Emily wasn't the one on trial, that sort of thing. But then I *am* rational. Who knows what this maniac might have read into anything? Obviously, she summed up at the end, giving the jury guidance on the law. You know, the usual thing – how they should weigh the evidence, what reasonable doubt means. She absolutely didn't lead or direct them, but I suppose if you're twisted enough..."

"Do you remember who the judge was?"

"Yes. It was Judge Sara Wright."

"Then we'd best make sure she's safe. Can you think of anyone else at all he might target?"

"No one I'm aware of. Although..."

"Go on," he urged. "Anything, however off the wall."

"Her tattoo. The lipstick kiss. Woodley made a lot of that. Asked her what it meant, whether it was supposed to represent her flirty, sexually provocative nature. It was just a little tattoo, for Christ's sake, and he made it look like a fucking neon sign, shouting, 'COME AND GET ME!' I mean, he didn't actually say she was asking for it..."

"Hang on," Quarrel said. "So basically, if she hadn't had that tattoo, that would have been one less thing Woodley could have twisted against her?"

"Well, yeah."

"Oh, Christ." He slammed the heel of his hand against his forehead. "The tattooist."

"I suppose it's possible."

He thought about it. "It could fit, you know. Her name's Tabitha Hunt. We had her down as a possible suspect, but the fact is, the night there was no murder, she was ill in bed and not answering the door to anyone. What if it should have been her turn to die and, when Parker couldn't get to her, he simply skipped her?"

Comprehension dawned in Michelle's eyes. "So he got back on track with Ben Newell last night, but you're thinking this Tabitha could be unfinished business?"

"That's exactly what I'm thinking." He felt the blood draining from his face. "I only hope we're not too late."

*

Despite the initially frosty reception he and Katie got from Tabitha, having dragged her from her sick bed again, Quarrel offered up a prayer of thanks that she was home and safe. And her mood changed once they'd explained the purpose of their visit.

"This psycho thinks, because of Emily's tattoo, I'm partly to blame for her killing herself?" She barked a laugh that turned into a cough. "What a prick. I mean, I knew the defence had managed to drag the tattoo into it. Making it something dirty. It still makes me angry. It was a really sweet tattoo. A lipstick kiss – what's not to like?" She blew her nose on a tissue. "Well, if this Parker character comes near me, he'll be messing with the wrong girl. Did I tell you I box?"

"No," Quarrel had said.

"Just for exercise, but you don't want to piss me off. You don't want to get on the wrong side of my self-defence spray either."

He blinked. "You do know mace and pepper sprays are offensive weapons in the UK and illegal to carry?"

"Chill," she said. "I've got the legal kind, with the coloured gel. Disorientates them for a few seconds and dyes their face and hands for up to a week. I'll make damn sure I have it handy."

He sighed. He should ask what it was and check its legality, or just attempt to confiscate it. Instead, "I might have to forget you told me that," he decided. "Just don't go looking for trouble."

"I'm not stupid, and I'm going nowhere with this bug. Besides, I'll be getting round the clock protection, right?"

"I'd like to say yes, but you're not the only potential target, I'm afraid."

Maybe at one time every potential target could have had a patrol car stationed outside their door, but modern budgets and resourcing simply didn't stretch that far in most cases.

"What we will do is make regular phone calls and have a patrol car pass your door at regular intervals."

Similar arrangements were being put in place for the judge in the rape trial, who was also being warned to be vigilant, along with Emily's parents and ex-colleagues. But it was impossible to protect everyone, nor to be a hundred per cent sure all the bases had been covered.

"Cool," Tabitha had said. "At least you'll be able to pinpoint what time I was abducted or murdered."

"I'm sorry." And he was.

She'd flashed a rare smile. "Don't worry about it. I won't be opening the door to anyone and I'll keep my spray about my person. Just let me know when it's safe, preferably before I run out of chocolate and teabags."

For all they knew, Howard Parker was holed up miles away, or he'd somehow managed to get out of the country. He could be simply waiting for the fuss to die down before resuming his mission.

The uncertainty was killing Quarrel. What if they were still missing something obvious? A fifth victim they hadn't thought of, or maybe an obvious hiding place for Parker?

He called Katie into his office and ran through his worries.

"If only we could be sure where he might strike next," he said. "Really get a step ahead of him. This extra design is a real wild card. It could be just to throw us off, but that doesn't sound like him at all."

"I've been grappling with the same thing," she said. "Trying to think how it might fit his master plan, in case anything shakes loose. I can see a few possibilities."

"Go on."

"First, suppose Parker's actually been working the chronology of the case backwards? He starts with the jury verdict – Alastair Murdoch. That's actually the end of the case. Then there's the defence counsel, Michael Woodley, who must have done some sort of summing up. Then the damning evidence – Megan Jacobs. Then to the alleged rape by Ben Newell."

"Hold on though. You're forgetting that one-night gap between Megan's murder and the attempt on Ben."

"I know, but it works if something simply interrupted his plans that night. Perhaps he's watching Ben, sees us when we go to warn him and gets spooked. He has to regroup and try again next day."

It was possible, he supposed. "Say that's what happened. How does that help us with the fifth victim?"

"It would have to do with something even before the alleged rape."

"Like Tabitha doing the tattoo?"

"That would fit," Katie said. Then she grimaced. "But so would a whole lot of other things, maybe. For example, if someone had known what Ben was capable of and said nothing."

"Like who?"

"Another colleague he'd tried it on with, maybe? Someone who confided in Emily when it was too late, and Howie somehow found out? Maybe he'd blame them even more than Ben himself."

He nodded, seeing the logic. "We'll speak to Chantelle Price again. And your other scenarios?"

"Okay, try this: he's killing them in order of how much he blames them for Emily's death. Maybe Ben Newell *isn't* the ultimate victim here. What if there's someone he blames even more, and he's saving them for last."

"More than her alleged rapist? Like who?"

"Maybe her family, for not noticing she was suicidal?"

"That's more than one victim, surely. And does that fit in with what we know about The Moon card?"

"It might, if he thinks they were guilty of deluding themselves about Emily's situation. Letting their emotions blind them to what was under their noses because they didn't want to believe she was capable of harming herself. Maybe he even had plans for several Moon tattoos."

"Any other candidates for ultimate victim?"

She shook her head. "Is it worth going back to Michelle McGrath and asking her again? Just in case something suddenly shakes loose?"

"Nothing to lose. Any other ideas?"

She smiled. "Something more like we've been thinking. He'd picked out a day for Tabitha or whoever, and for some reason he couldn't get to them. So he simply moved on to the next name on his list. Then, rather than try to get back on track the next day, he just rolled his whole plan forward and left the one who got away as a loose end to be tied up."

"That makes a kind of a bonkers sense," he admitted. "He might have even thought that going off-piste would help throw us off the trail."

"It's possible, isn't it?"

"It's also possible that, now we're onto him, he'll have abandoned The Moon for now and is concentrating on evading capture."

"That would be good, wouldn't it?"

He nodded, although his gut was telling him otherwise. "We can but hope."

*

The team had worked tirelessly through the day, but with no return for their efforts. Emily Snow's rape and Ben Newell's trial had been filleted and filleted again, but with no real sense that they were any closer to knowing who Howard Parker's intended fifth victim had been, nor where the killer might be. At 7pm, DI Quarrel had announced that there was nothing to be gained by everyone sitting around the station any longer. He sent them all home, with the proviso that they kept their mobiles on and they kept them close.

Izzy Cole stepped out of the station, tired but elated. Quarrel had taken the trouble to call her into his office and tell her what a good job she'd been doing.

"You've got good instincts, Izzy," he'd told her. "Have you thought about a career in CID?"

"It's what I want," she'd admitted.

"Well, I think you'd be good. Your thinking about that white van – that our so-called witness's story didn't add up – was what ultimately put us on to Howard Parker. If you're really interested in detective work, I can see if we can get you attached to my team as a Trainee Investigator."

TIs built up a portfolio of relevant experience and developed their skills and knowledge to prepare them for the detective exam.

"Wow," she'd said. "That would be great. Thank you, sir."

"Well, we've still got a killer to catch, but when this is over I'll see what we can do about that."

It had certainly taken the edge off her disappointment earlier when Matt had texted to say he had to be away one more night to tie some things up, but would call her over the weekend.

She got in the car, trying to keep her feet on the ground, but wondering if this week would turn out to have been a turning point in her career. She felt a little celebration was called for and, if Matt wasn't around, there was always her best friend.

"Ah, sorry, Iz," Bethany said. "I've got this stinking cold."

"No worries, I'll come round with a takeaway and a bottle of fizz. Kill or cure?"

"Nah, I'd be really rubbish company, and I'm probably hideously contagious. I feel like an extra from *The Walking Dead*."

Izzy hung up and started her car, frustrated that she had no one to share her little moment of pleasure with, but also sorry for her friend. As she turned out of the car park, it occurred to her that, even if Bethany didn't want company, she could at least do something to cheer her up.

Less than an hour later, she was driving into the Buckinghamshire village of Cheddington, just five or six miles from Tring. A get-well card, a half-bottle of Prosecco and a box of Bethany's favourite M&S chocolates were on the seat beside her. She'd drop them off and be on her way.

Bethany lived in a small close not far from the village green. A good degree had earned her a well-paid job in the city, and her salary, plus some help from her parents, had given her an early leg-up on the property ladder. Izzy envied her in some ways, but didn't regret her change of career direction. Especially on days like this.

She pulled up outside Bethany's house, started to get out, and then froze. Her friend's open-plan frontage had hardstanding for two cars, and there were two cars parked there. One was Bethany's mini.

The other was Matt's BMW.

She stayed like that, half-in and half-out of her vehicle, trying to rationalise it. But she couldn't. If this was a rom-com, they'd be secretly plotting a surprise birthday party for her. But her birthday wasn't for months.

Matt had said he had to be away tonight. Bethany was claiming to be at death's door.

She didn't need to hone those promising detective skills DI Quarrel had spoken of to see what was going on here. Bethany had said Matt was a keeper. She just hadn't mentioned that *she* fancied doing the keeping.

March up to the door? Ring the bell, hammer on the door if necessary, until they opened up? Confront them?

No. She was due in the office early tomorrow, and making a scene now wasn't going to make her feel any better. Let them think they'd got away with it. DI Quarrel was handing her an opportunity to make her dreams come true, and those conniving, two-faced people she'd thought she could trust the most in the world weren't going to fuck it up for her.

Tonight she'd go home, drink the Prosecco and eat the chocolates herself and, yes, probably, cry a lot.

Tomorrow she'd be back trying to help her team catch a killer.

31

Saturday morning. A time when most people would be enjoying a well-earned break. For Quarrel's team, there was no such luxury. The budget might not stretch to overtime, but no one was grumbling. Everyone was focused on catching Howard Parker before he struck again.

If the nation's media had been interested in the events in West Hertfordshire before, the circus had really come to town since yesterday's press conference, especially after the connection between the victims had finally leaked. Superintendent Taylor was spitting blood, but Rachel Sharp had persuaded him that they had higher priorities than trying to identify the source. She shared Quarrel's trust in his team and agreed with his assessment that most likely a victim's family had spoken to the press – as was their right, even though they'd been asked not to.

However the story had got out, it had elevated the enquiry to front page news. A juicy rape case and a vengeful serial killer on the run were all the ingredients the tabloids needed for lurid headlines, and the broadsheets were only relatively more restrained. Hemel and Tring in particular had been invaded by a battery of outside broadcast vans. People with cameras and microphones seemed to be everywhere.

"We might have been able to talk the Super out of a witch-hunt for the moment," Sharp told Quarrel in his office, "but he wants a result and he wants it now. He's gone from us doing great work identifying Parker as our prime suspect, and saving Ben Newell, to us having spectacularly screwed up in letting Parker get away."

"That's a bit unfair."

"Yes it is. But you know and I know that Ian Taylor's main focus is always about climbing the greasy pole. He probably feels the media spotlight's on him personally, so he's already thinking of scapegoats. Because, if Parker kills again, the shit's really going to fly."

"No pressure then."

She grinned at him. "All you have to do is deliver Howard Parker, tied up in pink ribbon, by teatime. At least no one's asking you to get Brexit done."

"The Government should be pleased with us. At least we've got their daily dramas out of the headlines for a while."

There was a tap on the door. Quarrel raised an eyebrow to Sharp, who shrugged.

"Come in," he said.

Katie entered with Aliya Nazir in tow. "Sorry to disturb you, but there's a couple of bits of news."

"Good news, I hope."

"A bit mixed, actually. First of all, Conor Burke was burgled last night."

"His flat?"

Aliya shook her head. "The shop, guv. Equipment, including a tattoo machine, inks and some ThermoFlex paper."

"ThermoFlex?"

"It's for transferring the tattoo design from paper to skin."

The implication was obvious. "You think it was Parker?" Sharp asked.

"Got to be," said Quarrel. "He's preparing for his next victim and he left his tools behind when he fled. Except, of all the shops to choose from, why that one, with its connections to Emily Snow? You'd think he'd have chosen somewhere more random."

"I'm guessing he's passed by there, seen it's sealed off, and spotted the opportunity," said Katie. "The irony is, the CSIs were going to give Conor the all clear to move back in and open up today. The thief broke in through the back door. Smashed the glass."

"No alarm?"

"There is, but Conor hasn't been there to set it, and none of our guys has the code."

"Marvellous," Sharp muttered. "So, wherever he is, he's probably back in business, and we're back to square one."

"What's the other news?" Quarrel's mood had taken a gloomier turn, and it hadn't been great before.

"We've had a response to our media appeal," Katie said. "We might just have a sighting in an all-night Tesco."

"*Might* have?"

"The lad who served him, just before midnight, says this customer had longer, lighter hair than our picture, and glasses, but he remembers him because he bought a weird collection of stuff and paid cash. Cereal, milk, a load of snacks and bottled water. A duvet and pillow. And duct tape, string, a cheap screwdriver set. The kid remembered joking with a colleague that maybe he was planning on taking a hostage. Then he saw our appeal and thought it was the same man, in disguise. He reckons he's good with faces."

"How sure are we that he's not just looking for five minutes of fame?"

"I spoke to him myself," Aliya said. "He seemed pretty straight, but who knows?"

"And a *duvet*?" Sharp looked puzzled. "What do we make of that?"

"Not sure."

"Maybe he's hiding out somewhere unfurnished," Katie offered.

"Like an empty house?" Quarrel wondered.

"Maybe."

"Let's come back to that then. I take it they have CCTV at the store. Do we have this guy on camera? I'm still worried this is just a timewaster with an over-fertile imagination. I'd like to see for myself."

"Ricky's on his way over there now. We're also thinking we might catch his bike on camera and get the number plate."

"Yes. Although he's going to struggle with all the stuff he's supposed to have bought on a bike. Maybe he's got access to a car after all."

"Yeah, Ricky's going to look at all that too."

"Good. Are CSI on their way back to Conor Burke's tattoo shop? I suspect Parker's been his usual careful self, but you never know."

"Izzy's gone over there, and I spoke to Debbie Brown before I came to update you. She's going to scramble a team."

"Good again."

"There's one thing, guv," Aliya said. "If it was him at that supermarket, and we're right in assuming he broke into the tattoo shop... well, he's almost certainly somewhere in the borough still."

"Or not far outside it, I guess," Sharp said. "Still a bit of a needle in a haystack. We need a break."

*

Ricky James had found the supermarket where Parker had been identified extremely helpful. They'd thought ahead and, by the time he arrived, they'd already gone through their CCTV footage, not only finding images of the suspect several times, but also capturing him loading his purchases into the boot of an old Saab 900.

Ricky returned to the office with the footage and a few stills. These days, good quality CCTV equipment produced decent results, and a couple of the stills showed the man's face fairly clearly. Everyone who was available compared that face to photos they already had of Howard Parker. The consensus was that it could very well be the same person. The more they looked at the hair, the more unnatural it seemed. It did alter the shape of Parker's face, and the spectacles obscured the top half of the face still more.

But the nose, mouth and jaw were there to compare, and that was where strong resemblances were observed. In addition, Aliya Nazir pointed out further similarities in stance, gait and mannerisms to the Howard Parker captured on the station's CCTV when, in the guise of Harry Baker, he'd come in to make his bogus witness statement.

For Quarrel, though, the clincher was the car. Ricky James pointed out that no Saab 900s had been manufactured since the late 1990s, and a DVLA check confirmed that the 03 plate on this car didn't belong to that make or model.

"Good work, Ricky," he said. "Now we need ANPR to find that plate. Parker's been careful about cameras in the past, but if he's getting desperate…"

"He could make mistakes. On it, guv."

"Get someone to check out the cameras in Tring, especially near to Conor Burke's shop. If we're right, we'll find that car was in the area last night, when the shop was raided."

"We'll also see where it is now, if we're really lucky," Katie said.

"That would be good," said Quarrel. "We need to move fast now. He's got the tools he needs to make a tattoo again, and we can be sure he intends to use them."

Katie shrugged. "If Tabitha *is* his target, I think he's going to be out of luck."

"That's true, Katie, but that's a bigger 'if' than I'd like. What if he's set his sights on someone we haven't thought of? By the way, did you touch base with Michelle McGrath?"

"Not yet. I'll get on it now."

"No mad rush. I dare say she's been thinking about the case. If anything comes to her, I'm sure she'll be on to us."

*

Izzy Cole stuck her head round Quarrel's door. "Sir, I might have something useful."

He was getting used to the look of serious enthusiasm that she wore on her face now. At a time when self-doubt was chewing away at him like a ravenous rat, he could at least congratulate himself on getting this excellent young cop on board. She'd fitted so seamlessly into the team that she could have been here for years, had fine instincts, and certainly wasn't afraid of hard work. He hoped he'd be able to keep her when all this was over.

"Come in and grab a seat. I could do with something useful."

He thought she looked a little pale and noticed her eyes were somewhat red-rimmed, as if she'd been crying.

"Are you okay?"

"I'm fine, thank you, sir. I think I maybe got some dust in my eyes out in the car park. It'll pass."

He wasn't convinced, but didn't want to pry. "So what have we got?"

"Well, it could be use*less*, but I thought I'd bring it to you." She sat. "So here's the thing. We thought Parker was using an old Saab with fake plates and I wondered if maybe he'd simply stolen it. We know older cars are easier to get into, and to hotwire. So I thought I'd check whether one had been stolen locally in the last couple of days."

"And?"

"And yes. A guy called Alex Chapman from Newford Close reported his 900 stolen yesterday morning. It had been outside his house Thursday evening but was gone in the morning."

"Colour?"

"Blue."

"Same as the car we think Howard Parker had at the supermarket. Well done, Izzy. At least there's a good chance we now know where he got it from, for what that's worth."

"Oh, but there's more. Quite a bit more."

He caught the hint of excitement in her voice.

"Tell me."

"Alex Chapman reports his car stolen, gets a case number from us for his insurance and then decides to get the bus to work. He's walking down Wood Lane End towards the bus stop and he happens to glance down Masons Road and spots what looks like his car. He walks down to it and, would you believe, it is!"

He looked at her. "Masons Road is what? A block away from Newford Close, where the owner lives?"

"Yep. It had been hotwired all right, but apparently it was otherwise fine."

"And did it have the fake 03 plates on?"

"No, the originals."

He felt his enthusiasm waning. "So it could just be joyriders."

"It could, although the make, model and colour is a bit of a coincidence, isn't it?"

"Fair point." He rubbed his tired eyes. The ongoing threat from Parker, and finally speaking to his estranged mother was all taking a toll on his sleep. He'd spent much of last night staring through the darkness.

"Anyway, there's something else," Izzy said.

"Go on."

"So last night an old black Ford Focus was stolen from Wood End Close, same area again. I asked Ricky if I could look at the CCTV footage he's got from last night, especially that near Conor Burke's tattoo parlour. There are no cameras covering the actual shop, but you do see a black Focus drive past the nearest one. I checked the plates against DVLA and they're wrong too."

He felt a little surge of adrenaline. "The same 03 plates that were on the Saab?"

"No. But they don't go with the car either. These are 96 plates. The Focus didn't come in until 98. The car that was stolen, was originally a 99 plate."

"Do you think he's still using it?"

"I think it'll turn up somewhere near where he took it from with the original plates back in place. I think he's using the cars once only, and he has at least two sets of fake plates. He's probably banking that, once the cars are found close to home, we'll have better things to do with our time than try and find out who stole them."

Quarrel found himself grinning. "Maybe he's too much of a planner, and he's been over-thinking on this. I want you to check whether any cars have been reported stolen this morning."

She grinned back. "Already done. There's a few. Including one from Hales Park."

"Which is?"

"A block away from Wood End Close."

"So off Wood Lane End yet again?" It couldn't be a coincidence. "He must be hiding out somewhere in the area.

And I'm betting that he's using that stolen car even as we speak, possibly even for his next abduction. What's the car?"

"Vauxhall Carlton estate, 1993. Silver."

"Okay, I want ANPR searching for the two fake plate numbers we know of, plus the actual number of that Carlton. Especially near Tabitha Hunt's home. Liaise with Ricky on that."

"He's already on it."

"Great. And I want an unmarked car across the road from Tabitha, with eyes open for that car. If Parker shows up, we can't lose him again."

"I'll get that sorted, sir."

"Great. When you've done that, come back with Katie."

*

Quarrel, Katie and Izzy were gathered around a map, printed from the Internet, that included the locations that both the cars Parker was known to have stolen had been taken from, where they had been dumped, and where the Carlton that Sophie suspected he was now using had last been seen.

Quarrel had enclosed all five locations within a circle of black marker.

"We've got to think like him," he urged. "He must have yet another property somewhere around this area. But where?" He glanced from one woman to the other. "Ideas?"

"I assume we're looking for a house," Katie said. "Not flats. Let's get the street view up on your computer. Detached houses are good, I suppose. Less likely neighbours would see or hear anything. I wonder if he'd want a basement again?"

Izzy deftly pulled up a map and switched the street plan to satellite view. "A fair few detached houses in the area. Mostly quite new looking, so basements unlikely." She frowned. "We'd need to go door to door, surely, over quite a concentration."

"Even then, not everyone's going to be at home on a Saturday," Katie observed. "If Parker's behind one of those doors, all he has to do is not open it. We can hardly break down every door where we get no answer."

Quarrel tried to fight down feelings of despair. Were they going to be too late again?

Even Ben Newell's life had only been saved after he'd been disfigured by Parker's tattoo gun. Now he felt someone else could die and he'd be powerless to prevent it.

What if Tabitha Hunt wasn't Parker's next intended victim at all? What if stealing cars from the same area had been a sleight of hand to deflect them from where the killer was really hiding out? How long before he abducted his next victim? And how long would they have to live?

"Sir?" Izzy said, and he realised he'd zoned out for a moment.

"Sorry, Izzy. I was thinking," he said lamely.

"I said, maybe it's not a house. Those streets where he took and dumped the cars – this industrial estate runs right through it."

"Maylands Avenue." He stared at the map. "You think he might own, or be renting, a factory? Or offices?"

"A factory's not a bad base for what he's been doing," Katie commented.

"I suppose not." Other factories nearby, machinery making plenty of noise by day to drown out any sounds from Parker's victim – who would almost certainly be gagged anyway – and from his own equipment. Izzy already had the satellite street view up and was navigating the estate. So many buildings.

"Christ," Quarrel said. "That's a lot of real estate. Checking out who owns what, especially on a weekend... we might not have time."

"There must be a fair few cameras," Katie persisted. "We're looking for two, maybe three cars, if he took that Vauxhall. We should narrow the search to the estate."

Depression, panic and the sense of impending failure were making him stupid, Quarrel realised. Thank God for these two.

"Let's do it," he said. "I mean, it's all guesswork, but what else do we have? Surely we're due a break." He drew a breath. "Izzy, could you work on this? Get Sophie Monaghan to help. And good thinking."

Izzy was been halfway to the door when Aliya Nazir burst in.

"Guv, a woman's been abducted in Gadebridge Park. Looks like it might be Howard Parker again."

Time seemed to stand still. "Do we know who the woman is?" Quarrel heard himself ask.

Grim-faced, Aliya told him.

The stakes had just been raised.

32

Michelle McGrath's world swam back into focus. She still felt groggy and disorientated. What the hell had happened? This had been supposed to be a normal Saturday, her routine reassuringly predictable. The weekly supermarket shop with John, then her Saturday run round Gadebridge Park. A bit of time for herself, a chance to clear some head space. She'd finished her run, jogged back to the car park, and then what? She'd been attacked. A man. Some sort of cloth over her face. Whatever she'd breathed in, it had cut off her fightback almost before she'd begun.

She thought about moving, but immediately realised she was totally restrained, sat up against a wall. She could just about see her ankles, strapped together with duct tape. Her wrists were similarly bound behind her back. There was more tape over her mouth, and she couldn't move her head. Her forehead and neck were somehow attached to the wall. With more tape, she thought, but something else, too. Some kind of cord? She fancied it was cutting into her throat.

Oh, God, was she slowly strangling?

No. No, she could breathe easily enough. So whoever had abducted her didn't want her to die, not yet, anyway. They had other plans for her.

It wasn't hard to work out what those plans might be.

The Tarot card killer immobilised his victims' heads, she knew. Ben Newell had been strapped to a bench, his head in a vice. But Howard Parker had left both bench and vice behind when he fled his Boxmoor lair, and had been forced to improvise here.

And it had to be Parker, and she thought she knew why. Her best guess at the last outstanding victim had been Tabitha Hunt, over the innocuous tattoo that Michael Woodley had somehow managed to twist into a metaphor for casual sexual availability.

She'd realised someone else could be in Parker's sights, but never for a moment had she imagined she'd be on his kill list. So why was she? That card, the one she now knew was reserved for her – The Moon? Something about not going with what your instincts told you? What was that all about?

Parker had boldly abducted her in a public car park, in broad daylight, she realised. The struggle before she'd passed out had been violent, desperate. Surely someone had seen what happened? Had they noted the registration number on Parker's car?

That didn't matter, she realised. She was pretty sure there was CCTV in the car park. Provided someone called it in, the whole thing would have been captured on camera. With any luck, it wouldn't take too long for her colleagues either to recognise her or identify her from her own car. And they'd be using ANPR to try and track Parker's vehicle.

Except she knew he was pretty good at knowing where cameras were and avoiding them as much as possible. It could take time to track him, time she might not have, and she wondered how close they'd manage to get to where she was being held.

And, since *she* had no idea where that was, how was anyone else supposed to find her?

*

Since the shocking news of Michelle's abduction had come in, the team had pieced together what had happened from eyewitness accounts. By Parker's previous standards, it had been pretty reckless. There had been people in the car park at the time. Some ran to help, some had stood watching in disbelief. One or two had filmed it on their mobile phones.

One would-be rescuer had stepped into the path of the stolen Carlton, but the driver had floored the accelerator. The man had thrown himself aside, but not quite quickly enough. The estate had caught him a glancing blow, cracking his hip, before roaring out of the car park.

Witnesses had reported the incident, but the first thought on the switchboard had been that it was some sort of domestic incident, or perhaps a reckless sex attack. So valuable time had ticked by while another team examined the scene, ordered CCTV footage, and checked out what appeared to be the victim's car. Even so, the facts fell into place fairly quickly. The victim was one of their own, Michelle McGrath. The abductor matched the photograph of a disguised Howard Parker that was in circulation, and the estate was carrying plates last seen on a blue Saab.

Quarrel had forced himself to ignore the horror squirming inside him. Michelle had been a friend to so many sexual assault victims over the years, and she had clearly felt outrage at Ben Newell's acquittal, for a crime she was convinced he'd committed. Her anger at the perceived injustice, her loathing of the man, and her sense of guilt about the tragic aftermath of the case was palpable.

Yet, too late, Quarrel could see why Parker would view her in a different light. Snatches of conversation played over in his mind. Emily's parents saying their daughter had regretted going ahead with her complaint. The fact that she'd put herself through the whole ordeal partly to protect other women Newell might attack. Michelle herself commenting that the young woman had 'had some wobbles' and been 'brave'.

Had Emily felt in some way pressured by Michelle to keep going, against her urge to run away from the prosecution? Had that feeling reached Howard Parker's ears?

A fresh wave of despair washed over him. All the time they'd been fighting to identify the final victim on Parker's list, even consulting Michelle McGrath herself, and the truth had been right under his nose. How had he been so blind, so stupid?

And now Michelle could already be paying the price of that stupidity. Quarrel suspected she had, at best, only hours to live – the time it would take Parker to complete his final tattoo, in all likelihood. The fact that he had stolen tattooing equipment from Conor Burke's premises gave some reassurance on that point. Parker might be hunted and possibly desperate – the comparatively reckless way he had snatched his latest prey showed that – but he clearly meant to see through his plans to tattoo the face of every one of his victims.

That meant there might still be time. But that time was running out like melting snow.

33

Michelle had been trying to work out what this place was. The constraint of her head seriously reduced her field of vision, but she had worked out that it was an empty building – no sign of any kind of furniture, or fixtures and fittings. And she thought it was either new or freshly refurbished. There was a whiff of recent paintwork, mingled with a hint of cement dust.

Her impression was that the ceiling was high, too high for most residential properties. Maybe a factory or warehouse. But where?

She was trying, hopelessly, to work her wrists free from the tape that bound them when she heard a door open in the building. Footsteps were approaching, quickly, purposefully, echoing in the emptiness.

She closed her eyes and let her body go limp. She knew what Parker would have in mind for her. She had no idea what his exact process was, but she was fairly confident that he would want her conscious for it. Pretending she hadn't yet come round from whatever chemical he'd used to knock her out would maybe buy her a little time. Somehow, she had to control her terror and put on the acting performance of her life.

Her wrists were sore from fruitless chafing, and her head ached where he'd slammed it against the car during their brief struggle. She tried to ignore it all. They were the least of her worries.

The footsteps came closer. She sensed that they'd stopped just in front of her.

"Michelle?" A man's voice. "Michelle!" More insistent.

A handful of her hair was grasped, and her head was forced back. She managed not to wince. Regulated her breathing, simulating sleep. He patted her cheek a couple of times, just short of a slap. "Come on, Michelle."

He let her head drop. "Damn. They've never been out this long before."

He paced around a bit, then came close again. She sensed him hunkering down. She could smell slightly stale breath. "All right, sleepyhead, I'll give you a little longer. Not too long, though. If I have to wake you up, I'll find a way of doing it. I might have to hurt you."

The footsteps receded. The echoes suggested he had left the room. Only when she was sure he'd gone did she allow a whimper of fear to escape her.

*

Quarrel had made himself a mug of strong coffee in the nearby kitchenette, and had used it to wash down a couple of paracetamol. Stress and tiredness had brought on the early signs of one of the massive, debilitating headaches he sometimes suffered. If he got one now, he could kiss goodbye to any hope of clear thought for the rest of the day, and Michelle McGrath needed him.

He stared again at the map of the Maylands industrial estate, and surrounding residential roads. They were basing an awful lot on where a few cars had been stolen from, but it really was all they had. If that hunch was wrong, Howard Parker could have Michelle anywhere, and this deadly race against time would surely be lost.

Meanwhile, Michelle's husband, John, was being kept in the loop by Libby Statham. By all accounts, he was trying to keep calm for the sake of the children, but Libby didn't know how long it would be before he crumbled.

For all it was worth, Debbie Brown had sent a substance found in Parker's basement for urgent analysis, and she'd reported back that the main ingredient was belladonna, also known as deadly nightshade. Although it was technically a poison, it had a number of medical uses, including as a sedative. Brown believed it had been used to sedate Parker's victims. Belladonna was a toxin that wouldn't have shown up on a typical tox screen, so further tests had now been ordered to confirm the theory.

It was a piece of the jigsaw, but hardly one that was going to help locate Parker or Michelle.

Quarrel's frustration was growing. He had to *do* something. He wasn't prepared for his colleague to be just one more death he'd failed to prevent. And a feeling was nagging away at him. There was a flaw in their thinking, he was sure of it.

The Maylands estate. Wood End Lane. He knew, just knew, that Michelle was being held somewhere in that area, but where? Get every keyholder to open up every business unit until they got lucky? Parker could get wind of something going on, scrap the tattoo, and simply suffocate Michelle before making a run for it.

He sat back, tapping a pen on his desk. What did they know?

Well, they knew that Parker had been planning this campaign for a long time, probably since Ben Newell's acquittal. He'd learned to tattoo, and to do it well. He'd kitted out the basement at Cowper Road as a killing room. He'd almost certainly studied his victims, learning their routes and habits, before finally making his move, his entire grisly body of work scheduled for completion within a single week.

And he'd thought ahead, too, with contingency plans in place: the rear exit from the Cowper Road basement, the fake number plates ready to attach to stolen cars.

And yet, the thought struck him, Parker wasn't the perfect planner after all. Because he'd had to steal tattooing equipment after he'd been forced to abandon Cowper Road. Was that the bum note in the symphony?

They'd been assuming he had premises, another bolt-hole, somewhere, to run to if Cowper Road was compromised. But why, if he had such a place at his disposal, wouldn't he have a backup set of kit already there?

In fact, he'd only got lucky with Conor Burke's premises at all because the Tring tattooist had come under suspicion and the place had been empty while CSIs checked it out.

No, Quarrel realised, Parker's forward planning related entirely to the escape. Since then, he'd been making up his final attack – on Michelle McGrath – on the fly. He was almost certainly holed up somewhere, with a new killing room in place, but he'd found it quickly, without going through the usual channels for obtaining a house, a factory, some other sort of building.

He'd broken in somewhere. Somewhere empty, surely.

He called Katie Gray, and she came straight to his office.

"Any joy?" he asked her.

She looked gloomy. "We're all treading water, to be honest. Even if we're right about the area he's in, he's still a bit of a needle in a haystack."

"I agree. What if we were able to reduce the amount of hay?"

"I don't follow."

"We're scratching our heads over a shedload of buildings that he might or might not have access to. But if he didn't have access to anything – not legally, I mean…"

"Then maybe he'd do it *ill*egally?"

He nodded. "That's what I'm thinking. Something empty. And you were liking a factory."

"Even more so, now you say that. With residential property, if someone's suddenly in the house next door, however discreet, you *will* notice. A factory, maybe not so much so."

"How easily can we get a list of empty factories on that estate, I wonder?"

Katie grinned. It felt like the first time any of them had smiled today.

34

All that Michelle had succeeded in doing in Howard Parker's absence was chafing her wrists raw in her attempts to get them free from their bonds. After he'd gone, she'd felt around within the limits of her movement for something sharp enough to make an impression on the tape. At first she'd despaired, but then she'd found a screw head, standing proud slightly from the skirting board behind her. It wasn't much and, so far, it wasn't making much of an impression, but it was all she had.

She knew her 'still drugged' act wouldn't fool him for much longer. Her only hope was that Nathan Quarrel would find her in time, and that seemed like a very slim hope indeed. It was down to her to gain them as much time as she was able. And, if it came to it, she had to find some way, helpless as she was, to fight for her survival.

Her head and neck were immobilised, her hands and feet restrained, but her torso and legs were free to move, within limitations. It wasn't much, but it wasn't nothing, either.

She was starving, and parched, she realised. All she'd had all day was some toast and coffee for breakfast and another coffee and a couple of biscuits after the supermarket.

How long ago had that been? She had no idea. John must be frantic by now. So must the kids. What if she never saw any of them again? Never saw her children finish their education, have careers, fall in love, maybe have children of their own?

The thought that she probably wasn't coming out of this alive brought tears to her eyes, but it also strengthened her will. If Howard Parker thought she'd go down without a struggle, he was mistaken.

She heard footsteps approaching again, and she allowed herself to go limp once more as the door opened.

"Still out?" he said. "I can't believe that."

She knew he was coming closer. Abruptly, fingers closed around her left earlobe and twisted hard. She couldn't help crying out in pain. She stared at him, angry.

The wig he'd worn in the car park had gone, and so had the glasses. His hair was dark and close-cropped, his eyes mournful.

"Sorry," he said, "I hate to hurt a woman, but we have a lot of work to do."

She glared at him.

"I imagine, being police, you know who I am, what I've been doing, and why," he said.

Was the fucker actually trying to justify himself to her? She rolled her eyes. She wondered if she could rile him. Riled people could get careless.

He shrugged. "I suppose, despite all the stuff in the media, and all the fine words from your top brass, rape victims are a lot of bother to you lot. Hard to prove, and better things to do with your resources, right?"

She smiled with her eyes.

"Christ, you don't even care, do you? I bet you hardly even noticed when Emily Snow took her own life. She did the right thing, reporting Ben Newell's attack on her so he couldn't do it to anyone else. I bet you were happy enough for her to put herself through all that. Where were you after the case failed? Well, someone has to speak out for Emily. You might think all this is about revenge. But it isn't. It's about justice."

Behind the tape gag, she made herself laugh as if he'd made the most hilarious joke she'd heard.

The first flash of anger showed in his eyes. Good.

"You think that's funny?" He stepped over and ripped the tape off her mouth. It hurt, but she wasn't about to let him know that.

"Scream away," he said. "No one'll hear you."

She managed a shrug.

"So what's funny?" he demanded.

She licked her parched lips. "*You* are, *Howard.* You think you're on this big moral crusade. You think because you slap a symbolic Tarot card on someone before you kill them, that gives it all a higher purpose. Well, I've got news for you, mate."

"Oh, yeah?"

"Yeah. You're just another poor, messed up sicko, my friend. I sincerely hate that our system still allows sex crime victims to be put on trial. But it's the shitty system I have to work with. I tell you what, though."

He looked almost amused. "I can't wait."

"No one made Emily kill herself. I know her life was in a really bad place, but it would have got better eventually. It always does, even if things are never the same. If only she'd given it time."

"Christ," he said. "You're blaming her? You really are a piece of work, aren't you?"

"And you're not? Three people are dead, Howard. Every one of them had a life. Family, friends. You lost Emily. What about those people? You punched a gaping great hole in their lives. Don't they matter? *Their* loss?"

He'd already broken eye contact. "You're just trying to talk your way out of this."

She rolled her eyes again. "Have you even been listening? I've got a husband, who's a really good man. I've got two teenagers at crucial stages in their education. They need their mum. If they lose me, it'll destroy them and probably ruin their life chances."

"I liked you better when you were gagged."

"You don't have to do this, Howard."

"Oh, but I do. I can't quit now." He looked her in the eyes again. "Shall I show you what your tattoo's going to look like?"

She affected a yawn. "The Moon, right?"

He looked surprised for an instant, then nodded. "They found my templates?"

"Of course they did, you idiot. Might as well be Mickey Mouse, though. We both know this is a vanity project. You care more about wallowing in fake grief than you ever cared about Emily."

"You know nothing about it."

"I know more about your motivation than you know about Tarot. You might have learned tattooing, but you never really bothered to study the cards, did you? You made do with casting around on the Internet for card readings you could contort to fit your narrative. If Emily's looking down on you, I bet she'd be embarrassed."

"You talk too much!" he snapped. "In fact, I think I'll shut you up."

He moved across the room, out of her field of vision. She heard the unmistakeable sound of tape being unwound from a roll. Moments later, he was back with a piece in his hands. He walked towards her, obviously planning on sticking the tape across her mouth.

It might be her one chance. As he passed her legs, she pushed down with her hands, steadying herself as best she could, and swung from the hips, sweeping his feet from under him. The cord around her neck took much of her weight, choking her. As she scrabbled with her feet to push herself up again, Parker, taken by surprise, fell over backwards, arms windmilling. He went down hard on the concrete floor.

The crack his head made as it hit the solid surface seemed to resound around the room, loud as a pistol shot.

Then silence.

*

Quarrel's team had hardly been blessed with good fortune on this case, he thought, but maybe the tide was turning. The husband of one of Katie Gray's friends had been looking for premises for his expanding business a couple of years ago and found what he was looking for via a nationwide website advertising commercial properties to let. A couple of phone calls later and Katie had not only those details, but also links to other sites of interest.

In total, there were seven factory units for rent on the Maylands estate, including a new four-unit development offering immediate availability.

"What do you think?" Katie said. "Autumn Place. No neighbours to hear you or observe your movements. We can try and focus in on CCTV footage nearby."

It felt right. "No time. I'm going over there."

"What about backup?"

"You can sort that while I'm on my way. I want to save Michelle's life, if I can. Maybe even get to her before he starts tattooing."

"I'm coming with you."

"No, you—"

"It's not the start of a debate, Nate."

He knew when not to argue. "Then get Aliya to organise backup for us."

No one had to be told twice what Quarrel and Katie needed them to do. Quarrel drove. It was less than ten minutes' drive to the industrial estate. He prayed he'd be in time.

*

Howard Parker lay very still. Michelle wondered if he'd fractured his skull. Perhaps he was dead. Part of her almost hoped he was, even though she was trussed up in an empty factory without food or water, and there was every chance that no one was going to find her any time soon. She seemed to remember reading that you could survive without water for about three days, although she thought organ failure and other damage might start to occur sooner than that.

For all that, she still thought she stood more chance of survival than she would if Parker was alive and conscious.

She considered yelling for help, but suspected that was probably a waste of time, breath and energy. It was most unlikely anyone would hear her. No, her best hope was that Quarrel would somehow find her. And that could prove a faint hope.

She looked at the motionless Parker again. Was his chest rising and falling? If it was, his breathing was shallow at best.

She started working on the tape around her wrists again, rubbing them on the screw in the skirting. Bit by bit, she had been making little tears in the tape, but the progress was very gradual, and she found it impossible to judge how long it would take before she could free herself

She racked her brains for quicker ways of getting herself free. How had the cord securing her head and neck been fixed to the wall? She forced herself to think, really think. If it was a solid wall, he'd have most likely used screws. Could they be worked loose?

She tapped her bound hands against the wall behind her. The sound they made was inconclusive. Solid wall, or hollow with plasterboard? If plasterboard, would it be possible to somehow break it? John was the practical one, he'd know. But, even if it was theoretically possible, how could she do it in her present situation?

She remembered the choking sensation when she'd used her legs to trip Parker. It would have been ironic if she'd put him out of action only to wind up inadvertently throttling herself.

She went back to rubbing the tape on the screw. Another nick. Another.

Her joints had been aching for ages. Now her shoulders and elbows felt as if they were on fire, and she was getting cold. She was still in her running gear, it was only March, and there was no heating in the factory. The light was fading, and with it any warmth the day held was starting to leach away.

Her thoughts were interrupted by a faint groan. Her breath caught and she looked at Parker. He was starting to stir. A few moments later, he had moved onto his front and was slowly raising himself to his knees. He touched a hand to the back of his head and examined his palm. Michelle could see that it was bloody.

He looked her way. "You bitch. You tripped me. God, my head."

"Does it hurt? Good."

"At my own place, I had a proper bench. I had to improvise here. I can see now I should have secured your legs to something."

She raised her legs from the floor. "Come and try it. I'll kick you in the balls."

He burst out laughing. "I bet you would, too. Not that you're in a great position to fight, are you?"

"Try me."

He shoved his hands in his pockets. "I thought this was going to work, but now I can see it's not going to be so easy." He sighed. "I think I might have to adjust the plan. When I first started planning this, I loved the idea of using Emily's interest in Tarot to brand each of you for what you are and then leave you in her favourite places for all to see. To avenge her and honour her."

How he loved to talk. She carried on working at the tape.

"I know," she said, seeing another chance to goad him. "I heard you were a bit of a nerd. You're not so much the Tarot Killer though, as the Nerdy Killer. Even serial murder is some sort of geeky obsession for you, isn't it?"

"Do you have any idea how long one of those tattoos can take? I went to Birmingham for a two-year apprenticeship, so I wouldn't be registered anywhere near here. But, even now I've had plenty of practice, it's still hours." He rubbed the back of his head again. "Thing is, Michelle, they could have been extra hours for you to live, but you know what? I think you've just talked yourself out of that time. Maybe I'll just move straight to killing you and do the tattoo afterwards."

Oh, God, no. This wasn't what she'd had in mind when she set out to provoke him.

"But what about your ritual?" She had to buy as much time as possible. "I thought it was important to you."

"Oh, I see." He was grinning. "Not so nerdy now, am I? Well, yes, I always loved that moment when I held a mirror up for them to see my work, but it doesn't really matter. Don't worry. The actual killing isn't a big deal for me. Think of it as an execution. It won't hurt too much."

35

"There," Katie said. "Autumn Place."

A dull, grey, functional row of industrial buildings.

The light was fading fast now. In less than half an hour, twilight would have given way to darkness.

"If he's working on a tattoo in there, how can he see what he's doing?" Quarrel wondered as he pulled up just past the silent block. "I mean, he's got quite an intricate tattoo to do."

"Maybe he's at the back of whichever building he's in, with some sort of lamp set up."

"Or maybe he did the work when there was still natural light," he said grimly. "Maybe he's already gone and is dumping Michelle's body somewhere."

"We can only hope not."

"I know." They got out of the Volvo. "I still think it would be one of the middle units, and I'm guessing he'd have broken in somehow. Unless he's really good, there should be some evidence."

"Okay. How about you check the one on the right and I check the one on the left?"

"That works for me. Come and get me if you find anything, and we'll go in together."

*

Parker returned with a pillow under his arm. Michelle sat watchful, knowing what was coming, wondering how she could prevent it with only her legs free. If he came at her from the side, he'd be able to push the pillow over her face, and there'd be nothing she could do about it.

In his absence, fighting back equal measures of terror and frustration, she'd started making one last attempt to free her sore, chafed wrists, and she suddenly felt a little give in the tape. It was definitely parting. She sensed that the tape might rip, if she only had time.

"This has never been about violence," he was saying.

"Of course not," she said, trying to work one wrist free from the tape, finding that she could get some real movement now, and hoping he didn't get wind of what she was doing. "Jabbing sharp needles all over people's faces, making a load of open wounds, then smothering them with a pillow? Why would anyone describe that as violent? You really think suffocation is painless?"

As she had feared, he approached her from the side, avoiding her legs.

"Just give in to it," he said. "It'll be quicker and easier."

He moved the pillow towards her face and that was when the tape finally parted and she managed to pull her right wrist free. She brought that arm from behind her back, her bicep stiff and protesting, to lash out at him. She caught him a glancing blow on the side of his face.

Swearing, he threw the pillow aside and grabbed her by the ankles, yanking her away from the wall, raising her buttocks so the cord around her neck was taking all her weight. The more her torso was pulled towards him, the more she felt the cord tighten across her throat.

Panicking, she wrenched her left arm round, bringing both hands up to scrabble at the cord. As she'd feared, it was covered with duct tape. She couldn't get her fingers inside it. She was choking, her airway restricted. She tried to kick out, to dislodge him, but Parker hung on grimly. He was panting with the exertion, all thought of so-called non-violence apparently fled.

As she pushed against the floor with her hands, trying to take the strain and raise herself up, she could hear herself making gagging noises as she attempted to draw in air that was already out of reach. The pain of the cord biting into her throat was intense.

As consciousness slid away, she thought of her family.

*

Quarrel watched Katie start off, then moved towards the centre-right building, which turned out to be Unit 3. There was no sign of tampering at the front. He put an ear to the shuttered door, but could hear nothing.

He turned towards Katie and saw her hurrying back in his direction. He met her halfway.

"The locking mechanism's been broken," she said. "Pretty crudely, too. And I swear I can hear something in there."

"Then let's go in, quiet as we can. I don't want to spook him into harming Michelle."

He walked back to the shutter. It was on a simple roller mechanism, and its newness proved to be a bonus, as it slid up almost soundlessly. The door opened inwards, equally smoothly on well-oiled hinges. As Quarrel stepped over the threshold, he heard sounds of a scuffle. Ahead was a large open space, semi-dark. A couple of doors led off, but he had eyes only for the figures at the far wall. One, clearly a male, presumably Howard Parker, held the other by the legs. The second person's head seemed somehow connected to the wall itself.

The first figure turned towards them.

"Police," Quarrel barked. "Let her go, Howard."

He began to sprint towards them. Parker dropped the woman's ankles and ran towards one of the doors. Katie, fitter and faster than Quarrel, cut him off, tackled him to the ground and twisted one arm behind his back. As she cuffed him, Quarrel ran to where Michelle McGrath lay motionless. He could see that her neck had been tied to the wall. He checked for a pulse and found none.

No.

He felt a howl building inside him. All through his life, starting with his father, when he was a child, people had died and he'd been unable to help them. Now he was failing again.

He manoeuvred Michelle's body into more of a sitting position, lessening the pressure on her throat. Her mouth was open, tongue protruding, face suffused. Tape and string also held her upper head to the wall, but he found that relatively easy to push away.

The ends of the tape were simply pressed onto the wall. He peeled them back and managed to uncover simple string, knotted at one side. He fumbled with large, awkward fingers, finding that his hands were trembling.

"Katie!" he said urgently, "Is he cuffed?"

"Yep."

"I need you. Quickly."

She hurried over and he pointed to the knot.

"She's not breathing, and I need your smaller fingers to undo that."

She hesitated, that familiar squeamish look on her face.

"Fuck's sake, Katie, this is Michelle."

She was a shade paler, but nodded and got to work on the tight knot. Quarrel called an ambulance.

"Almost there," she said, as he came off the phone. She released the string. Michelle's body went limp, and he took the strain.

"Let's lay her down," Katie instructed him. "I'll try CPR."

They laid the unbreathing woman on her back and the DS went to work, counting chest compressions. He realised how scantily dressed Michelle was – John had said she'd gone to the park for a run – so he slipped off his jacket, ready to cover her.

Abruptly, he heard a noise behind him and turned his head. Parker had somehow managed to get to his feet, despite his hands being cuffed behind his back. He began running for the exit.

"No you don't!" shouted Quarrel, bolting after him.

Parker got through the door, running awkwardly but quickly towards the road, Quarrel gaining on him.

As Parker hit the tarmac road, a dark van hurtled around the corner. The driver slammed on the brakes, but he never stood a chance. There was a sickening thud as the van hit the killer full-on.

The driver of the armed response van got out, looking pale. He looked down at the broken figure, blood pooling around the head.

"Oh, Jesus," he said. "There was nothing I could do."

Quarrel shrugged, knowing he ought to hate the twinge of satisfaction he was feeling. "Not your fault. See if there's anything you can do for him. There's already an ambulance on its way."

"Is that the suspect?"

"He's a dangerous killer, yes. Or at least he was."

36

Quarrel had been relieved to find that Michelle McGrath was breathing again when he returned to the factory floor. She was conscious and even talking to Katie in raspy tones. She was taken to hospital, where it was decided to keep her in overnight, but she was expected to be discharged on Sunday morning. The mental effects of her ordeal might take longer to emerge and to deal with.

Howard Parker had a number of fractures, including to his skull. Amazingly, he was alive, but in an induced coma. Doctors were putting his survival chances at 50/50. When he was able to think objectively, Quarrel had decided that he hoped Parker lived to stand trial.

Quarrel himself arrived home just before midnight, to find Laura still up.

"You hungry?" she asked. "I did something I can bung in the microwave."

"In a bit."

"Glass of wine?"

"Now you're talking."

He watched her taking out glasses and pouring generous measures of blood-red liquid.

"Shouldn't you be in bed? Don't you start day shift tomorrow?"

"Don't worry about me." She brought the drinks over. "I heard the news. You got your man and rescued someone?"

"We barely rescued her. She was a policewoman." He gave her the bare details.

"See?" She smiled. "You *can* save people some of the time."

"Katie Gray did CPR. She was really calm. I would have messed up. I was shaking. I couldn't even undo the string around her neck. A few more minutes…"

"You got there in time." She raised her glass. "To a result."

They clinked glasses. She looked suddenly serious.

She put her glass down and said, "Look, I've been thinking about the other night, and I'm really sorry. I mean, I know we made up, but I think I screwed up. Inviting Sandra in. It wasn't my decision to take, was it?"

He looked at her. "No, it wasn't. But I understand why you did it. And I think it was the right thing to do."

"Truly?"

He leaned over and kissed her. "Truly."

She kissed him back. "I love you, Nate. I do. But, right from that day we met, at the reservoir, there's always been something broken in you. Something missing. All those letters you shredded. And then she was there on the doorstep, and I thought if I invited her in, you'd finally have to speak to each other, for good or ill. I just hoped maybe finally confronting her, and what happened when you were a kid, might help to finally fix it."

"I'm not sure it works that way. I don't know. Maybe... maybe something..." He shook his head, unable to articulate his feelings. "I don't know," he said.

"Have you given any thought to her case files. Maybe taking a look at them?"

He took a couple of sips of his wine. "Yeah, but what's the point? All I know about the day my dad died – the day she killed him – is second-hand knowledge. What am I going to find in those files that didn't come out at the time? "

She looked him in the eye. "Will you look, though?"

He gazed into his glass. "I've never told this to anyone before," he said. "Not even you. But one thing did come back to me when I was talking to my mother." He hesitated. Did he really want to talk about this? He'd never said much, even to Laura, about the murder, mostly because he had no memory of it – but now he knew there was another reason.

It was time to tell the whole truth.

"My grandparents waited until I was twelve to tell me what had happened between my parents – how my dad was dead and my mother was serving a life sentence for his murder. There was no instant restoration of memory, although it did explain the flashbacks I'd always had. What I never told them, or anyone else, is this. The more I brooded on it, the more I believed I was to blame for what happened."

"You?" Laura blinked. "You were six. How could you be to blame?"

He leaned back in his chair, suddenly bone-tired. "There are two versions to the story. The one my mother told the court, and the one the jury believed. But they both have the same bare facts in common. My mother stabbed my father to death."

Red on white.

"And that was your fault because…?"

"I keep thinking, what might I have done to make it all right?"

She came over and knelt beside his chair, taking his hand.

"You listen to me, Nate Quarrel. What *could* you do? However it really happened, it was an ugly situation. You were a little boy. You weren't supposed to somehow stop it. How could you? For all you know, if you'd tried, maybe you wouldn't even be here now."

"That's what I'd tell me if I was in your shoes. But I can't shake the feeling that my life's fucked up because I wasn't brave enough to do something. I don't know what, because I don't *remember*. It's probably why I find it so hard to let people in, or to trust them. Because, since my grandparents told me what happened, I haven't thought I deserve love or friendship. Christ, Laura, I've even kept this from you until now. What does that say?"

She squeezed his hand. "You're telling me now. Maybe getting it out in the open is a first step."

"I'm so tired," he said. "We *will* talk more about this, I promise we will. But I need to go to bed."

She took the glass away from him and set it down. "You don't want to eat?"

"Maybe I'll have a glass of milk and a couple of biscuits."

"I'll bring them. You go up."

He unfolded himself from the chair, stood up. Paused for balance. Then he headed for the stairs.

"By the way," she said, "Aldbury Church is having a small memorial service for Alastair Murdoch tomorrow. It was on the local news. That model, Anthea Swallow, will be reading a poem."

The early stages of the case, when Anthea and her husband, Jimmy Steele, had been viewed as possible suspects, seemed an age ago now.

"I might go," he said. "Pay my respects."

*

Monday morning.
Izzy Cole left DI Quarrel's office with a spring in her step. She would be returning to Tring soon, but he'd wanted to emphasise her contributions to cracking the case and assure her he'd do all he could to get her back as a TI. The rest was up to her.

She'd had some thinking space on Sunday, and she'd concluded that, for all the shock and hurt of discovering that Matt and Bethany were seeing each other behind her back, neither of those things was as important to her as getting back to this team and working her way towards becoming a DC, and beyond. And that seemed within her grasp.

She'd realised something else, too. The thing she'd had with Matt hadn't ever felt like the real thing. They'd never properly got to know each other as people. With both their jobs getting in the way too often, when they did get together, a lot of it was about the sex.

And the sex was good. But there was a better than evens chance the relationship – if that was what it had even been – would have petered out in a few more weeks or years.

Much more painful was the betrayal by Bethany, the friend Izzy had been there for so many times, the friend she'd thought she could tell anything. Maybe Matt enjoyed having two women on a string. Maybe it fed his ego. Certainly he'd phoned yesterday, smarming and suggesting he came over. She'd put him off, claiming work pressures. She hadn't yet decided what she wanted to do about the situation.

The thing was, though, Bethany had apparently been okay with it, complicit in his two-timing. The only person in this triangle who hadn't known it *was* a triangle had been Izzy. She imagined the two of them laughing at her. It made her angry.

She could just confront them. Dump them both and walk away with as much dignity intact as possible. Or she could bide her time and devise something a little more satisfying.

There was no rush, no rush at all. She had plenty of time.

*

Quarrel had spent much of Sunday on the aftermath of Howard Parker's arrest. The circumstances of Parker's injuries were being considered by local brass for a voluntary referral to the Independent Office for Police Conduct, both because Quarrel had 'chased the helpless suspect into the road' and because the driver 'might not have been paying due care and attention'.

Quarrel prayed it wouldn't come to that. He knew Parker had brought what had happened upon himself. It was not that he believed police were above the law or needed to close ranks at the first sign of criticism. In his opinion, IOPC investigations were a necessary evil, both to root out the bad cops, and to learn from mistakes. But Parker had all but thrown himself in front of the van whilst fleeing the scene of his crime. An investigation would unjustly stick mud to Quarrel and the driver and waste a lot of valuable time.

He'd attended Alastair Murdoch's memorial service and seen first-hand how loved the man had been. Even Jimmy Steele was there, ostensibly supporting Anthea.

"I suppose Alastair wasn't such a bad guy," he told Quarrel outside the church. "I just like my own way. I'm glad you caught his killer."

Last night he'd done his Sunday ritual of sitting at his desk, making a 'to do' list for the coming week. He was in the habit of colour-coding the list with highlighter pens, so he'd fumbled in a desk drawer for them. His hand brushed the receipt his mother had given him, with her mobile number written on. The sooner he destroyed that, the better.

But not tonight.

Now he sat at his desk in the station, all the events of the past week playing in his mind. It should have been all about the Howard Parker case, but personal matters kept intruding.

He sighed and entered some words in the search box of his Internet browser. A little while later, hesitant but resolved, he dialled a number. Told the switchboard who he'd like to speak to.

He was put through and the call was answered on the sixth ring.

"Good morning," he returned the responder's greeting. "This is DI Nathan Quarrel from Hertfordshire Constabulary. I was wondering if there was any way I could get sight of an old case file... What's going on? Best I don't say for now. It could be nothing."

The woman on the other end asked which file he was interested in, and he told her.

"Sandra Bowman?" He could imagine her frowning. "Doesn't ring a bell."

"It was over thirty years ago."

"Give me a number and I'll get back to you."

He recited it.

"And your name again?"

"My name? It's Nathan Quarrel."

THE END

ACKNOWLEDGEMENTS

First of all, my thanks to you for reading *In Ink*. It's been quite a while since I've created a new protagonist and a whole new cast of characters, and it's been fun getting to know Nathan Quarrel and his colleagues.

As any writer will tell you, books don't write themselves, but it also takes so much more than just the author to make a book the best it can be. As always, my insightful and (sometimes painfully) critical beta readers, Chris Sivers and Debbie Porteous read *In Ink* early on and suggested ways I could make it much better. The eagle-eyed Helen Baggott helped me to give it a final polish.

I'm always delighted and deeply grateful for the kindness of experts who freely share their knowledge to help me sound as if I know what I'm talking about. Thanks are due to real-life CSI Clare Heron and to Rosie Claverton for their professional guidance; to Chris Moseley for guiding me through the mysteries of Tarot; and to Ammar Farah at Sons of Ink in Tring, who gave me invaluable information about tattooing and the tattoo business. Any mistakes are either intentional in the interests of the story, or my boo-boo.

Writing can be a lonely business. The support and friendship of all my wonderful mates in the crime writing business – too many to name, but they know who they are – as well as the Oxford Crime Writers, Chiltern Writers, and my friends and followers on social media, all help to keep me going.

A big shout out too to my two cheerleaders in chief – to my dad and to the very lovely Jane Lord, both of whom never miss an opportunity to tell people about my books.

And finally, my thanks and love to my wife, Chris, whose support, encouragement and love mean the world to me.

Buckinghamshire, 2020
www.davesivers.co.uk
Twitter: @davesivers
Facebook: @davesiversauthor1

Printed in Great Britain
by Amazon